PAYING FOR IT

PAYING FOR IT

Tony Black

preface
publishing

Published by Preface 2008

2 4 6 8 10 9 7 5 3 1

The extract on p186 is from the short story 'What She Offered' by Thomas H. Cook
from the the anthology *Dangerous Women* (Arrow Books, 2007) and is reproduced by
kind permission of Thomas H. Cook.

First published in Great Britain in 2008 by
Preface
1 Queen Annes Gate
London SW1H 9BU

www.rbooks.co.uk
www.prefacepublishing.co.uk

Addresses for companies within The Random House Group Limited
can be found at:
www.randomhouse.co.uk/offices.htm

The Random House Group Limited Reg. No. 954009

A CIP catalogue record for this book is available from the British Library

Hardback ISBN 9781848090200
Trade Paperback ISBN 9781848090217

Typeset by Palimpsest Book Production Limited,
Grangemouth, Stirlingshire

Printed and bound in Australia by Griffin Press

For Madeline

FUNERALS MAKE MY EYES WATER. Don't get me wrong, not in the 'Oh, he was a lovely fellah taken from us too soon' sense. That stuff, I can handle. Old ladies with waterbag legs shoving egg-mayonnaise sandwiches at you, I can just about manage. Slipping them in the pocket beside the scoosh bottle is no problem for me. That type, they never listen to a word you say anyway. Fire out 'Is that right?', or 'Really? No, really?', and they're happy as Larry. Just don't stray into the 'And how's your Finlay doing in New Zealand?' minefield. Uh-uh. That can spell catastrophe.

It's details like cause of death that have me filling up. Send me reaching for the twelve-year-old Macallan they roll out for such occasions. And hitting it hard. Not just because that's what drinkers do. But because I know that, in my racket, it doesn't look good to be moved by things like funerals and death.

It's when death comes so close to home, stamps on your doorstep, then invites itself in that I wince. Really wince. I mean, who wouldn't wince at something like this?

'Gus. Gusgo. Gusie boy . . .'

The skill of the man, pure piss-artistry, to make poetry with my name like that.

'Gus, did you hear what happened before the . . . you know . . . ?' Malky Conroy, one of Edinburgh's widest gobshites, weighed his hands out in the air like he had hold of a mortar launcher.

'Booka-booka,' it was a pathetic attempt at gangster patter.

I tried to keep my tone serious. I mean, we were talking about a man's death here. A man I barely knew, granted. I had met him twice, tops. But out of respect to his father I wasn't going to mess about at Billy Boy's funeral.

'It's the noise a shotgun makes,' said Malky, 'when it goes off, like.'

I gave him a nod, straightened my back. 'Got ya.' I tipped back the last of my Red Eye laced coffee, crushed the Styrofoam cup.

For reasons best kept between Billy and the grave, the poor lad found himself on the wrong end of a sawn-off shotgun one evening. One evening, sounds so civilised, doesn't it? Not in the least. Unless you call finding a lad, barely into his twenties, with both barrels emptied in his face, civilised.

That's the sight that greeted some old biddie walking her Westie at the foot of Arthur's Seat one morning. The official verdict was suicide, but nobody was buying that.

'Like I was saying,' Malky crouched over, leaned into my lapels, 'before they, like . . .' He tried to whisper but in his pissed state it came out too loud. I moved my face away from the gobs of spit he flung from his mouth. 'Well, you know what they did in the end. But before that, there was . . .'

Malky straightened himself and shuffled back a few steps. His Hush Puppies squeaked on the church hall's laminate flooring. And then he did it. I couldn't believe he did it, but he did . . . he touched the side of his nose and gave me a little wink.

It seemed a moment like no other. Make this a movie – that's your Oscar clip right there. He felt on form, in his own mind. This was the juiciest slice of gossip he'd had in years and he itched to serve it up.

He shuffled again, got right up close. God, he looked rough, like Johnny Cash circa 2008. A white ring of dried spit sat around Malky's mouth, catching in the corners, like the Mekong Delta . . . Jeez, you could have stripped the Forth Bridge with this guy's breath.

'Now, Gus, you never heard it from me,' he said, 'but I know for a fact there was . . .' he looked over his shoulder, and then, he did it again, winked, 'there was torture, his father told me so.'

'Spill it, Malky,' I said. Immediately, I regretted this, he belched up a wet sliver of lager-perfumed bile onto my tie. 'Man, be careful there,' I yelled, loosening the knot and tugging the wet loop of cloth over my head. 'It's ruined, Malky!'

'Sorry, it's the emotion.'

Emotion my arse, unless they're selling emotion in six packs these days.

'That poor boy ... that poor bloody boy,' he said.

'*What?*' Steering a drunk to his point, without having taken a good bucket yourself, is a task and a half. I felt ready to give up, try the sausage rolls. Then he hit me with it.

'His fingernails, and his toenails – they were pulled out,' said Malky. 'Blood everywhere.'

'*Christ!*'

'Can you imagine the pain of that, Gus? Hell, it's sore as buggery just catching one of those wee hangnails.'

I didn't need convincing.

'Plod said it was suicide, Malky.'

'My arse! He moved in some shady circles, our young Billy.'

I felt loath to admit it, but Malky had my attention now. 'Was that it, just the nails?'

'If only it was, Gus. God, I hear they did his teeth as well.'

'Pulled them?'

'Think so. They say there wasn't much to go on after the gun went off in his face. Must have pissed off some serious people.'

'Have the filth any ...' I needed to use the word – no other came to mind – but it stung my lips as it passed, made me sound like a character from *The Bill*, '*leads?*'

'They could give a tinker's toss. He was mixing it with gangsters, man. I kid you not, he was into all sorts. One less for them to worry about now, though.'

'What *was* he into?' I couldn't believe Billy had the marbles to ... Hang on, it was precisely because he didn't have any nous that Billy *would* get involved with this kind of thing.

Malky shrugged. He remembered who he was talking to. The shoulder movement wasn't welcome and his frame looked fit to collapse before me. I felt glad, really. I'd no desire to hear any more. It sounded like a tragedy of the type to make you want to pack up and leave this troubled city.

As if I needed to look for reasons.

I KNEW GUS DURY WHEN ... *when*? When he held down a job? When he still had a wife? When he never drank himself to oblivion every night? I knew that's what they said, once Billy got put in the ground, and everyone ended up back at Col's pub.

The Wall, or the Holy Wall as Col's mates called it, is a bit different to the usual Edinburgh watering hole. There's no polished granite bar, Baccardi Breezers, or rocket salad on the menu. Down at heel is the way the ad agency ponytails might describe the Holy Wall. The floor's linoleum, the seats, PVC. There are so many layers of nicotine in the joint you'd get a decent rollie out the woodchips. It's rough beyond belief. Just my style.

The name suits too; you see Col has faith. The Big Faith. And faith in me. Don't know why, he just does. He says he sees something in me. I suspect it's the Grouse and Black. Col doesn't drink, but for me it's a full-time job.

'I was sorry to hear about how Billy . . . you know, went, Col. Really very sorry,' I mumbled, broke up my words and choked on ciggie smoke. This was something I'd wanted to say from the heart, but it got slopped out. 'Malky – y'know the wideo – he gave me the rundown. I'm so sorry, Col. Really very sorry.'

Col placed a hand on my shoulder, 'You heard all about it, did you?'

I lowered my brows; gave a brief nod.

'My Billy shouldn't have went like that. He was talking about making it big the last time we spoke – he was full of grand plans, you know.'

Col trembled, stammered on his words. He seemed to age decades before my eyes.

'He was full of talk about making his pile, Gus, but he went wrong somewhere. His mother's beside herself, the house is a total midden – you should see the state of it!'

I felt taken aback, but I saw he'd only reverted to type, tried to cover his feelings with humour.

I joined him, said, 'I don't do dusting, Col.'

Laughter.

We'd lightened the tone. Col tried a weak smile. 'I have no work for you in that line, but there *is* something you could do for me.'

He leaned on the bar. His eyes widened, showing their whites, but the dark centres haunted. 'You know about this kind of thing, don't you?'

I tried to look away but his eyes left me nowhere to hide.

'Col, I'm out the game.'

'But you have the form. This kind of thing's just your line.'

I knew what he meant, but that felt like another lifetime ago.

I raised my glass, drained it. 'This is my line now.'

'Gus, c'mon, you forget I knew you before.'

I knew what *before* meant right away.

The thing is, I owe Col. Not in a debt sense, just – well – morally. He's been good to me since my troubles started, a bit like a father figure. Not like my father though. Uh-uh. The mighty Cannis Dury has few to match him. You might say it's because Col is so unlike my old man that I feel he deserves my respect.

'I'd like to help, I really would, but what could I do?'

'Same as before when we had that spot of bother.'

When everything went tits up for me, Col helped out. Some of his employees thought they'd been recruited on two hundred a week and all they could pilfer. He gave me the security gig and a roof over my head. I felt very grateful. Still do.

'That was a different matter entirely.' On-site snoop to jumped-up gumshoe looked quite a leap to me. I felt happy enough with our current arrangement – free flat, only a stumble from the bar.

'Just have a look around in the city, go to your old mates and do some sniffing about.'

'Hacks have no mates, Col.'

'You're no hack – quality you are boyo!'

I laughed. 'Half right. I'm no hack any more.'

I raised my glass, motioned to the whisky on the shelf. Col fired off a refill, planted it in front of me. His eyes widened again. When I looked in them I saw they'd grown rimmed in red. I saw the worry there. Genuine grief. I knew the territory.

'No promises,' I said.

He smiled, and those eyes of his shone like headlamps. 'It's a deal. Gus, I could ask no more. You've no idea what this means to me. The father–son bond is a very precious thing.'

'Tell me about it,' I said.

I DON'T KNOW HOW LONG I've been soaking up dosser life. A year anyway, maybe longer. Most of my time's been spent at the Holy Wall, listening to Col's sermons, but never acting on them. He's funny that way: deep in his religion. It's like we're both a world apart, which truth be told, is probably just what I need.

I know his heart's in the right place. He wants to motivate me, get me back into the life. But I already know I don't want it. I haven't the stomach for it. All I want now is a few beers of an evening, plenty of whisky chasers. Some good books would be nice, and maybe a dog. Would have to be a mutt, a real mongrel. Mutts are definitely the most loyal.

'You can keep the rest – possessions, people, respect,' I thought as I strolled through the city.

Everywhere the old place was being torn down, brand new glass and chrome apartments going up in place of memories. I just didn't buy into this new lifestyle thing. I aimed for an anti-lifestyle. Trendy magazines weren't queuing up to feature my idea of happiness in their glossy pages.

I headed up Abbeyhill in the East End, on my way to Calton Hill. It's the place they put on all the postcards. Edinburgh – the place to be, huh? City of spires and cobbled streets. Tartan and bagpipes. A culture capital, a gourmet's delight . . . don't get me started: I know the real story.

Now, with most days to myself, I like to take to the high ground and look down. Just watch the place. Think about the time I played a role in the mess, before I fell off the merry-go-round.

Seagulls squawked overhead, threatened to shit on me. I looked up, shouted, 'Bugger off, would you?'

Bloody vermin. Rats with wings, that's what they are. Birds and me don't get on, just ask my soon to be ex-wife.

'Piss off, vermin,' I yelled.

An old woman stuck out her bobble-hatted head.

'Sorry, missus,' I said. A killer frown fired at me. 'Sorry, again.'

I slunk off to a bench. Dipped into my mobile mini-bar. It's very mini – I only carry the basics – quarter bottle of scoosh in a brown paper bag.

I know, I know. A real jakey look with the bag. But I like it. There's an honesty about it. The first time I bought a quarter bottle and the bloke in Booze and News put it in a brown bag I thought, 'No way.' Simply too dero, even for me.

I carried it about, rustling inside my pocket for hours before I could touch it. But when I did, it felt like I'd put on a badge of honour that read: 'I drink! Get over it!'

A few quick shots settled me down. Always does the trick. Nothing like it for cooling the blood.

I tucked away the scoosh and ferreted for a piece of paper with some details from Col. 'What am I getting into now?' I thought. I'd enough to deal with on my own without taking on someone else's problems. But like they say, I could hardly say no.

The note was written on Basildon Bond. Col's careful copperplate handwriting listed some of the people I should talk to about Billy. People who knew him before his very public demise.

I scanned the names. 'Christ, Billy, you were a silly boy, weren't you?' I whispered.

The list read like a police round-up. I knew some of old. Mostly, they were small-time crims and hard men. Knuckle breakers and old pugs. I wouldn't be too keen to drop in on any for a chat.

Some of the names made me think. Made me think I wanted to fire down some more whisky. It's the drinker's way: it burns, so you drink and it doesn't. But this was Col's gig. The holding-folding in my pocket was for finding his boy's killer, not pissing up the wall.

I got moving.

Started to roll over what Col had told me.

There was a girl in the picture, her name was Nadja, and she gave Col what the Scots call the bowk. For a placid guy he'd got pretty steamed up at the mention of her. I reckoned her to be a long shot to begin with, but Col supplied a number for her, and I had to start somewhere.

I picked up my mobi. It stank of fags: Benson's.

'Hello? Hello there, my name's Gus Dury.'

Silence.

I heard breathing on the other end of the line.

'Hello,' I said again, 'I was wondering if . . . Look, is this Nadja? Billy's father, Col, gave me your number.'

'This is Nadja.' The accent sounded thick, Eastern European. She reminded me of the Bond character Onatop. I hoped she wasn't going to be as much trouble.

I kept it brief. 'I wondered if we could meet. I'd like to talk to you about Billy.'

I expected a few tears. Word shuffling at least, but got, 'I have no-thing to say.'

I moved the phone to my other hand. 'Look, I knew Billy a bit, and I really think—'

She cut me off. 'That means no-thing to me.' The phone got shuffled, hand to hand. 'You are finished, yes?'

I drew in the big guns, showed her I wasn't messing here. 'Look, lady, if I'm finished with you already, the filth's my next stop.'

Silence, again.

I pitched my tone to a whisper, got that edge of menace in there. 'You hearing me?'

She let that bounce about a bit, then the line fizzed from her end. 'There is a place, the Shandwick, do you know it?'

A hotel in the New Town, the classier end, green and tweeds territory. 'Yeah, George Street. Bit outta my league.'

'Be there at three.'

I put the phone down, the screen misted over. My mind felt pretty cloudy too.

I had a few hours to play with so trailed the cobbles down to Leith Walk and on to the Bull's Head. Inside I ordered a Jim Beam and chased it with another. Felt the fire of it settle my insides and raised the glass again. The heavy barman, gut like a wrecking ball, promptly filled up.

A danger sign flashed in my mind, 'Steady, Gus.' A siren wailed, but got howled out by a gale of cravings. In the mirror over the bar I caught sight of someone I half recognised. His skin looked white as a maggot, his eyes dipped in mustard. I took a drink and instantly felt just like when you're in the station and the train next to yours starts to move.

I stared at myself some more. I looked rough as guts and only half as welcoming. I thought, 'I wouldn't like to bump into myself on a dark night.'

My hair looked too long and I had the bloated Jim Morrison, Paris '71 look about me – the way he looked on four packs of Marlboro and a couple of bottles of brandy a day.

I kept hearing 'The End'. Round and round in my head, 'This is the e-e-end'. After a power of drink I passed out. Came to with bats swooping me. My hands shook so badly I missed with every swipe at them. But they soon left. They never last long. And anyway, it's the buzzards you really need to worry about.

I glanced up at the barman; he polished a pint glass, arm rested on his gut. He'd missed my blackout and I didn't want to stay for him to catch the next one. I got up to leave.

In the daylight outside, I squinted. The sun started to creep through the clouds. I stumbled into the touristy centre of the city. Kilted mannequins strayed from every shop front and cutsey Greyfriars Bobby dogs begged to be picked up and drop-kicked into touch.

'Enough's enough,' I thought. 'Get me back to the East End and some blue-collar bliss.'

The Scott Monument looked black against the skyline, casting a shadow toward the tightly packed tenements of the Old Town. A breeze brought up the city smog, blew it down Princes Street. Diesel fumes, strong enough to taste, swirled about. The only thing that knocks out those babies is the brewery fumes. I thanked Christ for their absence.

I felt no joy to be this deep in the heart of a chocolate box. A crippling embarrassment crept up on me, and I pulled up my collar. All very Mel Gibson in *Conspiracy Theory* – but who was I kidding?

'The way you look, Dury, your own mother would be lucky to pick you,' I told myself.

On the pavement an American tourist stopped me. He looked like he'd just walked from the pages of a Ralph Lauren catalogue. All veneered teeth and spray-on tan. Hitting fifty, but fighting it. He smarmed at me; I expected to be asked something as dumb and inane as all Americans ask when they stop you on Princes Street. Something like: 'Can you tell me how to get to Rabbi Burns' synagogue?'

I tried a side step. Tourist was light on his feet, obviously working out too. He jumped before me and produced a Groucho Marx style cigar. 'Have you a match, buddy?' he said.

I looked him in the eye and hit him with: 'Not since Errol Flynn died!'

He stepped back to let me pass. As I walked off, I glanced round to catch him put his mouth into an O and remove the cigar, stupefied.

Some people are so easy to set straight. But something told me Nadja might not be such a pushover.

THE SHANDWICK LOOKED PLUSH. Billy's girl obviously had a taste for the finer things in life. I'd passed the place many times but had never been in. I'd promised Debs to visit as a treat one of these days, but that seemed like a long time ago, before we started communicating through lawyers.

Col had given me a description of Nadja, he said she looked classy, but was 'A little gold-digger'. Straight away, I saw he was wrong on one count, either that or Col and I had different ideas of class.

She had the standard footballer's wife look: peroxide blonde, shag-me boots, what the Scots call 'All fur coat and nae knickers'.

I took a chair at her table on the back veranda and introduced myself. 'I'm Gus Dury,' I said.

'Should the name mean something to me?' said Nadja, as she pinched her lips into a little red cupid's bow. 'Very cute,' I thought.

I hit back. 'Maybe once.' I mean, who was I? A nobody? Well, yes, but *she* didn't need to know that.

She paused, lit a cigarette, Dunhill, asked, 'Why are you here, Mr Dury?'

Starting early, eh? I matched her with: 'I think we both know why.'

A smooth blue trail of smoke left her lips as the waiter arrived, with a menu as thick as the phonebook.

'Will you be having lunch with us, sir?'

I had to do a double take. Couldn't remember being called that for a long time. 'Eh, no.' Wasn't planning to stay long. 'Nothing, thanks.' I felt ready to drink the place dry, but kept focused.

Nadja raised her heavily mascaraed eyes. 'Bring him a tea . . . Earl Grey.'

She waved him off, I stuck my hand in front of him. 'Better make it an Earl Brown, pal!'

'Excuse me, sir?'

'I don't do tea. I'll settle for hot chocolate, though.'

Nadja shooed the waiter away with an impatient flurry of her carefully manicured mitts. 'Who sent you?' she said.

'Sorry, no can do. Client confidentiality.' It felt good taking the reins. 'I need to know a few things like, for a kick-off, when did you last see Billy – features intact?' What the hell, she didn't seem to need pussy footing around.

'I have no idea,' she snapped. She looked rattled, puffed briskly on her Dunhill, 'Maybe it is three weeks.'

'That's a long time. What did the police say to that?'

Her expression hardened at the mention of the filth, but her voice somehow managed to soften, 'Business quite often took Billy away for long periods of time.'

Business. The last time I clapped eyes on the lad his business was collecting football stickers and looking for swaps. He'd barely hit twenty. Now I know this is a moneyed old town and people can rise faster than Basil's hackles, but something didn't quite square with the Billy I knew.

'What business?' I said.

She looked away, avoiding eye contact. She took a brief glance at her watch and a flash of tongue came out to moisten her lips. 'I have no idea.'

'You've already used that one.' I wasn't buying it a second time.

Nadja leaned forward, drew deeply on the Dunhill, and then flung back her carefully layered blonde hair as she wet her lips again.

'Mr Dury, I understand perfectly that you have a job to do,' she smiled at me, showing off a set of teeth that seemed far too white and far too straight to be this far from LA, 'but could you keep me out of your . . . investigation?' She whispered her last word with a pout.

I had her pegged.

'That'll never happen,' I snarled. The words sounded just as harsh as

I'd hoped they would. I even managed a rasping, throaty little alkie's cough at the end, just to ram home how immune I was to her charms. 'You're out, plod's in – that's the deal, and believe me, I'm a lot easier to get on with.'

She quickly stubbed out the cigarette. It snapped off at the filter. She started firing out words at me: 'He worked for a man called Benny Zalinskas. He has some properties that Billy looked after. You know, keeping tenants happy, that kind of thing. He took care of Benny's business. Now, is there anything else you need to know? Or can I let you get on with . . . whatever.' She threw herself back in the chair, arms raised to the ceiling in exasperation. It seemed an overly theatrical gesture for these genteel surroundings; Edinburgh ladies who lunch don't generally raise more than a pinkie in company.

I pressed harder. 'And what else does Benny do?'

Col had told me that Billy started out driving a van, humping furniture from one gaff to another. It seemed a big jump to hear he'd been running the show. I'd known people to make big jumps in this city before, but generally not from so far down.

'I do not understand. What is it that you mean?' said Nadja.

'Any work that might not be so . . . above board?'

She shook her head wildly. A loud huff pulled in a few more glances, and then she stood up to leave.

'I don't think I can be of any more help to you,' she said, bringing her heels down hard on the Shandwick's expensive quarry tiles.

I frowned. Looked down at her seat and motioned, sit. I was ice. God knows where I found this line in cool.

'I'm gonna need names, numbers and addresses,' I said. 'Unless you'd sooner deal with plod.'

IT TURNED OUT BILLY COLLECTED his wages from an East End kip house run by Benny Zalinskas. I liked the sound of the place, Brigadoon House. But when I checked it out, I found a better name would have been Fallingdoon.

The man on the desk turned out to be a Russian with a thick accent. I smiled and joked with him, then handed over a wodge of cash, said, 'Tell me when that runs out.'

I'd seen this done on *Miami Blues* and always wanted to try it. Alec Baldwin could make any line sound cool back then before he piled on the pounds, and totally lost it, dumped Kim Basinger.

The cash before me got counted faster than any bank teller's effort. The Russian's smile disappeared faster yet. 'Monday,' he said.

Now I was in *Miami Blues*, had to fight saying, 'Get me a girl, Pablo.' Went with: 'You jest.'

His eyes widened. I figured he wasn't kidding. I stayed at the counter for a moment, then carried my bag to the room.

He shouted at my back, 'No drinking and no drugs on the premises.'

I turned around and gave my best dagger-throwing stare. I knew the words, 'Know you bloody Scots,' would be muttered under breath soon. It was one of the side effects of the city's drive to embrace multiculturalism; we were the minority in some places.

I dumped my bag in the room. I'd been kipping above Col's bar for the last three months or so. The tiny flat was crammed in above the gents and reeked like the Waverley Steps at chucking out time. My new room looked small, shabby in the extreme, but it seemed like a step up for me.

I checked myself in the mirror: faded denim jacket, slightly more faded 501s, torn at knee, and my crowning glory, cherry Docs, scuffed all to hell. I looked like Jim from *Taxi*, the spaced-out one.

Something needed to give. I'd been getting looks on the street. The kind of loser stares that shout, 'Get a job, you bum!' They set me right off. That kinda thing, it hits at the core of me. I knew I needed to smarten up my act.

I splashed water on my face. Ran fingers through my hair. It was so long it sat back without trouble. I needed some serious grooming attention, but fought the urge to begin right away.

I filled up the kettle, one of those jug types. Ripped open a sachet of Nescafé. I felt ready for a caffeine hit. I felt ready for something stronger to tell the truth, but that would have to wait.

The cup barely touched my mouth when the door went. A delicate little knock like a child, or maybe, if my luck was in, a woman. I opened up. In the jamb stood a small old man, hunched over and as frail as lace.

He rubbed at his fingers, said, 'I hate that, the knocking plays terror on me hands.'

I looked down. His fingers seemed to be folded at right angles. Great bulges of bone stuck out where arthritis twisted its way through them.

'Howya, I'm Milo,' he said holding out a hand, bravely, I thought.

'Pleased to meet you.' I hardly touched his two most prominent fingers. They felt soft and cold. Skin as smooth as a baby's, nothing like they looked. 'I'm Gus,' I said.

'I heard you come in, heard the *no drink* speech. Thought you might be from the Old Country. I'm a Limerick man m'self – you?'

'Eh no, I'm a Leith boy, through and through.' I caught a deck at the disappointment in the old man's eyes. He looked lonely. I felt the misery waft out of him, it kicked my heart like Bruce Lee in slow mo. 'Look, the kettle's just boiled. Can I get you a coffee?'

'Have you tea?'

I looked on the tray by the kettle. 'Eh, no. Sorry.'

'I'm a tea man really. I'd have taken a sup o' tea with ye – coffee does my insides great distress.' He sat himself down by the wall in the room's only chair. 'Are ye with the Trust?'

'The Trust?'

'Christian Fellowship. They put me up here. It's a bastard of a place really.'

'Brigadoon?'

'Brigadoon my arse! It's run by Russkies. They're all over the place hereabouts, it's like Red Square, I tell ye.'

I ventured a laugh.

'Do they look after you, Milo?'

'They could care less.' He raised a gnarled thumb over his shoulder. 'Yon Stalin's a cute hoor.'

'*Stalin?*'

'It's what I call him – yer man what runs the place, he's as sour as all get out. Him and the rest. Has roughnecks in and out at all hours. Still, I guess they won't have me here for much longer.'

'On the move?'

He laughed like a roar. Went into a hacking cough and had to wipe his eyes. 'I'm eighty-seven, my next move will be my last, son.'

I smiled. My stomach fluttered when he called me son. 'You're wearing well for your years, Milo.'

He started up again, laughing into tears. 'Jaysus, isn't that the best yet. You're a terrible liar, my friend.'

I felt embarrassed. Heat rose on my face. I hoped I hadn't offended him. I really liked the old boy, said, 'Don't they say there's many a good tune played on an old fiddle, though.'

His eyes sparkled. They matched the coldest of blue, but beyond them I saw he was still a young man. 'Aren't ye a ticket, Gus . . . Gus what is it, now?'

'Dury.'

'I've enjoyed your company, Gus Dury, but I won't keep you. Only wanted to stick my head in and say hello.' He stood up, it seemed to take him an age. And then he made for the door. I grabbed the handle and prised it open for him. He nodded graciously. 'I knew a Dury once – a Kerry man – have ye roots in Kerry?'

'No, sorry.'

'That's good. Wasn't he a prick entirely!'

I laughed out and placed a hand delicately on Milo's back. 'See you again.'

I watched him shuffle across the hall and struggle with the key in the lock. It dug in my heart like a pick handle, but I knew he'd be too proud to accept any help.

'I'll get some tea in,' I shouted at his back.

He raised a crippled hand above his head in a wave, and then vanished back into his lonely world.

Alone, I lay down on the bed and started to think. Always dangerous territory for a drinker. Wondered would I reach Milo's age? Never. Dylan Thomas's last words were: 'Eighteen whiskies, I think that's the record.' He was thirty-nine when he died.

I did the math: it gave me three years to beat Dylan's best effort.

'The way I'm going,' I thought, 'I probably won't need that long.'

DOWN TIME.

I lay on the bed stacking up my prospects. Didn't take long to count to zip. I felt a serious need for distraction. I knew by agreeing to help Col I'd put myself in danger of resurrecting some ghosts, but somehow managed to push it to the back of my mind. A friend in need and all that – but was I really being selfless? A pop psychologist inside me wondered: 'Are there demons you have to confront, Gus Dury?'

Bollocks. If there were demons, they ran the show.

I sparked up a Marlboro red top, as near to a crack pipe as you can buy over the counter, a proper lung-bleeder. I got the Docs loosened off, kicked them on to the floor. I balanced a heavy smoked-glass ashtray on my chest and flicked away at the grey as it mounted on the tab's end.

Jesus, did I really think I had a chance of tracking down who'd done in Col's boy? I tried to shut it out, but a quote, Wilde I think, went round and round in my mind: 'Experience is the name a man gives to his mistakes.'

I had plenty of experience. It flooded back to me now, thick and fast.

I'd held down a top job. Handled the big stories. Had been a name.

'When does this Dury sleep?' I'd overheard the paper's chairman say to the editor once. Mr Bacon, or Rasher, as I called the boss, appeared underwhelmed – as he always did. It made no odds to me, though, because my self-destruct switch had already been flipped. For some of us, it's never far out of reach.

I had been assigned to a press call at the new parliament building, the half-a-billion-pound fiasco. Some junior government bod stepped forward to talk about immigration, as the whole country became gripped by rabid nationalism. Living in fear of Johnnie Foreigner flooding through the Channel tunnel to steal our jobs. The tweedy arse-wipe Alisdair Cardownie, Assistant Minister for Immigration, jumped right on the vibe of hatred. Talking tough on an emotive issue to boost his profile. I'd seen it a million times before. Truth told, I cared less about the ramblings of another slack-jowled, in-bred son of privilege.

It felt cold out and I fought off a killer hangover: a real shades on a grey day scenario. My snapper, Ronnie, bought me a quarter of Black Bush to steady my nerves, said, 'Here he comes, you set, Gus?'

I nodded. Tanned most of the bottle in one.

The chauffeur pulled up and some overpaid flunkey ran out like a doorman at Harrods who's just spotted Elton John getting out the back of a Bentley.

'Holy shit! Did you see that?' I said.

'Steady,' said Ronnie. He hunkered down and started firing off some shots.

I approached with my Dictaphone outstretched. 'Minister, could I ask a few questions?'

Banal looks, pointed in my direction.

'Minister, if you don't mind?' I kept it polite, but frustration brewed. I mean, his lot had called us here, it wasn't for me to do the running. I stepped up a gear, leaned forward. 'If you don't mind, Minister, I'd just like to ask about your plans to close down the people smugglers?'

I felt an arm on my chest. Another, with an open palm on the end, thrust in my face. 'No interviews,' said the flunkey. I couldn't see the flunkey's face, only the junior minister's hiding behind a group of cling-ons. He wore a satisfied, smug, you-can't-touch-me look I'd seen before.

'*What?*' I said.

'No interviews,' repeated the flunkey.

'What do you mean no interviews? It's a press call for Chrissake!' I felt close to losing it, big time. And then this little mollycoddled arse-wipe of a minister got my goat. He led it out before me on a bit of rope and kicked it in the bollocks. In the next second he clicked his fingers like Brando in *The Freshman* and a shower of suited-up grunts man-handled me like crowd controllers.

'Get your fucking hands off me,' I shouted.

I felt the blood start to pump inside my head. I saw Ronnie covering his eyes like he didn't want to look, and then, something clicked. My throat went dry . . . and I let out a haymaker right.

'Oh God!' I heard Ronnie scream.

My punch caught no one but threw me off balance so much that I lunged forward, head first chasing its grand arc. Suddenly the minister loomed before me and, in no time at all, my brow connected cleanly with his nose.

It was the kind of diving header that might have graced the dying moments of a European Cup final. I must have looked fearless. Like some mad pogoing skin out on the lash. But it was totally unintentional.

'My nose, my nose,' the minister whined.

People gathered around, said:

'Tip back your head.'

'Take this handkerchief.'

'Put a key down his back.'

Ronnie just about cried. 'What have you done, Gus?' he said.

'It was just a tap. A tap, that's all it was,' I said.

I couldn't believe the fuss. Then the cuffs came out, and I felt the heat of a thousand camera flashes go off.

I made all the evening news broadcasts. A career first. And last. Rasher had my desk cleared while I sat in a cell. I'd left the office for the last time. I had no plans to return.

I stubbed the Marlboro. It lay flat in the ashtray, stray insect legs of tobacco squashed under it. I got to my feet and searched the room.

'Paper. Where is it?' I said.

I pulled open a few drawers. Hissed at a Gideon Bible, then: 'Bingo!'

Hardly the Dorchester on the heading but, never mind, it would have to do. I began to compose a letter to Debs. If she was gonna send me any more mail from her lawyer, she'd better have some facts.

I AWOKE WITH A START, loud Irish curses filled the air all around me. I heard a thud, then another. For a moment I thought I'd returned to my childhood, my father after me with his razor strop, then reality flooded in.

'It's fucked entirely, man, have ye not the sense God gave ye?' Milo's voice berated all hell out of somebody. I reached for my 501s. They felt soft, smooth as velvet after a thousand visits to the laundrette. I rushed in with my big toe and caught a hole in the knee, stretched a tear near halfway down the leg, said, 'Christ on a bike!' This was all I needed; I'd a busy day ahead.

When I looked down the hallway I saw straight into Milo's little world. 'Can I get you a hammer?' I said.

'Ah, Mr Dury, it's your bold self.' His face lit up like a Chinese lantern. 'And how are we this grand morning?'

'I'd be better for a bit of sleep, to tell you the truth.'

'Sleep, bollocks. A youngster like ye should be up and about, availing yourself of all the wonders of this fine morn.'

Another thud sounded behind him, Milo turned back towards the source of it. 'Walloping's not going to mend the thing! Would ye ever fecking listen?' He shook his head, turned back to me, raised eyes aloft, said, 'Eejit.'

'Trouble?'

'Telly's on the blink. Yon Russki thinks kicking the shite out of it's the answer – I tell you, it's Stalingrad all over!'

I laughed and gave Milo an understanding nod, then turned back to my room. As I closed the door I heard him cheer. I'm sure Anne Robinson blasted a contestant on *The Weakest Link* for all of a millisecond, before banging on the TV resumed.

I mouthed, 'Nut house,' and looked to the heavens.

Got booted and suited. Grabbed my jacket. Checked the pocket – I still had some holding-folding. Col had seen me right so far but I would need to tap some more expenses soon.

On the way out Milo roared like Doran's ass. I heard him as I hit the street and pulled up my collar. It felt cold enough to grate cheese on my pods. Shit, it was Edinburgh, but nice to be out as Kelly Jones says.

Cars clogged up the crossroads at the top of Easter Road. I choked on the fumes from the school-run mums in their Stockbridge tractors. It was too early a start for me. I usually miss all this mayhem. The days when I needed to be at a desk by nine sharp were long gone.

I watched the pinstriped yuppies power walking towards fifty-grand-a-year, superannuation and medical benefits – would need to come with a crate load of Prozac to get me interested. The big thing with the suits this season appeared to be massive collars and cuffs. Real Harry Hill jobs. They made me laugh, the bloody comedians.

Beyond the grass embankment on London Road, a drinking school knocked the froth off a few cans of Special Brew. The Flower of Scotland got its first airing of the day. Never ceases to amaze me, it's always time for a celebration with this crew. The desk jockeys shirked past them, eyes down, upping their pace till a few steps clear, then they dropped down a gear.

I let out a wide smile on my way past. I ventured brief applause when the performance finished. They loved it. Thing is, I know my own coat's hung on a slack hook as well.

I headed on past the cottagers' cludgie. Too early to see any Careless Fisters, as they'd been renamed following the George Michael contretemps.

Every manor has its Huggy Bear. Just like the character from *Starsky and Hutch*, they know the lot. I figured if any theories on Billy's demise had been put about the East End then Mac the Knife would know.

Mac's a character. What his native Glaswegians call a chib man. Very handy with a knife, until he landed a score at Her Majesty's extreme displeasure. After the best part of eight years in the Riddrie Hilton, Mac fled to Edinburgh and never looked back. Now he'd turned his attention to the more mundane task of hairdressing. He'd seen to my short back and sides for more than a year before I got the story behind his half Chelsea smile. I've never watched a barber more closely since.

A bell chimed and a Super Mario lookalike greeted me with a black robe at the ready. 'Is it yourself under all that?'

'The very same.'

Mac flung the robe over his shoulder, a silver comb in one hand and a set of scissors in the other, he stretched out his arms to hug me. I leaned forward, watched my back in the floor to ceiling mirrors.

'It's good tae see you, pal,' he said. 'Come in, come in. Get yourself oot the cold.'

Mac's patter hadn't changed in years. By the look of him neither had his T-shirt – an early eighties job with the words 'I Came On Eileen' printed across the front.

I said, 'Thanks,' took him up on the offer of a coffee.

Mac looked to be aiming for a more up-market clientele than usual. The way this city was headed, he'd no choice, but it seemed like a struggle against the grain. Especially as the waft of Brut 33 still filled the joint.

The coffee came with a wafer and a little bunch of grapes, three to be precise, on the side.

'What the hell's this?' I said.

'Call it a wee garnish, eh.'

'I'll call it what it is – bloody pretentious!'

'Pretentious . . . *moi*? You say the most hurtful things.' Mac smiled at me in the mirror. 'Right, what can I do for you, big man?'

'Information.'

His comb hovered above my head, he shifted it sideways, said, 'I meant the haircut, pal.'

'Short, very. And lose the beard.'

He ruffled my mullet in progress, grabbed up a sizeable ponytail. 'Do you want your hair cut round the back?'

I joked with him: 'Why? Have you no room in the shop?'

'Ha-ha. Funny man.'

He started cutting.

I started probing. 'Billy Thompson.'

'Uh-hu.' Mac looked unfazed. Always his way of doing things. If he knew something, it needed teasing out of him. Though he hadn't been part of a firm for decades, he still liked to be seen as part of the life, a man in the know.

'Shame for the boy,' I said.

'Och, we're all headed the same road, Gus.'

'Some quicker than others.'

'True. True.'

I upped the ante. 'Mac, his family's ruined. Have you a family of your own?'

'Gus . . .' He stopped cutting and looked at me over the comb. 'You know I've a family.'

I snapped, 'Well, stop buggering about and tell me what you know.'

Mac looked in the mirror. His mouth became a taut wire. 'Relax, would you?' he said softly. This Weejie obviously took notes in the anger-management classes. I pulled out my cigarettes and showed Mac the packet.

'Oh, go on then, haven't had a red top since Adam was a boy in Dumbarton Rock.'

We sparked up and started to fill the small shop with smoke. It seemed to relax us both.

Mac said, 'He was an early riser.'

'What – from his pit in the mornings?'

'No. No. He was on the up.' Mac raised his hands, crossed his brows, then continued, 'The last time I saw Billy Boy he was driving about in a Merc, not any Merc, a fifty-grander. Don't think it was his, mind.'

'Benny Zalinskas?'

Mac's eyes widened. Then they dropped like lead weights. He turned quickly back to the job at hand. 'I don't know.'

'Mac, come on, you can't kid a kidder.'

'I really don't know. Probably was the Bullfrog's, he didn't say.'

'Whoa, whoa, back up there. The Bullfrog?'

'Aye, that's his handle. Benny the Bullfrog.'

I laughed. 'Nice one – so, so scary!'

Mac smirked, then the smirk trailed off and his face changed. Suddenly a grey pallor settled on him. A real shit-stopping seriousness.

'Gus, that whole firm's bad news,' he said. 'You don't want to get involved.'

'Then put me off,' I said.

'I don't know what to say. I'm well out of it . . . *Christ*, in my day carving seemed scary enough, these days all the firms have shooters coming out their arses, but nobody messes with Benny's mob.'

'Why? You telling me he just got off the plane from Moscow one day, took over a well-established patch and nobody said boo to him?'

'He has the numbers. He's well big, Gus – the Edinburgh firm's a minor spoke in his wheel.' Mac pointed the scissors at me. 'This guy's fucking Blockbusters, do you get me?'

'Whatever you say.'

'I mean it, stay away.'

'And what do I tell Billy's family? I got scared off so your boy's murderer is just gonna be left to walk the streets. No can do, Mac. I owe his father answers.'

Mac threw up his hands once again, said, 'You're done.'

'Come again?'

'That'll be five fifty.'

'But what about the beard?'

ON THE WAY OUT MAC'S door I bumped into someone I'd been meaning to call.

'I might have guessed you'd be headed in there. Is this the *on trend* clientele Mac's going for?'

'Bollocks to that, he owes me big time. Who you think splashed for the decor?'

'Decor – Christ, you're getting la-de-fucking-da, Hod.'

A smile. Laughs.

'It's business speak. You know me.'

'Aye, into everything bar a shit sandwich.'

'That's about right – anyway, what about that room I offered you?'

Hod was an old, old friend. One I'd kind of let slide, since letting things slide became my way of life. To his credit, he'd kept up, even offered to dig me out of a few holes.

'Yeah, I'm all for it. Just give me a couple of days to get sorted and I'll bell you.'

'No worries.'

Hod turned, swaggered through Mac's door like John Wayne, testing the hinges. Mac waved me off again, I wasn't done with him, but he was a slow burner. I knew I'd have to let him think I really needed him before he'd come up with the goods. If I was lucky, I'd sown enough seeds. Mac's type love to be useful, just can't help themselves.

I took a stroll down Princes Street. One messed-up main drag if ever there was one. They say the tills ring up more moolah here than any other street in Scotland. That's no mean feat, especially when you consider there's only shops on one side of the road. On the other, there's a gigantic medieval castle complete with cannons and crumbling battlements. There's a stretch of grass at the foot of it that we call the Gardens. Its 24–7 soundtrack is the skirl of bagpipes; strictly for the city-breakers.

I stuck to the right side of the road. The place seemed to be awash with trendy types. Everyone looked the same – I just don't get fifty-somethings dressing like beat boys. No matter how trendy it becomes, I won't be carrying a manbag; I won't be wearing shoes that curl up like Ali Baba's slippers; and the day you see me in a hoodie and Kappa cap, I'm on my way to put a gun to my head.

Still, my look played on my mind. After a few brews I cared less, but now I had people to impress. I checked myself in Currys shop window. Sorry, Currys.digital. Sure that dot makes all the difference to the paying public. Mac had done a beast of a job with my barnet, cropped to the wood but with a little weight on top. I looked halfway to respectable.

As I stared, something caught my eye inside the shop. A face I recognised appeared on the wall of television screens. I went inside to catch the verbals, it turned out to be a man I knew well. The Right Honourable Alisdair Cardownie MSP.

He banged on about stemming the tide of illegal immigration. I raised a laugh. Couldn't help but remember the time he was hardly able to stem the tide of his own nosebleed.

A title flashed up below his name, 'Minister for Immigration'. So he'd moved on then, landed the top job. A shudder jolted through me. Since our last meeting, I'd taken the opposite direction on the career ladder.

A voice from nowhere, a thick Geordie accent, suddenly landed within earshot, 'Is it a flatscreen you're after, sir?'

I turned round to see an acne-covered yoof. A mess of angry red plooks shone on his nose, so much gel slapped on his head he looked like the victim of a water-bombing prank.

'What?'

'The Sharp's our top seller. Is it for your living room?'

He started to fiddle with a little control panel hidden in the side of the telly. 'It's a great picture. I can really recommend the Sharp. I've got one myself. I bought it when they first came out and no one could believe the picture quality, it's so, *sharp*, I suppose. Would you like me to get one from the back?'

'Whoa now, catch your breath there . . . Mark.' I flicked his name tag. 'Can't a man look in this shop?'

He smiled. Showed off a row of grey teeth in need of severe grouting and repointing. I saw my accent had him beat.

In this city there's two types of shop assistant: the demonic home-grown variety and the deeply confused imported ones, like young Mark. You see, the sucking-up gene – a necessity of the salesman's trade – missed the Scots entirely. We don't do pleasant. Perhaps that's why, most of the time, the man with the tag's a southerner.

The yoof sized me up, went for a catch-all. 'You won't find much better than the Sharp in this range, sir. But if you were looking to go to the next level, we have— sir, sir!'

I left him standing.

Shop workers like young Mark just won't get off your case these days. Despite the fact I was obviously talking Mandarin to a satsuma, he was still gonna try and flog me a telly. A curt turn on the heels is the only language they understand. Was a time when 'Just browsing' got shot of them. Now it's like they're trained by the Japanese military. A whole generation on a mission. And taking no prisoners. How the likes of my dear old mother deals with them I'll never know. She has the patience of Job, Christ she needed it with my family, but things like patience and manners are a weakness you can't afford to show nowadays. Leastwise some butt-munch will walk all over you, and try to sell you a flatscreen telly.

I felt riled.

My temper spiked, to tell the truth. I'd purchases to make, couldn't expect to be taken seriously looking like Jim from *Taxi*, but I wasn't spending any of Col's hard earned on the high street.

I took my makeover down market, found a charity store, Save the Children. Bought up a pinstripe jacket, black 501s (very black) and a blue shirt with French collar.

I tried the lot on and looked the ticket. Bit like Paul Weller in his Jam days but updated for the twenty-first century.

I caught the old dear behind the counter smiling at me and laughed.

'What you need's a nice tie to go with it,' she said.

She'd a drawer full of them, great florid numbers and a few tartans thrown in.

'Eh, no thanks. I don't do ties.'

'Shame. I like a man in a tie.'

She looked morose, like she might go tearful on me at any minute.

'My Maurice always used to wear a tie,' she said, 'every day of his life, he wore a tie.'

Christ, now I felt bad. 'Okay, pick me out a tie – a nice one mind. I'm relying on your judgement and good taste to win the day for me.'

She smiled like a hyena and avidly rummaged among the ties. She picked out a horrendous turquoise and lavender swirl-effect number. It looked a real seventies kipper too. Totally bust the look.

'Perfect,' I said.

'You think so?'

'I love it. You couldn't have done any better. Those colours are just grand.'

'I'm glad you like it. It'll match the pinstripes.' She held it up to my new jacket.

'Well, wrap it up then,' I said.

A shake of the head. 'Och no, you have to put it on and let me see it with the outfit.'

I felt an involuntary wince creep onto my face. I chased it off with a broad grin. 'Right-oh.'

She watched me do up the tie and rang up my total on the till. I got change from twenty sheets.

'Thanks, then. I'll be seeing you,' I said, trying to appear truly grateful.

Outside I gave a wave. Turned and nearly knocked a young girl off her feet.

'Gus!' she said. She stared at the tie. 'Nice neckwear. Very . . . retro.'

BACK IN THE DAY, WHEN I had a name, I'd occasionally agree to take on keen youngsters looking for work experience. I'd a test, got the idea from Rabbitte, the band manager in The Commitments, asked: 'Who are your influences?'

Any mention of Pilger, they got shown the door.

Amy, on the other hand, came up with this ripper: 'Lois Lane!'

I thought she must have imagination or at least ambition. All she did have, however, was a burning desire to find her Superman. In the end she got shown the door. An Übermensch, I wasn't. But in those days she was jail bait, and I was very married. The girl before me now had, how can I put it, developed.

I pulled off the tie. Felt fortunate to be standing beside a bin, said, 'It wasn't my idea.'

Amy laughed. 'Hello Gus – you look great.' She gave me a smile. One of those welcoming, from the heart jobs. It made me melt.

'Thanks. You're a great liar.'

The headlight smile came on again. She gave off an air of total calm. I wondered if this was really the same Amy who had once been walked out the office by a security guard after a foot-stamping display of undying love for me before the entire newsroom.

'I'm on my way to a lecture,' she said, 'but it would be nice to, you know, catch up over coffee some time.'

'You're a student, then.'

'Sorta – it's art school.'

It sounded just the thing for Amy, put her excess energy to use. 'Art, wow . . . you look so focused now.'

A laugh. 'Changed days, eh?'

'No, I didn't mean . . . I wasn't trying to have a go.'

She reached over, touched my arm. 'Gus, I know. I'm only messing.'

'Sorry.'

'So, coffee then?'

I hesitated, then thought, why not? I had little else in my life. 'Okay. Great.'

She rummaged in a huge bag and produced what looked to be a complicated phone, said, 'Can I beam you?'

'Come again?'

'Have you got Bluetooth?'

'God no! I've a pen.'

She rolled up her sleeve. 'Write your number on there.'

As I wrote I felt suddenly self-conscious, like I was being watched. I shook it off, thought it was probably just nothing but when I raised my head I got a definite eyeball from a man in the street.

He was short, heavy in the build, a cube of a man carrying a three-day growth. As I caught his eye he took a newspaper out of his back pocket and started to read, leaning up against a lamp post, far too casually I thought.

'Friend of yours?' I asked Amy.

'No. Never seen him before. You okay for about five?'

'I'm good for five,' I said dipping into *Friends* speak. I blushed, then said, 'Er, five o'clock's fine.'

'Great. I'll text you to make sure, but will we say in there?' She pointed to a Starbucks, one of about fifty that seemed to have sprung up in Edinburgh in the last year or so.

'Christ, do we have to?'

'They do good coffee. You've not gone all health-nutty in your old age, have you?'

'That'll be right – Starbucks it is, then.'

She leant over and gave me a peck on the cheek. 'It's really good to see you again, Gus. It'll be good to talk – you know, clear the air as it were.' She turned quickly and gave a childish little wave as she went.

When I looked around the man with the newspaper had gone.

I CROSSED THE ROAD AT the lights and jumped on a number 11, heading down to Leith. The bus driver looked like a time-warped old Teddy boy with his greasy quiff and a swallow tattooed on his neck. His watch strap had studs in it like a pit bull's collar. Even though it felt about four below he was in shirt sleeves, and sweated like a pig on speed. Two big purple pools under his arms and a skitter down his back that looked like it'd just been shat out of his duck's arse. Public transport – no wonder the roads are clogged with cars.

A group of young yobs made a racket on the back seat, cursing strong enough to shame navvies. I gave them a stare. In my younger days an adult gave out a stare on a bus, you shat bricks. To this lot it was incitement.

A hail of little rolled-up newspaper pellets started to make their way in my direction. I turned round and saw old women, too scared to look, sat between us. I felt sorry for them, the old women, but more so the yobs.

I checked round the bus for interfering types. Only one college day-releaser. None likely to hold me back. I stood up and approached the funny boys. A few giggles started up, then their eyes trained on the windows.

I planted my foot on the seat of the ring leader, a pencil-neck with a bleached-in badger stripe circling his barnet, said, 'See that?'

He smirked out the side of his mouth. 'Aye, it's a foot – you've another one there, look.'

A peal of laughter burst out from his little crowd of admirers. I cut it short. Grabbed the yob by the ear, forced him to re-examine his response. 'Take a closer look.' I pushed his head onto my toe. 'That boot's coming between you and your first ride if I hear another crack out of you, geddit?'

He whimpered, but said nothing. So I twisted his ear tighter than a wing nut.

'Ah, right, right. Sorry mister. Sorry n'all that, eh!'

Kids today. No respect. On my way back to my seat I smiled at one of the old women, said, 'I blame the parents.'

Got nods all round.

The rest of the journey passed in silence. I felt glad to have the time to gather my thoughts. Mac wasn't my only source in this town; I still had a few favours due. And some open to persuasion by other means.

As I jumped off the bus a Rasta played Bob Marley. The travelling public weren't impressed. Too early to be jammin' – and his voice sounded like a Wookie being molested.

I walked down the maze of bustling streets at this end of the city to a little greasy-spoon café I knew. It served up killer bacon and egg rolls, smothered in onions, dripping with brown sauce. If you talked nicely to the old girl behind the counter she'd even trim the fat off the rashers.

I ordered up a bellyful. One roll, heavy on the onions. Coffee, mug of, very sweet. And a pack of Rothmans, for afters.

I took the *Sun* down from the rack. It looked to be full of nothing but celebrity gossip. Half the pictures, I didn't even know the people. There was a time when to be in the paper meant something. You'd done something or had a talent. Now, fame – everyone's at it. You shag a footballer, tug-off a pig, and suddenly the world's hanging on your every breath. Riches and the whole nine yards to follow.

The waitress came over with my roll. She was near to retirement and world weary. Must have discovered blow-drying at some time in the eighties – her hairstyle wouldn't have looked out of place on the pages of *Smash Hits*. She said, 'It's all a bloody joke, isn't it?'

I started to agree, thought she was talking generally, and then she tapped the pages of the *Sun*. The picture showed Bob Geldof addressing a group of politicians, and, of course, some celebrity un-worthies. He was on the tap for more cash for the developing world.

'I wonder how many African babies that suit would have immunised?' said the waitress.

I nodded, tried to appear interested.

She fumed on. 'I don't see the likes of him using our lousy health service or hanging out for a pittance of a pension.'

I felt like I'd been trapped in the back of a taxi, listening to some cabbie's bigoted nonsense. I looked down at my roll. God, I felt hungry.

'It's a disgrace.' She added, 'Bono – he's another one. If they're so bothered about saving the world why don't they give their money away and come and live like the rest of us!'

'That would be a bit of a soberer for them,' I said.

She smiled at me. I saw I'd done enough to humour her.

'You better eat up, love, that roll will be going cold.'

As she turned away I flattened the newspaper, wiped the base of my cup on its cover. I raised my roll to take a bite, saw the rashers cold and grey within; then in walked plod.

He was bang on cue. 'Morning, Officer,' I said.

'Dury. By the cringe.' Fitz the Crime's eyes lit up like polished hubcaps.

'Can I buy you a pot of the usual?' I said.

He nodded, sat down, said, 'What you after?'

'Oh, and real nice to see you too, Fitz.'

He leant forward, went, 'Don't bollocks me, Dury.'

I stood up, called out, 'A pot of your finest, love.'

I felt a hand pull me back into my seat. I knew Fitz felt anxious, but he'd no need to be. Fitz and myself, we go way back.

'Jesus, what's with the animosity? I thought I was in your good books, after – y'know.'

Fitz squirmed, unbuttoned his overcoat, said, 'Look, Dury, that business is over with.'

He referred to the time I kept his name out the headlines. The filth may be prepared to turn a blind eye to one of its officer's peccadilloes, but they do tend to draw the line at it appearing in print for all the world to see. Examples have been known to be made in such cases. Fitz, however, merely lost his DI badge. Busted back to buck private as the Americans say.

'One good turn deserves another, wouldn't you agree?' I said.

'Piss off.'

'Now, now, Fitz, you never did pay me back.'

'Aye, and now you've nothing on me, Dury, and you're all washed up.'

'Is that so?'

'Aye, it is. Who would take the likes of you seriously?'

He sat back. A contented, smug grin crept up the side of his face. He looked like a lizard after its tongue has snapped an insect. I felt drawn to reaching across the table and smacking seven bells out of him. For years Fitz had been what is commonly called 'crooked as two left feet', and he knew it as well.

'Isn't that a risky strategy, Fitz?'

Cogs turned behind his eyes. I imagined a gerbil on a plastic wheel inside that great fat head of his. Who was he kidding? The only weight he brought to this table sat round his waist.

'Risky, you say?'

'Oh, I'd say very risky. Have you ever watched *The Blues Brothers*?'

'*You what?*'

'*The Blues Brothers* – you know Belushi and the other one.'

Fitz looked lost. Truly stupefied. I waited for a drool to start from the corner of his mouth.

'Anyway, in the movie they have this saying, "We're on a mission from God". Do you remember?'

He shook his head. He had the face of a saint . . . Bernard.

'No. Oh well, they did. It's what they said. But do you know what they were really saying? Deep down, what they were really trying to say with that statement, Fitz?'

I swear his mouth widened.

'What they were saying was – Don't fuck with us! . . . Fitz, let me tell you something – *I* am on a mission from God.'

'Fucking hell, you've cracked. You've finally cracked, Dury!' he roared.

The tea came, the waitress gently placed it on the table before us. Fitz rose to his feet.

'Shall, I be mother?' I said.

He put on his hat, hurriedly fastened up his overcoat.

'Fitz, I'm gonna be in touch soon. Real soon, about that favour.'

A CRUSTY-LOOKING GEEZER WITH a suitcase stopped me in the street.

'Wanna buy the latest U2?' he said.

I didn't want to buy the first. They've had one good album, maybe two, tops, said, 'Why would I?'

'Oasis?' he said.

'I still have *Revolver*, what's wrong with the real McCoy?'

He stood in front of me, held out his arms, tried not to let me past.

I stopped flat, said, 'That's a sure-fire way to get yourself hurt.'

He stepped aside. 'Okay, okay, I can tell you know your music – name it, I've probably got it, or can get it. Just name it!'

'Frenzal Rhomb.'

'What?'

'Australian punk outfit. Have you got *Sans Souci*? That's their best.'

I started singing from my favourite track, 'Russell Crowe's Band'.

He left, tapping the side of his head.

Back on the bus, my phone went, said, 'Amy?'

'Who's Amy?'

Turned out to be Col.

'Sorry. I thought you were someone else.'

'Obviously. I was calling to see how you were moving, but I see you've got your mind on other things.'

'No, Col. Shit no. I was just . . .'

'Distracted?'

'That's it.'

'Well don't be, Gus. Get your mind on the job I'm paying you for.'

'Sorry.'

'Did you speak to the tart?'

'I did.'

'And?'

'Like you said it.'

'But did she give you anything.'

'Hell no, no way. Col, I'm working here, what do you take me for?'

'I meant, information.'

'Oh, right. No, nothing really. Look, I've put out some feelers.'

'Any leads?'

'Leads? Christ, I'm not Eddie bloody Shoestring!'

'Okay. It's just, well, his mother – her heart is broken.'

I felt an almighty pang of guilt. It appeared there for no reason, I'd been doing my best. I knew there were words I should be searching for to comfort Col, but my mind flipped.

'There's no point thinking like that,' I said.

'I just wish you had something to go on, you know, so I could say to her – Gus's found this out, or what have you. Do you understand?'

'I do. As soon as I have any news I'll let you know.'

'Okay, son. We're all praying for you, you know that, don't you?'

'I do.'

'Good. Good. Well, I'll say goodbye then. God bless.'

I stopped in at the 7-Eleven on the way back to Fallingdoon House. Got stocked for a night in: six-pack of Murphy's (Guinness sold out), half of Grouse and a full bottle of Johnnie Walker Black Label.

I concealed the lot under my jacket on the way past Stalin. I'd got as far as my door when he shouted, 'Tomorrow's Monday.'

'Yeah, and . . . ?'

'You're not paid to be here by Tuesday.'

I shot him a glower, said, 'Tell me tomorrow.'

Inside I pulled the plug.

I shotgunned three cans in no time, then quickly necked half another, topped it up with the scoosh and gulped deep. I felt the hit coming on right away. I remembered reading one of Hemingway's books, the characters drank a few beers quickly and felt them go to their heads immediately. I hadn't felt that way for a long time. But to get lashed good and proper, definitely don't hang about.

I cracked the last can when the door went.

It was Milo. 'Howya.'

He had his head bowed, when he looked up I saw he carried a massive shiner. Bruno got off lighter from Tyson. I felt furious, immediately gripped with rage.

'What happened?'

'Arrah, it's nothing.'

'Milo, it's more than nothing. Have you had it seen to?' The eye bulged to the size of an egg, angry blood vessels had burst inside.

'Go way outta that, it's just a scratch.'

'What happened?'

'I . . . er . . . well it's embarrassing, really. I walked into a door.'

I don't know whether the drink or my instinctive trust of him let me believe this, but I bought it straight away. I watched him shuffle into my room and slowly lower himself down in a chair.

'Have ye tea yet?'

'Eh, no. Sorry, it's on my list. I've had a bit of a full day.'

'No matter. You have the telly, mine is still broke, can I watch with you?'

'Sure you can. Go ahead.'

River City polluted the airwaves.

'Bloody shite,' said Milo. 'Can't watch this, can you?'

'Never have.'

Milo flicked, settled on a doco, something about the Beats. Some dated footage showed Jack Kerouac reading from *On the Road*. He looked old and wasted. Alcohol oozed from his every pore.

Like most of my generation I'd read his books, once or twice, some more than that. There was a time when the whole Beat thing meant something to me. I swore it spoke to me, but not now.

I couldn't quite pin it down but somewhere in the last few years I'd lost all sense of idealism. The thought of cruising across the States with a bunch of dropouts seemed nothing more than a trip to me now. Not worth bothering about. And, no shit, I didn't have the energy.

After the doco, Milo muttered, 'You know, I've a notion to go and read that book.'

'I wouldn't bother.'

'You've read it then, *On the Road*.'

'I could tell you more about it than they're letting on. For starters, he didn't write it in three weeks flat the way they tell it. Oh no, there was about ten years' worth of rewrites before it made its way into print. But they like to keep quiet about that.'

'Ah, it removes some of the mystery the way you tell it.'

'No mystery, just plain old hype – gotta keep those tills ringing.'

'My, you're a cynic, Gus Dury. It's a cynic ye are.'

'I won't deny it.'

I broke the seal on the Johnnie Walker. 'Can I tempt you?'

'My stomach would never take it. 'Tis a terrible affliction I have these latter years.'

I thought, 'That's all the more for me then.'

'Sure I can't tempt you with even a small one – could water it down.'

'No thanks. I'm sure you'll manage fine on your own. Gus, do you mind me asking – how do you know all this stuff, are ye an educated man?'

'God, no. I just know books. I'm a reader for my sins. Since I was a boy, I've been bookish and solitary, scared the hell out of my father so it did.'

'Ah, 'tis the best time to start. I used to be a terror for the books m'self, until the old eyes went. Sure isn't the only education of any worth one that's burned in by lantern light!'

I nodded. 'I've always been a reader.'

Milo dropped his voice. 'And . . . have you always been a drinker?'

I didn't mind the question. After a few scoops I would talk the leg off an iron pot. And it mattered not an iota what I talked about.

'Can't say always, though maybe it was there at the back of me waiting to surface.'

'Most times there's a reason for it.'

'I've a million of those.'

Milo laughed. 'Jaysus, Gus, you're a rare character. Quite a combination, the reader and the drinker.'

'Just your average saloon bar Socrates.'

'Oh, you're above that.' He stood up slowly and let out a little laugh. 'We'll have to talk more another night.'

'If you like,' I said.

Milo tried to straighten himself but remained hunched over. 'Well, I'm obliged to you for letting me watch your television. 'Tis grand to have a bit of company of an evening as well.'

I took him to the door, saw him safely into his room. I swore sleep was already upon him, it scalded my heart to see his exhaustion.

I felt far from tired myself; my mind raced. There was a lot of stuff spinning about in there. The talk of childhood topped the bill. I've nothing but a pile of desperate memories left over from this time, which in darker moments will haunt me. It's always the way of it. The darker things look, the more I remember.

I heard my father's voice rise, the clang of smashed crockery, my mother's cries.

I hit the drink some more.

Started to think about that black eye of Milo's. I'd my suspicions it came from Stalin or one of his lot, and decided to go and find him. Knocked on doors about the hostel. Didn't feel in any condition to do much but, given half a chance, was ready to bury the bastard.

On the middle floors I got the trace of a foreign voice, it sounded Russian or something like it.

I banged on the door. 'Open up.'

No answer. Put my shoulder to the top panel. It didn't move, but pain shot through my arm and down my back like I'd been hit by lightning.

'Come on, I know you're in there, open this fucking door or I'm coming through it.'

I kicked out. The noise brought heads bobbing out all down the hall-way.

'Sorry – domestic dispute,' I told them. 'Nothing to worry about.'

I geared myself up for one mighty last charge when suddenly a little gap appeared in the door. A girl, no more than fourteen, peered out. Looked to all the world as terrified as a small animal in a snare.

I thought, 'The coward. He's sent his daughter out to face me, calm me down while he hides from me inside.'

'I'm having none of this,' I said. Grabbed the door in my hand and shoved it hard. Halfways to putting the girl on her backside, I stormed in.

Inside I got the shock of my life. More young girls filled the room, all as terrified as the first. They were dressed in little more than rags, old coats that looked like ex-army issue. Each one of them stared up at me and trembled. They held on to each other in desperate fear. Every face a sallow emaciated mess, but their eyes, to a one, sat wide open. They stared, searching for something.

For the life of me, I didn't know what to do. It looked like a scene from *Schindler's List*.

'What's going on in here?' I asked.

No answer. Not one of them dared speak.

I turned to the girl who opened the door, said, 'What is this? What's going on?'

She said nothing.

I got angry, it was frustration, the drink. I went over and grabbed her arm, ranted: 'What the hell's going on in here, a heap of girls dressed up like Belsen victims, half-starved and packed tighter than sardines – speak to me, would you? *Christ*, I'm not the enemy!'

She cried and tapped at her chest. In the machine-gun fire of her language, she uttered one word I understood: 'Latvia'.

I let down her arm, thought, 'Holy fuck.'

I left the room.

Downstairs I necked huge amounts of whisky. Right from the bottle. I tried to take in what I'd just seen. But my mind filled with visions of the young girls, crying and staring at me like I was their executioner. I knew it would take more than one bottle to erase a memory like that.

I looked around for my cigarettes, spotted them sitting on the windowledge with a book of matches tucked underneath. I sparked up and took a long draw, let the nicotine get deep into my lungs. I felt its calming warmth right away.

Tell me they're a killer, yeah, but what isn't? My nerves began to settle down from jangling like Sunday church bells to a susurration that whispered, 'Get a grip, Gus.'

I sat myself on the ledge and looked to the sky. Night stars, up and at 'em. Felt the religion of my childhood reach out to me. Old prayers said at the bedside returned. When the Presbyterianism raises its head, I know I'm in trouble.

I lowered my eyes, turned back to the earth.

I caught a hint of movement under the street lamp below. A man stood there. I clocked the scene before me, checked my facts, got all the data in order. Yes, a man stood in the street below, watching me.

I turned over the view once more. He smoked a cigarette, looked straight up at me. He saw me stood before him, mirroring his movements. For a moment we made eye contact and at once I knew where I'd seen him before. It was the cube-shaped bloke, the one with the newspaper who watched me with Amy earlier.

I stubbed the tab.

Ran for the door.

AS I REACHED THE END of the driveway the Cube took off. He ran like a Jawa, all stumpy legs and arms, thrusting away for dear life. I was onto him, 'Bang to rights', as they used to say on *The Sweeney*. He knew I wasn't hanging about. I followed him like bad luck. He turned round to grab glances at me again and again. His face as red as Hell Boy, cheeks puffed out like bellows. I saw his features clearly now and I wouldn't forget them.

'Right, you little prick, I have you,' I shouted after him.

I lunged out, grabbed him by the collar in a classic *Dixon of Dock Green* manner, no escaping the long arm of the—

'*Shit!*'

I stumbled. Took the Cube down with me. We rolled about on the wet pavement like pissed-up breakdancers. I managed a lame hold on him, yelled, 'Give it up!'

He went silent. I heard his breath grow heavy. It faltered with panic and carried a smell of menthol cigarettes.

The Cube wore a leather jacket and in the wetness it got too slippery to hold. 'Quit your struggling,' I shouted.

He paid no mind. Then, I took a sharp knee to the plums.

I let out a wail. The Cube seized his chance.

'Hey! Get back here y'bastard.'

Too late. As he ran from me, I caught a few glimpses of his back in the shadows, and then – nothing.

'Screw it,' I said. I stood up and limped back to the hotel.

Inside I threw myself on the bed. The room spun out of control, I couldn't take it. Once through the ringer was enough. I raised myself and returned to the Johnnie Walker.

I'd thought that doing Col's digging might bring me some trouble, but now I knew it. Somebody had taken a serious interest in me. I'd my suspicions who, but no clue as to why. I mean, what had I to offer? Nothing. I'd unearthed zip. Christ, most days, I could hardly find my arse with both hands.

I sat cross-legged on the floor, whisky in one hand, a tab in the other. None of it made sense, so I tried not to think. For a long time I'd wanted to be unthinking. That's what I use the sauce for – shutting out the noise, obviating the pain of existence. I downed more and more whisky until I felt myself slump and then fall.

Dean Martin once said: 'You're not drunk if you can lie on the floor without holding on.'

I was so drunk I couldn't even hold on.

I passed out, into brutal dreams.

I woke to my mobi ringing loudly, right at my earhole, croaked: 'Hello.'

A female voice, crotchety, said, 'You bastard.'

'Amy?'

'I thought we had a date.'

Confusion reigned, then long-term memory kicked in, I tried: 'A date . . . well, I don't know I'd exactly call it that.'

Her voice rose higher, she fumed at me: 'You utter, utter bastard!'

'Look, I'm really sorry, Amy – I got caught up in some other things.'

Silence, then a tut, followed closely by a pause. This was gonna cost me, I knew it.

'You can make it up to me, Gus,' she said.

'How?'

'There's a bit of a rave up at the students union this weekend.'

I thought, *students*, I don't know, said, 'Students?'

The critical intonation slipped in. Amy obviously picked up on it right away. 'Gus, I'm a *student*.'

Her tone carried accusation. Guilt flew in and settled on me once again.

'Okay, what time?'

'I'll call you this time – be ready!'

'Deal,' I said, and she hung up.

I put down the phone and wondered if my life would ever be my own again.

The room felt full of dead air. I opened the window, stuck my head out and got a waft of petrol fumes from the street below. God, did I ever need some fresh air in my lungs. This city would be the death of me, Debs had always said that.

I filled the sink with cold water, bathed my face. In the mirror I saw Mac's haircut was still sitting pretty, it only took a quick run through with a comb.

Got dressed in a beige shirt and Gap khakis. Checked myself out, said, 'Crikey!' reminded me of the late Steve Irwin. Pulled off the shirt and went with a white polo.

I felt rough, way rough.

Sparked up a Rothmans and immediately started a major coughing fit that shook my world. Would I venture some coffee? Would I ever.

The Nescafé instant sachets in the little basket seemed to have gone down. I'd need to tap Stalin for more. The thought of him suddenly brought the night before flooding back to me in brilliant Technicolor flashes.

I'd a few bones to pick with him. There was the Nescafé. Then Milo's eye. And of course, the room full of Latvian girls.

I made a second, weak cup of coffee with the dregs of granules spilled on the tray. Found the contents of a few previously torn-up sachets, tipped those in too.

I wanted to get my head in order before I sought out the cute hoor, as Milo called him. I knew the real answer was skipping out Stalin altogether and going straight to Benny the Bullfrog, but I needed to know more about him and his operation before I risked a foot in his direction.

Sure, questions needed to be asked, but without a bit of leverage I'd be as well keeping them to myself. I had a feeling that going to Zalinskas' lair unprepared would mean coming out feet first.

I stubbed the tab on the sole of my boot – the ashtray seemed to have gone walkabout. I hoped the cleaner might pick up on this and leave me another one.

It was a painful experience lacing up the Docs. My guts turned over; thought I might heave. It passed. I made a note to shop for some loafers, anything without laces.

In the hallway I listened at Milo's door – nothing. No sign of Stalin either. I'd got up early for me but the world looked to be well on with the day.

I took the stairs to the second floor, unsure of what I'd seen the night before. I wouldn't have put it past myself to have got it wrong completely. Drink, it'll mess you up that way.

I stumbled on the top step, said, 'Shit – get a grip, Gus.'

I found simple coordination difficult. But my mind played tricks on me too. It flashed up the faces of those young girls, huddled together, terrified. I imagined what grim fate awaited them. They were only children. What the hell were they doing in there? Where were their parents? My mind raced; the city was no place for them. With the streets awash with deros and criminals, what chance would they have? None, I knew it. They were easy meat. Pure and simple.

I stood outside the door I'd put my shoulder to the night before. It sat slightly open. A thin oblong of sunlight reached out over the floor towards me. I took a deep breath and went for the handle.

As I slowly stepped in, I remembered again the fear I'd created in those faces. God alone knew who they imagined me to be, or why they thought I'd suddenly appeared like that.

Inside I felt like I'd walked into the wrong room. It was empty. The bedding was straightened with great precision. Lamps, towels, kettle – everything neat as ninepins, as my mother would say. Only the window, slightly open, set the curtains dancing like ghosts.

I stood in the centre of the room in silence. I heard my heart beating, the blood circulating quickly in my veins. I put it down to my struggle up the stairs. Then I began to feel out of breath.

My head pounded now, but it wasn't the usual hangover. I felt rage. Those girls, this room, this whole place . . .

'What's going on?'

I lashed out with my boot and caught the door. It slammed loudly. A cloud of dust rose from above the frame.

I set about opening up drawers, wardrobe doors, bathroom cabinets. I checked them all but found nothing. I saw no trace of anyone ever having stayed there. It looked as innocuous as any other cheap hotel room in any other city. Then I heard a key in the lock.

I turned round to see the door open up. In walked Stalin, he eyed me calmly, then said, 'Why are you here?'

My fists clenched. I felt ready to beat some answers out of him. 'I'll ask the questions. First off, where're all the Latvian girls that were here last night?'

He stepped into the room. The door closed behind him and he folded his arms.

I said, 'I'll ask you again – the girls, where are they?'

He raised a hand, his index finger extended towards me. 'I have no idea what you are talking about.'

'Cute hoor,' I felt a bucket of adrenaline tip into my veins, 'that's what you are.'

I lunged towards him and caught him with a jaw breaker of an upper-cut. I instantly felt the heat of it in my knuckles. I stood over him where he lay on the floor. 'Feeling more talkative now?'

He crawled onto his knees and spat. A drool of blood spilled from his mouth. He watched me but said nothing. 'Someone once told me, never wrestle with pigs in shit. Do you know why?' I said.

He spat again.

'Because, you see, they enjoy the shit more than you.'

I kicked him in the head. I saw a flap of skin tear clear of his brow. More blood ran out. Lots this time. Looked like a coat-hanger abortion. He put both hands over his head.

'Think of me as a pig. You see, I enjoy this shit, I can keep it up for hours.'

I swear he whimpered. I'd expected more of a put up from a Russian. Maybe I was too sold on Arnie in *Red Heat*.

'The girls, fuckface. What happened to them?'

Finally, spluttering, answers: 'They've gone . . . gone, taken away.'

'Where?'

More whimpering, tears. 'I do not know . . . I do not.'

I drew back my fist, gritted my teeth, let him think I wanted another hit at his face.

'They come, they go. I can tell no more. The girls come here and then girls are taken away.'

'Who takes them?'

He cried now. Full-on tears, just like a nipper. 'They will kill me.'

Enough already, as the Americans say. I hit him again and opened a welt above his other eye. Not a matching pair, but near enough. He looked woozy, I thought I'd gone too far.

I let him breathe a while.

I filled a glass of water and threw it over him. Then I grabbed his hair in my hand and twisted, real hard.

'Now, my friend, they – whoever they are – may indeed kill you when they catch up with you, but sure as there's a hole in your arse, I'll kill you now if you don't tell me what I want to know.'

He spilled. 'A woman, she came for them early – she always come early. Drive them away. I just look after the hotel. It is not my business to know more.'

He was seriously panicked now. His breath grew patchy. I thought he might shit his pants, said, 'Name?'

'I . . . I . . . I do not know.'

'Somehow, I don't believe you.'

I lifted him on to his feet. He screamed as I pulled him towards the door by his long greasy hair. 'Maybe we'll pay a little visit to the roof top, must be some sights so high up. How would you like that?'

'Okay, okay . . . Her name is Nadja. I know nothing more. Nadja, that is all.'

I threw him onto the bed. He curled up like a beaten dog. The sight of him repulsed me. I saw how Billy had ascended the ranks so quickly if this was the piss-weak standard of Russian gangster he worked alongside.

'She's a tall blonde, yeah?'

'Yes.'

I took out a tab, lit it. The bitch, she'd held out on me.

I walked over to face Stalin. I crouched down and blew smoke in his face. 'If I find you're messing with me, I'll come back and cut out your kidneys.'

He looked away and his lip curled up like a spoilt child's. Then came more whimpering.

I grabbed his jaw and turned his eyes to me, said, 'This is separate.'

'What?' Fear latched onto him again. 'What . . . ? What . . . ?'

'Call it payback . . .'

I put my fist in his face, I heard the crack of bone and knew his nose had gone. He was out cold.

'For Milo.'

I TOOK MYSELF BACK TO the room. I needed to clear right out. My hands shook. Put it down to the sauce, but had a fear it might be something else.

I made time for a full Scottish breakfast: large Alka-Seltzer and two aspirin. Heard Dennis Hopper's immortal words racing around in my mind, 'Alcohol, there's no drug like it to take you so high . . . and drop you back down so low.'

My head spun, the hangover ramped up the revs. I had to find time to think, room to manoeuvre.

I ran into the street, over to the 7-Eleven. Grabbed two packs of tea – the good stuff, Twinings – and hoofed it back to Fallingdoon House.

'Milo? Are you up yet?' I stood in the hallway and banged on the door, all the while looking up the stairs for signs of Stalin.

'Milo? Are you . . . ?'

The lock turned and, slowly, the door widened to all of an inch.

'Ah, 'tis yourself,' said Milo. 'Come in, Mr Dury.'

Milo's movements seemed slower than usual. I saw his feet exposed, blue and gnarled on the cold floorboards. It nearly put my heart out.

'My, aren't we the early bird this morning. 'Tis, 'tis . . . 'tis the early bird ye are.' He seemed to hover above the bed, his sparrow-thin wrists looked like they might snap on contact with the soft mattress.

It took Milo for ever to lower himself; when he finally made it the pain drove two tractor tracks across his brow.

'I've brought this for you,' I said.

'Ah, Jaysus . . . ye shouldn't have.' Milo stretched, as near to a lunge as he was able. 'I'll get a pot boiling for some tay.'

'No –' I flagged him to sit, '– I can't stop, Milo.'

'I thought as much.' He looked up towards the cross above his bed, a large wooden effigy of Christ was in place, suffering for all our sins. 'Ye look, can I say it, a bit disturbed – Is it trouble yeer in?'

'I-I just have to go.'

'And when we were becoming such good friends as well.'

'The best of friends.'

He looked back at me, I caught the blue of his eyes as they shot into me.

'Look . . . I'll be back soon. Real soon. It's just . . . well, I guess you could say I've a spot of bother to see to.'

'Can I help?'

I nearly laughed out loud, the look of him.

'Thanks,' I said, 'but I can manage.'

I was out of words. We both were. I felt like I'd let the old boy down, abandoned him to grim fate.

'Milo, if there's any trouble from that prick Stalin, I want you to call me, you hear?' I scribbled down my mobile number on the back of the 7-Eleven receipt and tucked it under a glass at his bedside. 'You hear me, call – anything at all.'

He stared at the wall. There was nothing more to say. I felt there should be a handshake or, God forbid, a hug. But I just left him alone with his fears, as I carried off my guilt. I deserted him. Had I no spine?

I trudged back to the room and picked up my things, there wasn't much, it amounted to one bag, my denim jacket and a near empty bottle of Johnnie Walker. I had tabs and matches somewhere too, but bollocks to looking for them.

A sheet of horizontal rain hit me as I opened the door, the insidious Edinburgh type that chases you through the closes, makes you feel like you've got a personal rain cloud following. The brewery, in full swing, pumped out an overpowering stench. Mixed with grey skies and I understood why the streets looked so empty – save for one big biffer, stooped over with something behind his back.

'Dury?' he said.

He looked a useful pug, the sight of him put me on Defcom-Five.

'What's it to you?'

'What?'

'Look, fat boy – I only went with your mother 'cos she's dirty.' The old Happy Monday's lyric, first radge thing to come into my head as I squared my shoulders and put the bead on him. 'And I haven't got a decent bone in me, so come on and kill me!'

He reached behind him, I grabbed his arm. Swear I sensed a sawn-off, Stanley knife at the least.

'Try it!' I said.

'Jesus! Help! Help! I'm being attacked,' he roared.

I pulled his arm forward. There was no shooter, just a large red post sack.

'You're the postie!'

'Who did you think I was?' he bleated, breath heavy.

'You're the bloody postie!' I felt a flood of relief. 'Look, I'm sorry. I thought—'

'I don't care what you thought. I'm only trying to do my job here.' He shoved a pile of letters at me. I looked at him, feeling my face start to heat up, said, 'Look, I'm sorry, really . . . I didn't mean to—'

He pushed past me, bolted up the drive to Fallingdoon House. He fairly moved, a real 'Run Forrest, run,' scene.

At the door he shouted, 'You're crazy, do you know that?' His mail bag swung from side to side, nearly toppling him as he delved for a few stray envelopes that floated out. 'People like you need locking up!'

I couldn't fault him there.

'Sorry again. It's the lack of uniform! Posties used to wear uniforms.' I couldn't keep up with the pace of change. Time was when I knew my postie by name. 'When did you guys do away with the uniform?'

'Piss off!' he snapped.

I took the hint. Jesus, what kind of a life was I living?

I put my collar up as I walked into the rain. Would have liked to spark up but had left my smokes behind.

I looked over my shoulder as I hurried along the London Road. Kids on their way to school eyed me cautiously. They wore blazers and carried satchels – one tradition that hadn't died out in Edinburgh. To a one the kids looked dour. Put me in mind of myself at their age. I remembered how early we're all taught to be miserable. How we strangle the idea that life can be anything other than spiritless routine.

On this road I'd be at the Holy Wall for opening. The idea of a morning heart-starter jumped at me, but, I couldn't see it going down too well with Col. I pulled myself into a shop doorway and fired down some scoosh. I felt like street trash, a jakey, but I badly needed a hit.

I'd barely put the bottle away when a face appeared in the doorway.

'You coming in?' said an old woman turning over an 'open' sign. I looked above the door, I stood outside a greasy-spoon café.

'Eh . . . aye, all right then.'

Inside I shook off the rain, said, 'We'll pay for that summer yet!' I tell you, the Scots have a stock gambit for every occasion.

'Oh, I know, love – isn't it dreadful?' She seemed a nice old dear, salt of the earth, with the tabard to prove it. 'It's been like this for days as well, I don't know when I'm going to get a load of washing oot.'

I smiled, said, 'Och, maybe you'll have a lottery win and nip off to the Bahamas.'

'Chance would be a fine thing.' She laughed. 'What can I get you, love?'

'Coffee, black, please.'

'Something to eat?'

'No thanks.'

'You sure, son? You look like you could do with a square meal. I've seen more meat on a butcher's pencil.'

'Eh, no. Coffee's fine.'

She gave me a disapproving look, nothing nasty, motherly. It seared through me, reminded me I had some bridges to build in that territory.

The coffee arrived quickly and nearly took my breath away. Strong and hot, how I liked it, but I wanted something a bit more heavy duty. Under the table I took out the scoosh bottle, tipped a good measure in the cap, then poured it in my cup.

Bliss.

'Great coffee,' I called out to the waitress.

She smiled as she shuffled off for the back door, the Club king-size in her mouth turned like a rotor blade as she spoke: 'I do a good roll on sliced sausage as well, son, if ye fancy it.'

'Eh, no. Coffee's grand for now, thanks.'

'Don't know what you're missing!'

'Another day, perhaps.'

I spread out my mail on the table. Felt another pang of, was it guilt? Embarrassment? Probably both. But they soon gave way to the image of the postie yawing up that path, in full flight, with all the grace of a rickety whirligig. 'He'll get over it,' I thought. And sure, now he had a ripper of a story to tell the boys back at the depot.

The mail looked to be all the usual stuff addressed to no one: bank pushing loans; charity cash tap with bribe of a free pen; the latest offer from Branson's Virgin empire. And one formal-looking envelope addressed to me, Col's careful handwriting replacing the Wall's crossed-out address. I tore into it. The thick white paper inside felt expensive on my fingertips.

Dear Gus Dury

Bad start, preferred the old style. What's wrong with Dear Gus or Dear Mr Dury? These days, I tell you, we want to redesign the whole world from scratch, turn the lot into something trendy. I read on. One line stuck out:

Our client, Ms Deborah Ross seeks – following the recent completion of a trial separation – to instigate formal divorce proceedings.

So, she'd gone back to her old name already.

'She's not messing about,' I thought, as I scrunched the letter into a ball. My fist trembled as I threw it down. My knuckles turned white against the black of the plastic table top.

I LEFT A COUPLE OF quid by the cup and slid out the door. My self-esteem slid out beneath me. I felt lower than a snake's belly.

The Arc building hurt my eyes, reminded me how much Edinburgh had changed. If the city had sleepwalked through the planners' chrome and glass nightmare, this was the wake-up call. Some architect's Lego-brick piss-take. Painted turquoise.

A line of bills was fly-posted all the way to the foot of the Mile. Some drag act, I thought. Fifty casual glances later I pieced together that it was a Bowie tribute act, called Larry Stardust.

'Fuck me drunk!' I said. The Thin White Duke deserved more respect.

I wandered nowhere in particular. Just trying to clear my thoughts, but it proved difficult. I had too much going on, never a good state of affairs for a drinker.

For a long time I'd been living by Einstein's dictum: 'I never think about the future, it comes soon enough.' But here I was, being forced to do just that. The answers Col wanted wouldn't just turn up on their own. And neither would Debs' quickie divorce.

I walked on and on.

Tartan shops blasted teuchter music at every turn. I thought I'd grown immune to it until a Sikh, in a tartan turban, stopped me mid-stride.

'Would you like to try one, sir?' His accent was broader than mine, a grin wider than Jack Nicholson's Joker.

'Excuse me?'

'A wee nip?' he said.

I liked this guy a whole lot.

'Would I ever.'

A cheap blend, but what did I expect – Dalwhinnie?

'How is it?' he said.

'Hits the spot.'

'Glad you enjoyed it. Have a nice day, sir.'

I pressed out a smile, a thank you paired with a nod. 'Have a nice day.' I wondered when we all became so American? If you'd told me a few years ago I'd be served free scoosh in the street by a Sikh in a tartan turban I'd have been waiting for the punch line. Welcome to the new Scotland.

The nip lifted my mood, restarted the alcohol units I already carried, when my mobi rang. I developed a fit of the shakes and the phone slid from my hands onto the cobbles of the Royal Mile.

'Oh shit.'

I reached down and picked it up, but I was too late, it had gone to voicemail. The caller ID failed to recognise the number. For a moment I stared at the screen, then a superwoofer blasted out the 'Skyboat Song', and I got moving.

I put the phone back in my pocket. Right away, it began to ring again.

'Bloody hell.'

This time, I managed to keep hold of it, shouted, 'Hello!'

'Gus?'

'Yes. Who's this?'

A voice, barely a whisper, said, 'Gus, it's Mac.'

'Mac? Where are you ringing from?'

'Just about the waist down, son!' He raised his tone, 'But that's not pissing myself laughing, let me tell you!'

'What's up?'

'Your half-arsed attempt at playing Columbo.'

He sounded rattled. 'Isn't he dead?' I said.

'Aye, and you're not far behind him!'

'What? Mac, look, where are you?'

'I'm in a bloody call box. Do you know how long it is since I've said that? Took a bloody age for me to find this bastard. Where are you? We need to talk right a-fucking-way!'

'Have you got some information for me?'

'What did I say to you the last time we met? What did I say?'

He sounded highly rattled now.

For the first time I thought to weigh Mac's advice, but my need to find Billy's killer overrode any thoughts of danger to myself. Hell, what did I have to get up for anyway? Could maybe solve more than one problem at a time this way. 'Steer clear – those were the words you used, I think.'

'I wish you'd bloody well listened!'

'Look, Mac, what is this?'

'What is this? This is me, as your friend, putting my knackers on the block for you again!'

I got a definite bad vibe about this, said, 'You want to explain?'

'Well, no, not really. I'd sooner you'd listened the first time. I'd sooner I wasn't the one being hoicked out my bed in the wee hours by knuckle-breakers telling me to give you a message.'

'Oh.'

'Is that it? *Oh.* Is that all you've got to say?'

'Mac, did they . . . hurt you in any way?'

'No. But they gave me a pretty bloody graphic description of what they're capable of in that department.'

'Stay put. I'll come over.'

'No! Will you fuck! I'll tell you what to do, now, listen up . . .'

IT WAS THE FIRST GAME of the season, don't ask me which season. My old man's playing days of the seventies and eighties are a time I've tried to wipe from my mind. I say tried. If only I could.

There are some moments I'll never forget.

I'm about six when he comes in with a good bucket in him. I'm watching *The Six-Million Dollar Man* on telly. Steve Austin has just thrown some gadgie into a brick wall. I'm gripped by the slow-mo action but hit light speed when the mighty Cannis Dury announces himself – don't want to give him any ideas.

'Three fuckin' goals!' he says.

My mother smiles, rushes out of her seat. I know she's no idea what he's talking about, we both spent the afternoon at the park.

'Well, done!' she says placing a little kiss on his cheek, rubbing her hand on his back.

'*Well done?*' The smell of whisky fills the room with the rise of his voice. 'Is that it? Well-*fucking*-done? I put three goals past the league champions and I get this kinda shite from you. Look at you! Have you been sitting there all day in your baffies while I'm out running my arse into the ground?'

She shrinks back from him, but it's too late. The back of his hand knocks her over the coffee table. Her head lands in the fireplace, knocking out the bulbs behind the plastic coals.

'Get up!' he roars. He's taking off his jacket, rolling up his shirt sleeves. 'Get up you lazy bitch.'

I'm frozen still. I shut my eyes. Will he still see me if I do this?

'Get up!' There's anger pouring from him. His eyes are bulging, burning red, the same colour as my mother's blood on the white shag pile.

She struggles to her feet. I can see her trying to walk, but her steps are unsteady and she collapses on the couch.

'Up, up you useless bitch!' he shouts.

Flecks of spittle are pouring from him, they lash my face. I close my eyes again but I can still hear him yelling, roaring. The smell of whisky makes me feel sick. I'm trying not to move, but I know he's seen me.

'What are you looking at?' he says.

My heart quickens. In a second I'm running. I'm fast, round him and out the door in a flash. I feel the swish of his hand tracing my path, but he's missed me.

'Get back here, you wee bastard.'

'Cannis, no! Leave the laddie,' says my mother.

'Shut it!'

There's another sound – a hard fist connecting with my mother's face. Then the noise of her collapsing on the floor.

I run to my room and bury my head under the pillows on my bed. But I can still hear the yells.

'Three goals,' he's saying. 'Three goals . . . Three goals . . . '

I'm praying the Scotland call-up will come soon.

I MET MAC AT THE 'Big Foot', the Paolozzi sculpture on Leith Street.

'You hungry?' he said.

'Could eat a horse – and chase the rider!'

'Aye, well, keep that thought. You might not have such an appetite once you hear what I've got to tell you.'

We headed through Picardy Place, past the Sherlock Holmes statue, to the Walk. This part of the city is its schizoid heart. Where the New Town's rugby shirts and tweed caps give way to scores of tin-pot hard men and Staffies. I spotted three neds with fighting dogs in under a minute. Like the animal makes up for the undernourished frame, the coat-hanger shoulders, the general one-punch demeanour. Still, a merciful lack of shop fronts pushing shortbread and tartan down this way.

As we walked, Mac kept shtum. His front teeth nibbled on his lower lip.

'Are you going to tell me what this is about?'

'After.'

'After what?'

'After.'

I took his response for what it was, Scots for 'Don't fucking bother me right now.'

I saw Mac the Knife was on edge. I knew the signs. The Weejie stride was in place, chest out, in a dead heat with the spacehopper guttage.

What worried me, though, was the way he kept looking from side to side, and occasionally, over his shoulder. It wasn't fear. Not with Mac. This guy was a Bonnie Fechtir, take on all comers. It looked like serious caution, the act of an ex-crim who didn't want to go straight back inside.

Mac picked out a greasy spoon with an old barber's pole outside. Minimal attention to decor, less yet to the cleaning, I felt my Docs sliding on the oily linoleum. I was all for budget dining, but this place screamed 'salmonella to go'.

'Mac, are you sure about this joint?'

'What?'

'It's a bit rough, is it not?'

His lip curled, downward. 'Maybe you'd prefer the Shandwick.'

I pulled out an orange vinyl chair, tipped the covering of crumbs onto the floor.

'Aye, sit doon,' said Mac.

'What is this?'

'Eat!'

The waitress came, a hard-faced fifty-something. Running to retirement and dour as heartache. A fizz of ruined features, the rewards of a lifetime spent struggling for nothing.

I ordered up two eggs on toast. Smothered them in brown sauce and vinegar. Washed the lot down with coffee. In here I felt no shame filling the cup with the last of my scoosh.

'You still hitting that?' said Mac.

'Lecture time?'

'Stuff'll be the end of you!'

I drank deep. 'Trouble with the rest of the world is they're two drinks behind!'

'Bogart.'

'Bang on.' Felt he'd thawed, said, 'Have you something to say to me, Mac?'

He sat back in his chair. Leaned forward. Sat back again.

I prompted: '*Mac?*'

'Okay. Okay . . .' He reached below the table, took something from his belt. 'I want you to have this.'

I felt something touch my knee. Looked down to see a shooter, Browning 9mm, the type Canoe Reeves packed in *The Matrix*. Until now, that was the closest I'd come to one. 'Fuck that!'

Mac shook his head. 'Gus, I'm not messing about here.'

I rose to my feet. 'Forget it.'

'Sit down.' His voice sounded calm now, quiet almost. 'Look, Gus, this visit I got . . .'

I put the bead on him. 'Spill it.'

'I got a message to pass on to you.'

I'd strayed into some decidedly dodgy territory, I saw that now. My first thought was Stalin. Next, Nadja. The weak fuck had tipped her off to cover his own arse.

'So let's hear it.'

'You won't like it.'

Another thought entered my head: the Cube. 'Was this a stocky little shite, smoked Berkeley Menthols?'

'What? No. No fucking way, it was a hard-core thug, bling on his teeth, the lot – Gus, this is all the way from the top. I told you not to mess with this lot. The Bullfrog's spoken and he wants you to get out. To leave the city – now!'

'No way.' I had the murder to think about.

Mac shook his head again, it grated on my nerves. 'I thought that's what you'd say . . . so here.' He frowned, creased his mouth into a taut wire and pressed the gun into my leg again.

I needed to know what was going on, and just what the hell I'd gotten myself into. I had tapped into more than just the killing of a young lad who'd got himself into a bit of bother.

'What's this about? I don't see how Billy Boy suddenly becomes Billy the Kid over night.'

'I told you, Gus. I warned you. Didn't I warn you? Right from the start, I told you – don't mess with this mob. End of story. You just don't mess. They're into more shit than you ever dreamt of.'

'Is my name Horatio?'

'*What?*'

'Thanks for the tip, Mac.'

I got to my feet again, headed for the door.

'Gus – Gus, you bastard, we haven't got the bill yet!'

WAS IT WORTH THE TROUBLE?

'I mean what have you got?' I asked myself. Knew the answer – zip. I'd been flailing about, sticking my nose in, but had nothing to give Col. Except maybe, another funeral invitation. Real soon.

I turned into a newsagent's, bought up some smokes: Camels, the strong ones. Taste of them greeted me like a blessing. Truth be told, I felt ready for a bevvy, at least one or ten. But something, maybe Mac's warning, kept me walking.

My mind felt numb. I'd flitted between mental fireworks and virtual catatonia for so long that I wondered, 'Was I manic?' Sorry, that's bi-polar now, isn't it? I don't know . . . didn't even know how to pronounce Adidas these days.

'It's a kick up the arse you need!' The indistinct voice of Scots wisdom hit in.

The Scots don't do self-pity. Morbidity, yes. Drunken insensate, to block it all out, yes. But never self-pity. I put it down to the utter black-ness of Scottish history. The struggle to get by. The sheer suffering. I mean, how else do you convince a poor nation like this to drag itself up? The myth of dignity in suffering. Shovelling shite, filling your lungs with coal dust, good for your soul? Bollocks. Good for the plutocrats' bank balances more like.

Jumped the number 26 bus to the Wall.

I saw all the regulars propped up inside, got a few nods from the most familiar faces. The one I expected to greet me most enthusiastically, though, was goggle-eyed, staring at the telly.

'Col, how goes it?'

'Shush shush,' he said, the back of his hand flapping at me.

'Must be good, what's it, Debbie Does Dallas?'

Killer look fired on me. Frowns, the works.

I slunk back, settled myself at the bar. Col turned up the news bulletin, *Scotland Today*.

The outside broadcast came from the new parliament building. I shook my head. 'Bloody waste of money!'

Chorus of, 'Aye. Aye. Aye,' echoed round the bar.

'Did you hear this, mate?' Some gadgie I'd never seen in my puff approached me, his face a riot of red patches, a drinker's blue nose. 'They cannae even heat the thing, bloody spewing oot heat it is! See, they put one of them heat guns on it. Saw the pictures in the paper, what a bloody money pit!'

'Look, can you keep the noise down, *please*,' snapped Col.

I raised my eyebrows to the gadgie. He slumped off, old nineties track-suit dragging off him, pint spilling in his trembling hand. Acrylic and alcohol – a bad combination – he put himself in danger of going up like the Hindenburg with his next fag.

I turned back to the telly. The reporter looked about seventeen. How do they do it? In my day, the telly was a big gig. Went to the best hacks. Trained ones. Not some schoolie that looks like she'd been at her mum's dressing-up box.

'The protest started outside the parliament with people waving plac-ards . . .' she announced.

Incisive stuff. Top-notch journalism. 'Oh, bring back John Craven, please. It's *Newsround*, surely.'

The wind picked up at the reporter's back, I expected to hear a quick, 'and now back to the studio' to let in her make-up team. She went on: 'The protesters are asylum seekers, their families and supporters, who are opposed to the Scottish Executive's policies . . .'

They played some footage, the kind I knew would have news editors salivating. Early-morning raids with police battering down flats in Wester Hailes, the city's dumping ground for the dispossessed. They planned to turf out the illegals, quick smart.

They pixelated all the faces of the people being rounded up by plod. My mind played a trick on me, filled in the blanks with the faces I'd seen huddled in misery at Fallingdoon House.

'Joining us now is Minister for Immigration, Alisdair Cardownie, MSP,' said the reporter.

'Turn this up some more, Col,' I said.

'Good evening, Polly,' said Cardownie.

'*Wanker*!' I shouted at the screen.

'Minister, judging by the number of protesters, there seems to be quite a significant opposition to your party's policies on immigration.'

He put on a piranha smirk. 'Well, Polly, let's put things into perspective, a handful of very vocal protesters does not signify a backlash against the government. Let's not forget, we *are* the elected party. And, as the elected representatives of the people, can ipso facto claim some measure of assumed support for our policies.'

The schoolie looked dumbstruck. Swear a giggle came from her. Capitulation writ large on her peaches and cream complexion.

'But, well, why do you think these people are here, Minister?'

'A good question, Polly. And if I may, eloquently put. One can only assume that the overzealous actions of some rogue police officers has, rightly – I reiterate that point, rightly to my mind – raised the indignation of some sections of the populace.'

Col bridled. 'Fucking hypocrite!' he said.

I rocked on my heels, taken aback. I had never heard Col make such an outburst. Couldn't even remember hearing him swear.

'What's that, Col?'

He turned to me, eyes wide, said, 'Well, he's a politician, isn't he.'

I couldn't read Col's thoughts, but Cardownie got his goat, I saw that clearly enough.

'Yeah, like I say, a wanker. He's trying to put the blame on plod. Buck passer.'

I watched Cardownie smarm his way through the shitstorm with heart-stopping ease. Couldn't believe anyone bought this. Dredged up an adage from David Hume: 'Nothing appears more surprising to those who consider human affairs with a philosophical eye, than the ease with which the many are governed by the few.'

Suddenly, Col's interest shifted. He reached for the doofer, switched off the telly. 'Have you any news for me, Gus?'

I tapped the bar. 'Have you any booze for me, Col?'

COL TURNED TO HIS OPTICS, put a stare on me as he filled a shot glass with Jack Daniel's. Tennessee's finest, old-time number seven. Good old Col, he's got my number.

'Well?' he said, placing the whiskey in front of me.

'Go well with a pint.' After a comment like that, anyone else would have blown it, not Col. Cool as you like, he pulled down a pint glass.

'Guinness?'

'Nice and creamy.'

I will never tire of watching Col pour a pint of the black stuff. It's an art. Getting the consistency right is the first tester. Length of wait the next. The head requires a special kind of genius.

Col put the pint down, leaned on the bar. I knew he was desperate to prise information from me. I was desperate to avoid the subject. I had some details to give him, but I'd plenty more to leave out.

I avoided his gaze, grabbed up the telly doofer. *Doctor Who* had started.

'Never the same without Tom Baker.'

'What?' said Col.

'The Doctor – to me he's still Tom Baker, they can never replace him. Like Bond, you know, everyone has their Bond. It's a moment in time, a peak of interest, when the character first comes alive for you.'

Col returned to the Guinness. Worked on the final third of the pint. Minutes later he thunked down the glass. The shamrock drawn in the creamy head shuddered over the edge in the wake of his frustration.

'Thanks, Col,' I said. The taste danced on my lips. A joy like no other. I knew I'd delayed the inevitable long enough.

'Shall we, er, move to the snug?'

Three quick nods, a wipe of the bar, and Col led the way.

The snug was empty. At night time, you fight for a seat here. This time of the day, though, was for hard-core drinkers. The lonely looking for company. The dole moles.

The Wall felt like home, the snug, like my front room. Each name carved in the wood panelling as familiar as a family photo. The crushed and worn seat cushions were – what's the word? – cosy. You couldn't recreate the feel of this place with a million quid. Pubs like this, they need to evolve.

I drained my JD, fired right in. 'There's some . . . progress.'

'*Uh-huh.*'

'I don't know how to put this, Col, so I'm just going to tell it straight.'

Col's expression tightened. I traced the fine lines around his eyes, they crossed his cheekbones like girders on the Forth Bridge. 'I wouldn't want you to soft-soap me, Gus.'

'All right, but if you feel the need to, just stop me.'

'I won't!'

Took a breath, dived right in. 'Look, Col, I think Billy was involved with some very shady people.'

'I agree.'

'You do?'

'I've known for some time that that boy was no angel. If it wasn't for his mother—' Col broke off suddenly. 'Well, what have you to tell me?'

'The outfit he worked for are a heavy-duty Russian firm. We're not just talking about wee boys twoking car stereos here, Col.'

'What line are they in?'

I nearly laughed, he made it sound like we were two salesmen, bumping into each other in a Little Chef on the M8.

'I can't be sure of anything at this stage, but, and I think I'm only scratching the surface here, they look like people smugglers.' I took a deep breath. 'No, worse, it's young girls they're bringing in.'

'For what?'

73

'Hazard a guess.'

Col sat back in his chair. A pious look crossed his face. I wondered if he weighed what I said against his religion. I didn't think the good book had a section that read: 'Thou shalt not smuggle my poor European neighbours.' But what did I know about that?

'It's Nadja, isn't it?' said Col.

I nodded.

'I knew she was bad for him right from the start. I saw she was no good. I told him, Gus. I did.'

I couldn't muster the words. Col reeked hurt. There was nothing to be gained by telling him about the threat on my life. I didn't want to worry him, or worse, freak him out completely. I wasn't going to have Col pull me off the job. More than ever I felt the weight of duty pressing on me. The man looked ready to crumble into pieces.

'I just can't believe my Billy was involved.'

'Col . . .' He wasn't listening to me.

'I just, I just can't believe it.' He looked into me. 'Not my boy, not my son.'

'We don't know he was involved.'

'Oh he was.' Col sounded certain. 'I just need to know why.'

I wanted to tell him I'd do my best to find out; but I knew anything I said would sound trite. Went with, 'How's the wife coping?'

'She has her moments, y'know. I don't think she'll ever be the same. There's nothing I can do about that now.'

'Are you looking after her?' I'd blurted it out all wrong. Christ, why did you say that, Gus?

Col's eyes shone like match tips. 'Of course.'

'I didn't mean . . .'

'I know, I know. You're a good man, Gus. I can't tell you how much I— how much we both appreciate what you're doing.'

'I was just—'

He raised a hand. 'Look, there's no need. I want you to have no doubt about the debt I owe you for this. There is no one else can give me . . . closure.'

Closure. What was that? Jeez, I wanted a smoke.

'This smoking ban's a bastard, isn't it?' I said.

'Oh, sorry, you want a cigarette. Shall we go outside?'

'No, I'll go upstairs. I need to pack anyway.'

'Pack?'

'Yeah. I'll be moving out for a while.'

'But why? Where will you go?'

'I need to lie low for a time, Col. Don't worry, it's nothing to worry about. I just need to put a bit of distance between myself and this life for a while.'

'Are you in trouble, Gus?'

'No. God no. I just need to keep a bit of a low profile right now, if I'm to get close to this mob.'

'I see. You're going under cover.'

Under cover. Please. Saw myself on a stake-out with a bag of dough-nuts.

'Yeah. Kinda.'

ON THE WAY UPSTAIRS, I passed a picture hanging in the hall that grabbed my attention. 'Cannis Dury, Scottish Cup Final 1978', it said on the frame. How had I missed this? I stared at the photo for a full minute. He'd just scored. None of the Ryan Giggs making a lasso of his shirt. Was barely a glimmer of recognition in his eye. The only reason I knew he'd scored was that he had the ball under his arm. Back to the centre line, more work to do. No messing. That's how he played.

My father had a rep as a studs first sweeper; shouted himself silent every game. Would have made Vinnie Jones look like a shandy drinker. I once met one of his old adversaries, who summed him up in one word: 'Fierce.' I'd never been able to better that.

I turned the picture to face the wall.

I had the key to the flat in my hand as my mobile started ringing.

'Hello?'

'Ah, 'tis your bold self!'

'Milo?'

'Who did ye think it was? There's not many have the brogue as thick as me, not since Dave Allen passed, anyway.'

I gave a little laugh. 'It's good to hear from you.'

'Bollocks, isn't it the life of Riley you'll be living, not a care in the world, lest of all for an old pot-walloper like m'self.'

He had me, but I couldn't disguise how glad I was to hear his voice. 'So how are you, buddy?'

A hacking cough, chased by peals of laughter. 'Oh, grand, grand. Doctors reckon I've weeks ahead of me!'

His patter sounded tremendous for the age of him and the life he led. I couldn't admire him more. 'Stop, you're killing me!'

'I'll stop now, I will. To be serious for a second, Gus . . .' Milo's voice dropped to the pits of him, his words came like tremors to my ears, 'I was wondering, well, hoping really, if you could oblige me—'

I cut him off. 'Name it, Milo.'

'Well it's – you'll think I'm such an old fool.'

'Never.' He had me concerned, he began to sound so fearful. 'What is it?'

'If you had some time free, Gus, would you ever be able to pay me a little visit?'

'Sure I would. God, Milo, it would be a pleasure. Didn't I say I'd be round soon enough?'

'No, Gus, you misunderstand. I don't mean a social visit.'

'What?'

I heard him shuffle the phone from hand to hand, then his voice sank to barely a whisper, 'There are some very strange things afoot here.'

'You'll have to speak up, I can hardly hear you.'

More shuffling of the phone, then, 'Some very young women, pale as ghosts they were, and—' He stopped dead.

'Milo? Milo, you still there?'

'I can't really say any more – it's the cute hoor.'

'Gotcha. Stalin's about?'

'Ahem, yes, that's right.'

My mind flipped back to Milo's black eye. 'I swear, if that bastard has laid a finger on you—'

'No, Gus, sure I'm fine – right as rain!'

I sensed he overstated things, he sounded clearly distressed by something. 'I'll be round right away.'

'No! Jaysus, would ye ever listen? Amn't I fine? All I'm saying is I'd like to get your considered opinion on something.' He had started to choose his words too carefully for my liking, I could tell he feared they might land him in trouble. 'When ye have a moment, just drop by. I will look out for you. Goodbye for now.'

He hung up before I could say another word.

THE DOOR TO MY FLAT sat open. Right away, I thought it looked like the result of a blackout. Couldn't remember leaving the latch off, but hey, there's a lot of things I've lost to the drink. Inside I jolted: I'd have remembered this, surely.

The flat looked like a war zone. Bed thrown arseways. Mattress to the wall. Table, missing its legs, lay in bits under a pile of debris.

'C'mon, Gus – think.' It was no good. If I'd any part in this, it had left me.

My mind flipped into cartwheels.

I waded through the broken plates and torn cushions that covered the floor. Newspapers scattered to the four winds alongside a busted set of venetian blinds. My own cuttings, all my top scoops, ripped to bits. Every picture frame kicked cockeyed.

I did a circuit, picking up bits and pieces as I went. Was beginning to think this wasn't me. Much too comprehensive a going over for a start. I wouldn't have had the energy.

I pushed the door closed and saw it. Scrawled in foot-high lettering, 'GET OUT!'

Neat, almost stencilled, in block capitals. I went closer, looked like a magi-marker. 'What's wrong with the old spray can?' I wondered.

I did another lap of the joint. It all looked very strange. A textbook turnover for sure. But, who would do this? It wasn't gangster style. They'd have torched the place, or done my knees. Hadn't Benny the Bullfrog already given me one warning through Mac? A second would be verging on weakness. Either Zalinskas had turned soft, which I doubted, or someone else was also on my case.

A rap on the door stuck a needle in me. I turned quickly, grabbed up a broken table leg. A makeshift club, not quite the regulation baseball bat, but close enough to be in the ball park. I gripped tight, slapped the end of it into my open palm. Got set to knock seven bells out of all comers.

I walked to the door, called out, 'Who is it?'

'It's me. Who do you think it is?'

'Col, just a minute.' I wasn't about to let him see the state of the place. He had enough to worry about without this adding to his woes.

'I've brought you a wee bit of lunch.'

Heard a tray rattle. Shit. He wanted in.

'Eh, could you leave it outside? I'm just getting into the shower.'

A long pause, then I heard the tray rattle again.

'Suit yourself. But don't let it get cold. It's mince and stovies, thought you looked like you could do with a bit of fattening up.'

Another one, what was this?

I stuck my fingers down the sides of my jeans. They were 32s and loose. Maybe I'd missed the odd meal. Weight is a national obsession in Scotland, no one likes to see a skelf. In Edinburgh, since we got the tag 'Aids Capital of Europe', being a bit skelky wasn't a good look.

I waited till I heard Col's footsteps on the stairs, then I got the tray. Polished off the stovies in no time. Began to feel contented within myself, sat back and loosened off my top button. Then I remembered I wasn't staying. 'Don't get too comfortable, Gus,' I told myself.

It didn't take long to straighten out the flat. I picked up the cushions, put away the rest of the wreckage and hung a calendar over the warning notice.

I took out an old Lotto kit bag that I used for the gym when I was health conscious, employed, married . . . stable. Filled it with a few essentials from the wardrobe and a handful of books from the shelves. Some Hemingway and Steinbeck, to escape Edinburgh, and some Nietzsche to put my feet back on the ground.

In the bar, I caught Col's eye as he finished serving a punter. I saw he'd taken down the picture of my father and propped it against a box of smoky bacon crisps.

He caught me staring. 'I meant to take that down ages ago,' he said. 'Sorry, Gus ... but what with one thing and another, I must have forgotten.'

'Don't worry.'

'No. No. I know you told me to bin the lot of them after . . . Well, I just missed that one.'

'Col, it's your pub. I've no right to tell you what you can put on the wall.'

A long silence stretched between us. Col turned an open hand to the pumps. I shook my head.

'You must loathe the man,' he said.

'Got that right.'

'He's your father.'

'And . . . ?'

'Whatever he's done, nothing changes that, surely.'

I shot him a glower, then stared over his head to the line of mixers.

'I am only saying, Gus. Whatever he's done, could you not forgive him?'

I took my hands out of my pockets, reached down for the kit bag and swiftly lifted it from the bar stool before me.

'I'll have to be going,' I said.

I turned and walked to the door.

'Wait. Wait up,' shouted Col. He stopped me in the doorway, said, 'I've this for you.'

I didn't need to look, knew it had to be more money. A big wad of tens grabbed from the till, stuffed in an envelope.

'No, Col . . .'

'Don't go proud on me. We all need a lot more than we let on sometimes.'

I couldn't argue. 'Thanks.'

He lent me a smile and placed a hand on my shoulder. 'I, er, saw your mother the other day at the supermarket.'

'Yeah?'

'She says Cannis's not so well now.'

This again. I wasn't biting.

'Col, please, I know you think you're doing some good here, but don't use that man's name around me.'

'I was only saying . . . Your mother was asking for you, she wanted me to let you know.'

I sighed, said, 'Well, you've done it.'

SPENT THE NIGHT IN AN East End kip house. Came cheap, but none too cheerful. Knew I needed to make more permanent arrangements, and soon.

Going out the door my phone rang, was Amy. I said, 'Oh hi, was just about to give you a ring.'

'What kind – diamond?'

'Ha! Lot cheaper.'

'*Ruby*?'

'Closer, was thinking *Orange* – mobile.'

Loud sigh followed. 'At least I know you're not going to disappoint me tonight. We're still on, aren't we?'

I'd forgotten all about it, said, ''Course we are.'

'Great.' She sounded ecstatic, boosted my worth. 'Because I thought I might get my hooks into you a bit earlier, make sure you don't go AWOL on me again.'

This crushed me, I didn't want to be tied down by anybody. 'How early?'

'Like, now-ish.'

I looked at my watch. Wasn't yet nine, in the a.m. 'Where are you?'

Suddenly I felt a solid slap on my shoulder.

'Here!'

'Jesus! Are you trying to end me?'

She laughed like a drain. Amy looked luscious in tight white jeans, a kooky hip-hugging dress thrown over them. 'You're not quite in your heart attack years yet, Gus!'

'I'm a damn sight nearer after that, let me tell you. What are you playing at?'

'Thought I'd come and meet you.'

'How did you know where I'd be? I hardly know the answer to that one myself these days.'

'Impulse. Female intuition – call it what you like.'

'Stalking.'

The smile went. 'Not funny!'

'Touchy subject? The voice of experience?'

She grabbed my arm. 'Come on,' she said, 'and try to lighten up. Old, I can handle, old prick, no thanks.'

Thought about saying I was the same age all over, but left it.

There seemed to be something different about Amy today, but I couldn't place it. Truth was, I'd a distraction. Kept turning around to look for the Cube. Don't know why. I'd no reason to think he'd be following me at this moment, just a trick of the memory, I supposed. The first time he'd shown, Amy was in my company, but I'd nothing to suggest this was anything more than coincidence.

We got a rare blast of sun, grabbed some fruit smoothies and settled down in Holyrood Park. I ruined the healthy look with a Scotch pie – real cow-brain special.

'You should go veggie,' said Amy.

'I should do lots of things, going veggie's about bottom of the list.'

'Oh, whatever!' There it was again. Amy's vocabulary tripped across the Atlantic. Maybe there was hope for her generation to shake off some home-grown influences.

'Don't you mean, *like whatever*?'

'Eh?'

'No matter.' I felt bored with the conversation, changed tack. 'Amy, do you remember when I ran into you the other day?'

'With the tie. God, what was that like?'

'Yeah. Enough about the tie.' I shook my head. 'There was a guy, remember?'

'No, not really . . . well, maybe . . . You said something about a guy with a paper. Why?'

'He showed up again.'

'Freaky.'

'I thought so.'

'Is he, like, following you?'

'I'm pretty sure he's bloody following me. And some bastard turned over my gaff.'

'What? Like the movies? That's just mental.'

'Tell me.'

'Who do you think it is?'

I laid it all out for her: Billy's murder; the Latvian girls; the death threat. I left nothing out. I gave her an ideal opportunity to take off, run for the hills. But, all credit to her, she seemed concerned. Whether it came down to a lack of years or romantic idealism, her hackles seemed well and truly raised.

'Gus, this is just awful.'

I nodded into my smoothie.

'I wouldn't have believed . . .' She looked out into the road, an old woman struggled along with a shopping trolley. 'I mean, it all seems so normal out there.'

Her statement seemed absurd to me. I hadn't known normal for a very long time.

'What are you going to do?'

'What I have to – find Billy's killer.'

'I want to help.'

I smiled at her. She meant every word, but the idea that she could be any help to me was laughable and the exact opposite of what I'd hoped she'd say.

'You're doing that already – listening to this is a help, Amy. You're helping me get all this straight in my mind. It's a lot to carry around.'

'That's not what I meant. I meant proper help.'

'Like what?'

'I don't know. There's got to be something I could do.'

It crossed my mind that by keeping her around I'd take the edge off the danger – it might be tricky making a hit on me with a witness about. But I scrubbed the idea. She had to go, I knew it.

'The reason I told you all this wasn't to get you involved. I wanted to explain things, why I have to—'

'Oh, here it comes.' She flung back her head. A tremor of tiny ripples passed along the top of her smoothie.

'It's not like that.'

'No?'

'What I'm trying to tell you is that if you stick around me, you could be in danger. Maybe not as much as me, but there might be trouble.'

She stood up. 'You bastard.'

'*Sorry?*'

As I looked at her I became aware of what bugged me about her appearance. A new piercing sat above her lip, to the right.

'You've got a piercing?'

'Oh, so you noticed.'

'I did. I did. Look, sit back down, Amy.'

She calmed a bit. 'It's called a Monroe.'

'Why's that?'

'Marilyn *Monroe*.' Amy pointed to the shiny piece of silver above her lip. 'She had, like, a beauty spot or something about here.'

I liked the idea, said, 'Nice – I've climbed all the Munros, you know.'

She frowned on me. 'I think you've missed one!'

I PACKED AMY INTO A Joe Baxi. Things looked way too messy to have her around now. But something told me she wasn't just going to disappear.

The thought of putting her in danger was one of a million things whirring round in my mind right now. None of them nice. I caught myself biting on the inside of my cheek as I moved off. The pain nipped my nerves. 'Jeez, what doesn't these days?' I thought.

I jumped on the first bus that appeared.

Someone played Sting on their iPod. Me, I'm with Ozzy Osbourne, he said that no matter how grim things get, 'It could be worse, you could be Sting!'

I rolled this about for a while, to the soundtrack of 'Fields of Gold'. Christ, could have chucked up when it came on. That's the way with Sting. For me it's the whole 'save the planet' bollocks. He'll gad about on TV with some gadgie from the rainforest, while plugging Concorde and Jaguar at the same time. For Chrissake, a Jag's got two petrol tanks! Can't he see the contradiction?

I got off on Princes Street, immediately caught in the slipstream of shopping zombies. Was a no-brainer to just keep walking. My legs seemed to tap into the collective rhythm and before long I'd put myself right in the path of Fitz the Crime's patch.

'By the holy . . . I thought we'd said all we had to to each other,' he blasted coming round the corner of Montgomery Street and on to the Walk.

'That's not how we left it, Fitz.'

'Look, Dury—'

I cut him off, stepped up to face him. 'No, you look, Fitz. I'm not fucking about, hear me?'

Silence.

I started up again, 'I helped you out once and now you're going to settle the score.'

'Or else – Is that it?'

'Well . . .' I kept my tone threatening.

'I'm not a man to cross, Dury.'

'Neither am I.' I let that one register, shifted on to the front foot. 'I want the file on Billy Boy.'

'Are you out of your mind? Am I even hearing this?' Fitz tried to push past me, but I was too quick for him, blocked his path.

'I won't ask again, Fitz. The file on Billy.'

'Dury, you're cracked. Jesus! Have you any idea of the consequences?'

'Monday, Fitz.'

He lit up like a bonfire, his meaty neck quivered as he put his head down and walked right through me.

I decided to spend a few days in the West End. Thought it had to be the last place anyone would look for me.

Mostly, I don't get out this way, but I found a B&B. They charged like raging bulls, but it was getting dark and I needed to lie low for a while. Even managed to keep off the sauce. Kept playing Bob Dylan's advice: 'Alcohol will kill anything that's alive and preserve anything that's dead.'

I knew what he meant, but I wasn't ready to start drying out just yet. It was temporary; I needed a clear head.

Was tugging at the window, in preparation of a fly-smoke when my mobile went off.

'Dury.'

'You're an elusive fella, Mr Dury.'

It was Milo, but with none of his usual sparkle.

'Oh, Jeez, Milo. I'm sorry, I forgot to—'

''Tis fine, Gus. I know ye have a busy life to lead.'

'No, no – it's more than that. I had my flat broken into and, well, it's just been pretty full-on lately.'

'I understand.'

He might have understood, but I sure as hell didn't. What was I playing at? He'd asked me for some help, an old man with no one, and I'd let him down. I deserved flogging.

'Milo, are you okay?'

'Yes. I'm okay.'

'Are you sure about that? You sound tired.'

'Gus, I must be very frank with you—' He broke off, coughing and spluttering like he'd hit his death rattle.

'Milo? You still there?'

'Yes, I-I made the fatal mistake of travelling from home in the pissing rain, 'tis lashing!'

'What was wrong with the pay phone in the hallway?'

A long silence. I could hear him wheezing, breath a difficulty.

'Gus . . . I saw something very strange back there.'

I felt the muscles in my face twitch. 'The girls – is this about the girls, Milo? Look, I saw them too, and I'm all fired up to get to the bottom of it.'

''Tis depravity I saw. God, can I even say it?' His voice sounded flat of emotion; the words he usually packed with humour and meaning escaped him.

'Have you been hurt . . . threatened?'

'Not exactly.'

'Not exactly! Jesus, stay put. I'll be over right away.'

'No, Gus, please no.'

I could hear tears coming from him now.

'Milo?'

'Please, please. Don't come, not now.'

'What's up?'

'I'm sorry, I was wrong to call. I was wrong to involve you . . . only, haven't I no one else?'

His tears came faster. I could hear him croaking and trying hard to hold back the flow of hurt that came out of him.

'You have me! I'm here for you. Look, whatever the problem is, there's nothing I won't try to fix.'

I heard the heavy call-box receiver go down. My mind spun, my stomach followed it faster than getaway tyres. I ran to the other side of the room and picked up my jacket. My smokes fell from the pocket but I didn't stop to pick them up as I went to the door.

I yanked the handle and my heart rate suddenly dropped to nothing.

A face I hardly recognised stood in the hallway.

'Hello, Gus.'

'Debs! What are you doing here?'

A LENGTHY SILENCE FOLLOWED, LAID down a huge gap between us. This was crazy, we were still man and wife.

'How did you find me?'

'I went to your flat. Col said you were here.'

Good old Col, I had called to let him know where I was, but I could have done without her knowing I lived this way. Not exactly an advert for stability.

'I got your letter,' I said.

'That's good.'

'So, you're not messing about then, your lawyer's pushed the button.'

There it was, that gap again.

'Look, Gus, you knew this was coming. I told you.'

'I thought there might have been a bit more . . . discussion.'

A tut.

'We've done all the talking.'

I turned away, shook my head. 'Oh, have we now? You've decided. Deborah's made her mind up and that's all there is to it. If that's the case, then why are you here?'

A loud sigh, she shifted a hand to the bag strap over her shoulder, fiddled nervously with it. 'I see this might be a bit of a shock to you, Gus.'

'Oh, it's a shock all right – but don't pretend you care about my feelings. You'll be asking how I'm getting on next.'

Her hand jerked from the strap, slapped at her thigh. 'Look, if you're going to start getting aggressive . . .'

'You'll what? Get your lawyer to write me another threatening letter?'

'Okay. I can see there's not much point in pursuing this.'

She turned away from me, headed back towards the door. I locked myself down, this wasn't the way I'd wanted things to be between us. 'Sorry, I'm sorry, Debs . . . All this is doing my head in.'

She looked round, took her hand off the door handle. 'It's not easy for me, either.'

'I know, but I'm under a lot of pressure just now.'

'Are you drinking?'

'No. God, no – haven't touched a drop.'

'For how long?'

'Days.'

'How many – one, two?'

She had my number. Any more than that would be a new record; then, we might just have something to talk about.

'Does it matter? It's the fact that I'm cleaning up my act that's import-ant, surely.'

Another tut, softer this time, it arrived almost hidden under breath.

'What does that mean?' I said.

'Nothing.'

'No. No. Go on. Tell me what you mean.'

'There's no point.'

'There's every point, I want to know what you meant by that *tut*.'

'Gus, stop this.'

'I won't – I'll never get clean. That's what it means, isn't it? You've no faith in me, Debs, you never fucking have had!'

'Right, that's it. I'm not going to get drawn into another one of your stupid barnies. I had hoped we could resolve things amicably, but obvi-ously not.'

'Truth hurts too much, huh?'

'That's it, Gus. I told you the last time: I've had it with the rows, the recriminations – I'm not the enemy. I never was.'

Tut.

I turned the tables on her. It felt good, for all of a second.

'You pushed me away – just like you push everything else.'

'Yeah, yeah.'

'Keep pushing it. You're going to be left with nothing. Sad and lonely, staring into a bottle of whisky.' She upped the volume, her voice cracked, 'How could you think I could watch you do that to yourself?'

'Debs—'

'No, leave it.' I'd brought her to tears. 'It's over and the sooner you realise that the better. For crying out loud, just take a look at yourself. Not for the sake of this fucked-up marriage, for yourself.'

'Debs—'

'We're finished. I don't want you to call me again, do you understand?'

'What – why?'

'I mean it. If you've any more to say to me, call my lawyer.'

'Debs ... Debs ...'

I BEGAN TO THINK THE days without drink had left me damaged.

I took myself to a wine bar off Shandwick Place. These joints make me want to chuck. All the suits, designer mostly. Talk of blue-sky thinking and running ideas up the flagpole. Everyone looking so cocky, comfortable. I knew I despised them not only for what they were, but for what they had.

I could only stomach five minutes in the place. Long enough to drop two triples, and settle my shakes.

The bus out to the East End seemed slower than usual. Roads clogged up with taxis and teenage cruisers. When I finally made it to Fallingdoon House the whisky had hit in and sleep seemed ready to fall upon me.

Then I saw the blue lights. Police. Fire. Ambulance.

It took all my strength, but I managed to sprint the final few hundred yards.

The place was in disarray. Smoke billowed from a ground-floor window that had been smashed for the firemen to climb through. In the front yard the occupants stood in pyjamas and nighties, shivering and coughing their lungs up.

'What the hell's going on?' I shouted.

None of them answered, the look of shock on their faces said they knew as much as me.

I grabbed a cop. 'What's happened?'

'A fire.'

'Really?' I kept the no shit Sherlock to myself. 'Anyone hurt?'

The copper tipped his head back, looked at me from under the brim of his hat. 'Do you live here, sir?'

'No. Well, I used to.'

His head came forward, chased by a frown. 'Used to?'

'Look my friend lives here. Milo. Is he all right?'

'I've no idea. You'll have to ask the inspector.'

I left him standing with a thumb casually stuck in his belt, could think of a better place for it but let it slide.

Inside the house the walls were blackened. The floor squelched underfoot from the gallons of water that had been pumped in to put out the fire. It was impossible to say where the fire had been, but then I heard voices coming from Milo's room. I took off, sliding on the wet carpet and collecting black streaks of soot down my arms and hands as I tried to steady myself.

'What's happened?'

'Who the fuck are you?' said a trench coat, bald head and beaten-up features falling in behind.

'Dury. My friend lives here.'

He eyed me up and down. 'No one lives here. Not any more.'

'Come again?'

He turned away from me, spoke to one of the uniforms. As I stared at the back of his bald head I felt ready to rabbit-punch him through the wall.

'What do you mean, no one lives here any more?'

Trench coat flicked his head at the uniform and then turned to face me. He stuck his hands in his pockets as he started to speak, 'Look at that.'

His eyes pointed to a pile of empty bottles in the corner of the room; they were blackened and burned.

'Empties, so what?'

'No one lives here any more, because the old dosser who stayed in this room got tanked up on cheapo Vladivar and burnt himself the fuck alive!'

I felt suddenly drained of blood. My mouth dried up and a deadbolt twisted in my stomach.

'You see . . . that's the danger of smoking and drinking.' He pointed to a pile of charred mess in the corner, I could vaguely make out the iron bedstead where Milo laid his head every night, was that heap all that remained of him?

'Fucking silly old bastard,' he said.

'No. No! You've made a mistake. He didn't drink, and he sure as hell didn't smoke!'

I walked over to the broken window and grabbed for air. Outside the spinning lights of the fire engines slapped me senseless. I felt my knees weaken, I steadied myself on the ledge and prepared to fall.

'Mistake – bullshit. It's a no-brainer, seen it a million times before: some old jakey starts drinking to the old days, thinking he can still put it away and then – whoof! Probably didn't feel a thing.'

I turned round too fast, the room spun with me. 'No! You've got it wrong. This is murder! He called me to say there was something going on.'

'Murder? Don't make me laugh!'

I ran over and grabbed him by the lapels. 'I'm telling you – you've got to look into this properly.'

The jokey tone dropped from the trench coat's voice. 'Who the hell are you to be telling me my job?' As he spoke my arms got knocked into the air. It was just enough to set me off balance and drop me on the wet, soot-blackened floor.

'This is an open and shut case – the old jakey set himself alight after drinking all that shit. And by the smell of your breath, son, you could do with watching how much you're putting away.'

'But—'

'But fuck all. Get your arse out of my sight before I run you in for getting on my nerves. Now move it!'

FOR THE SECOND TIME IN less than a week I slung my bag onto my back and prepared to take up a new residence. Felt a strange sense of déjà vu out in the open. Couldn't place it. Had myself convinced Milo's ghost followed me around. Felt as good as a ghost myself.

I got an urge to turn around, and as I did so, saw I'd been off the mark, again.

The Cube stood across the road from me. He hid himself behind a *Daily Record*, but I'd have known that boxy frame anywhere.

'Right, you bastard,' I thought, 'this time you've had it.' Billy's death wasn't the only one I had to reckon with now; I'd be having some answers from this bastard.

I took off slowly. Sauntering pace. Right the way to Princes Street. I wanted to turn around, eyeball the Cube, but I knew better.

At Waterstone's, the first one on the main drag, I stood and stared in the window. I tried to get a view of the crowds in the reflection. Too hard to make anyone out, except a jakey wrapped up like Sherpa Tenzing. With his hand out, a blanket in the other flapped about as he tried some freestyling.

I said, 'Hey, Flavour Flav, come here.'

The jakey moved towards me. He looked to be one more purple tin away from sleeping in his own piss.

'Awright there, mister – price of a cuppa tea?'

I put my hand in my pocket, his whole head followed the movement.

'Right,' I said producing a five spot, 'this is yours if you can help me out.'

'Aw, for fucksake,' he said.

'Cool the beans. I only want you to tell me if there's a bloke with a copy of the *Daily Record* still standing over my shoulder?'

The jakey smiled. Showing a row of teeth with more gaps than a comb, looked like he'd been flossing with rope.

'Eh, aye,' he said. Then put his hand out.

'Not so fast. What's he look like?'

The jakey frowned. He grew agitated, but I saw he tasted that Tennent's Super already. I stepped in front of him. 'Make it look good too – don't want him to sus what I'm up to.'

A nod. Tap on the side of the nose. And another swatch at those teeth.

'Eh, he's a fat wee bastard!'

'What's he wearing?'

'Pair of trews and some manky auld leather.'

'That's my man!'

I handed over the fiver – he took the money and ran.

I set off in the opposite direction. Crossed at the lights. Took the path round the Gardens. Got halfway along when the one o'clock gun sounded at the castle.

At the Mound I shot up the steps to the Old Town. My heart thumped like a road drill. The sweat on my brow dripped in my eyes. I felt way out of shape. Not up to this. I hoped the Cube felt worse.

'Just keep up, Mr Cube,' I whispered, 'just keep up.'

At the top of the High Street, by the statue of David Hume, I spotted him skulking on the edge of the Lawnmarket, right where the scaffold once stood for public hangings. He'd no clue how close to a lynching he was himself.

I had him pegged: out of breath, fanning his chops with the pages of his paper.

I headed down the Royal Mile. Picked up my pace, worked through a stitch. I took a turn onto Cockburn Street. Just about heard the Cube panting at my back. My legs ached as I put in for a last spurt.

Head down, I tanked it up the steps of Fleshmarket Close.

At the top, I slumped. Back to the wall.

My chest wheezed. 'I am so, so shagged.'

I watched, moved into an empty shop front, and waited.

The Cube looked close to a coronary. He struggled to find the strength to drag his pudgy frame up another step. But, all credit to the man, he persisted.

As my breathing returned to normal, I felt an uncontrollable urge for nicotine. Sparked up a tab and drew deep. I relaxed at once. Flung back my head and waited.

On the final steps the Cube coughed and choked like a nag on the way to the glue factory.

As the top of his head came into view I stepped out in front of him. He hunched over, looked up, and I blew smoke in his face. 'Ta dah!' I said. 'And as if by magic, the shopkeeper suddenly appeared.'

THE CUBE MADE TO RUN.

He hobbled back down the steps, on his bandy legs, arms flailing. I let him open a dozen paces between us before I stubbed my tab and reached out to collar him.

'I think it's time you and I had a little chat,' I said, as I latched onto his throat.

He tried to speak, 'I-I-I . . .'

'Catch your breath, fuckhead, you've a lot of explaining to do.' I grabbed his paper, 'And you won't be needing the *Daily Ranger*!'

In the winding streets of the Old Town, it's never hard to find an empty vennel. Very few people stray from the well-trodden paths. I pushed the Cube through a set of rusty gates into a dark courtyard. A stack of mouldy crates fell with him as he tried to scramble to safety.

'No escape this time,' I said.

His eyes darted from left to right. I saw him toy with the idea of balling a fist. I didn't give him a chance. My right connected like a car crash. If pain was a target on his face, I'd hit the bullseye. Blood oozed from nose and mouth. He dropped like a telegraph pole in high wind. Soundless. Sprawled out on the ground, motionless.

'Is that it?' I thought.

A one-punch job.

I grabbed the collar of his mangy leather and sat him on his fat arse. He lolled woozily, but responded to a slap.

'Now, there's plenty more where that came from.' I felt fierce, I knew the territory. It didn't matter whether I was acting up, or it was real, either way, the Cube shat bricks.

'Spill,' I told him.

'What? What? I was just . . .'

Wrong answer. I drew up my elbow, the dumbfuck followed it. He caught a mouthful of bone.

'I can honestly say, I've never heard a grown man scream before.'

He spat blood, his face turned into a mask of agony.

'Are they tears?' I said. 'Are you crying?'

He said something, but I couldn't make a word of it.

I stepped back, lit a tab. I wondered if I'd gone too far. This guy looked to be in the wrong line.

As I knelt down beside him, he flinched.

'Okay. Maybe you've had enough – you ready to talk?'

He nodded feverishly. 'Yes. Yes. Yes.'

'Good.'

I drew on my tab, blew into the tip. Little orange sparks flew. Then I held it like a dart, close to his eye.

'Now, I am warning you, one word of a lie and you'll need a white stick and a Labrador to get out of here – understand?'

'Yes! God, yes! I'll tell you all you want to know, just leave me alone. God, you're insane!'

Too easy. Was I really this menacing? I'd need to hit some serious psychological tomes for the answer to that.

'Why are you following me?'

'It's a job – I'm on a job.'

'You're an investigator?'

'Aye!' He ferreted in his jacket, for his wallet. 'Look – look,' he said. He produced a stack of cards. Cheap printouts, poor quality. They all read Private Investigator. The address said Gorgie. He ran the show from a cold-water flat. Whoever hired him either worked to a budget or didn't know shit.

'Not exactly bloody Magnum PI are you?'

'I do all right.'

'Mate, believe me, you're far from fucking all right.' I pressed my knee in his back and grabbed a handful of hair. 'Now, who hired you?'

'Arghh . . . I can't.'

I tightened my grip, dug my knee into his shoulder blades. Felt the pressure mounting on my kneecap as he let out a scream.

'Okay – just let me go.'

'Name?'

'I don't have a name, she didn't give me a name.'

'*She?*'

'Aye. A woman, Russian – sounds it anyway. She just told me to follow you and report back to her at the Shandwick.'

Nadja. I didn't need to know any more.

'On your feet.'

'What?'

'Get on your fucking feet, now!'

He stood up; brushed at his backside. The way he looked, blood smeared on his face, hair sticking up like a duck's arse, he needn't have bothered.

'What are you going to do with me now?' he said.

I sooked the final draw out my tab and flicked the dowp into the alley. 'I'll ask the questions. Now, walk.'

'Where – where are we going?'

I prodded him in the back and pushed him into the close. 'To see your employer. I've words to have with Nadja.'

'But . . . why do you need me? Surely, I'm no use to you now.'

I held up one of his cheap cards, said, 'See that? I know where you live.' The Cube's eyes widened, like he'd been anally probed. 'One more word from you about leaving the party, I'll be on your doorstep with a machete. Am I making myself clear?'

Nods. Thick and fast.

'Glad we understand each other. Now move your lardy fucking arse.'

I HIT THE BAR WITH brass-knuckles. Wild Turkey. Pale ale. Burst of tequila slammers. Mixing like this, not a worry to me. Once, the volume of drink seemed all that mattered. As my alcoholism progressed, a different strategy became necessary.

That's the way it is with me. Swear, other alkies will tell you the same thing. It's not the drink. It's not the feeling, the taste, the debauchery. It's what Graham Greene called the battle against boredom. The need to escape yourself. After a while, any pressure from the outside world begs for the journey.

'Do you really need me here?' said the Cube. He watched me carefully. His shifty eyes took in the glass in my hand, then darted off to the exit.

'What we have here is a failure to communicate.'

'What?' said the Cube.

'Some men you just can't reach, so you get what we had here.'

'I don't . . . *What?*'

'It's the way he wants it. Well, he gets it and I don't like it any more than you.'

The Cube sat back in his seat, slowly his tongue appeared on his lips.

'You've never seen *Cool Hand Luke*, have you?' I said.

A shake of the head, finger in the collar.

'Shame. It's a classic. If you had seen it you'd know two things: one, if you move off that seat, I'll burst you. Two, sometimes nothing's a pretty cool hand.'

The Cube looked away. He lowered his head as if he was praying for an end to this insanity. Like I wasn't?

I flagged the waiter.

'Stick another in there, mate.'

'Excuse me?'

Looked up, had sat there so long there'd been a shift change. The waiter was now a waitress. Though, you'd need a magnifying glass to spot the difference. A hefty she-male with a short back and sides, tie and trousers, builder's arms, the lot.

'Er, it's Wild Turkey for me, please.'

Took a frown. My order got pushed down her 'to do' list, took second billing to changing the CD to kd lang.

'Here, I think that's her,' the Cube's voice lit up for a moment, then I heard his fear creep in, 'Who you're looking for.'

Nadja knew how to make an entrance. Carrying herself like royalty, she approached the front desk. Two arm-length gloves slapped on the marble. It looked like a non-verbal cue, but one I'd never had cause to decipher. To the concierge, however, it shouted: 'Action!' He scurried round to remove Nadja's coat, bowing and scraping like a coolie in the presence of the Raj.

'Take it to my room,' she said.

A near bow. Forelock tugging. 'Right away!'

The Cube looked at me, saw we thought the same thing: 'So this is how the other half lives?'

I got to my feet. From nowhere the Leither in me rose up. The ghost of Burns reminded me: 'The rank is but the guinea's stamp . . . a man's a man for a' that.'

She took a few steps into the elevator. I followed behind her, then pressed the hold button. The indignant look on her face seemed like incitement to me.

'Take her coat,' I told the Cube.

The concierge flustered, 'Really, I mean . . .'

'No, it's all right,' said Nadja. 'These men are . . . associates of mine.'

The doors closed.

The air inside the elevator felt thick with menace. A tinder-box waiting to explode. I'd happily be the spark.

'Associates?' I said.

'What is this?' said Nadja.

'I tried to—' said the Cube.

'Shut your fucking yap!' I said.

I moved towards Nadja. The closer I got, the more I became over-powered by the scent of her perfume. I looked her up and down. She recoiled from me. Guess I didn't smell quite as good. 'This, my dear lady, is the moment of truth.'

I stopped the elevator. Opened the door. 'Do one!' I grabbed Nadja's coat from the Cube, kicked his arse on the way into the hall, he'd served his purpose now. 'And remember – I wasn't kidding about the machete.'

As the elevator began its ascent, I eyeballed Nadja.

She held herself motionless. Wouldn't grant me so much as a stare. I felt a queue of my cloth-capped forebears forming behind me. Each one, prodding, demanding I do my bit for the class struggle. I fought them off as long as I could. Even after the caps came off and were trampled under tackity boots, I kept my cool.

When the elevator stopped Nadja looked through me. Something snapped.

I hit the door lock. Grabbed her face in my hand, said, 'Lose the high and mighty pose, lady.'

She tried to turn away, raised a neatly manicured set of claws to my eyes. In a second my forearm clicked into place, pressing her by the throat to the wall.

'This is the one and only warning you're going to get. Go down that route and you'll find out what a perfectly unreconstructed example of maledom I really am.'

Her face turned white. Even through the layers of expensive panstick I saw I had her beat.

'Now, we are going to walk out of here all nicey, nicey – understand?'

She couldn't move, but signalled her compliance with a flutter of long eyelashes.

I let her go. 'Don't test me. That would be a mistake you might not live to regret.'

I'D ONLY ONE WORD FOR the way I felt about the opulence of Nadja's room: appalled. I'm a working-class bloke, it's in the contract.

The carpet felt so soft that it added an extra layer to the air-cushioned soles of my Docs. But I couldn't feel comfortable here. I'd no place in my life for gilt mirrors and walnut marquetry. Tried to tot-up the cost of furnishing a room like this. Couldn't do it – had seen nothing like it in the Argos catalogue. All I did know, I'd need several lifetimes to afford one cabriole leg of the table Nadja treated like a piece of MFI flat-pack.

'I need a cigarette,' she said, slamming the drawer shut.

She seemed on edge – just how I wanted her.

I let her hang. Wandered about the place. Caught sight of a Peploe on one of the walls.

'You don't like the picture, Mr Dury?' said Nadja. She'd found some tabs, lit up and blew smoke in my direction.

'Not my style.'

'What is?'

'I'm more a "tennis player scratching her arse" kinda guy.'

She winced, found me coarse. I wasn't the type she usually dealt with. Thought, 'Tough shit.' She'd just have to get used to roughing it with the proles for a while.

'Do you plan to take me prisoner in my own suite, Mr Dury?'

I'd a mind to do much worse. A man had been killed, a man I'd got close to. The image of Milo's burned remains stabbed me, called for revenge, and the anger inside me wasn't choosy who paid.

'You really are quite a piece of work, aren't you, Nadja?' I said.

She hesitated, stalled with her cigarette halfway to her mouth. 'I'm quite sure I do not know what it is you mean.'

I walked over to the drinks cabinet, poured out a large Courvoisier, swirled it around in the bottom of the glass. When I turned round, Nadja had lowered herself onto the chaise. She crossed her long legs delicately in my direction. 'Please, give me one.'

I sighed. 'Sorry, but I've come out without my white gloves.'

She looked confused, but undeterred. Shot me a smile.

'Let's get something straight from the off,' I said. 'That kind of shit isn't going to cut any ice with me.'

'Excuse me?'

I fired down the brandy, said, 'I don't do fuckstruck.'

Her act slipped away. She sat forward, elbows on knees. 'What do you want?'

'I seem to remember telling you what I wanted some time ago.'

'And . . .'

'Here we are again.' I reloaded with brandy.

'Look, Mr Dury, when a man, a how do you say . . . private investigator, comes to ask the questions about my personal life I have little to say.'

I drained the glass, held it in my hand, some weight in these crystal jobs. As it hit the wall the noise came like gunshot.

'Okay – Okay,' said Nadja. 'I'll tell you what you want to know. I just had to be sure who you were before I could speak.'

'And, your little helper, he filled you in?'

'I wanted to know who you were working for. I couldn't trust that you might be from them.'

'*Them?*'

'From Zalinskas.'

She fell to bits. Head in hands. Tears. The works.

I moved a chair in front of her, turned it around, sat down.

'I know about the Latvian girls. My friend found out too – and they murdered him.'

'Yes. Yes . . .'

'You and the Bullfrog, you're in it together.'

'No – Yes. With Billy. It was his job.'

'Billy brought in the girls?'

'Yes. But, there were many things he did that I did not know of.'

I reached out, lifted up her head. 'Such as?'

'I do not know. Really, there were some things Billy wouldn't even speak to me about.'

I remembered Col's words, about Billy being close to making his pile. I wasn't buying that Nadja didn't have more to give.

'And Zalinskas, he knew all about Billy's . . . activities?'

Nadja looked towards the window, placed a curl of hair behind her ear. She shook her head.

'I see.' Now we were getting somewhere. 'So Billy was branching out on his own?'

She stood up, pressed down the sides of her skirt.

'Mr Dury, I shouldn't be telling you of this – any of it.'

'Why?'

'It will put me in danger.'

I stood up quickly, knocking over the chair. 'You're already in danger, don't forget that.'

'But these people – you do not understand. If they knew, they would kill me too.'

'Knew what?'

She turned away, started to move off. I grabbed her by the arm, stopping her in her tracks. 'Knew what?'

'Billy . . . he was talking about making a lot of money in a hurry, he was on to something.'

'On to what?'

'I do not know what, he had some information and I think Zalinskas thought he should not have it.'

I squeezed her wrist. 'What do you mean, information?'

'I do not know any more. I promise. I have told you everything. Oh, Mr Dury I promise you, this is all I know.'

I dropped her arm. She sobbed, placing a hand where I had gripped her.

She'd caved. She might still be useful to me, but there was nothing left in the well right now.

'Wait! Where are you going?' she yelled out.

I said nothing, walked to the door.

'Wait! Wait!' She ran after me, grabbed at my shoulder as I reached for the door handle. 'I'm scared!'

I unhooked her hand, said, 'So hire a bodyguard.'

ON GEORGE STREET I NOTICED that my knuckles were grazed. Told myself: 'You've been running around like a psycho, Gus.' Didn't feel too proud of myself. Walked about playing with pop psychology solutions to my 'life issues'. Christ, sounded like nonsense. Remembered Doddy once said: 'The trouble with Freud is that he never played the Glasgow Empire on Saturday night after Rangers and Celtic had both lost.'

Now that made sense.

I headed down the Mile, stopped to scratch my head at the concrete and glass fag packet added on to the side of John Knox's house. Oldest building in Edinburgh, ruined by some wanky architect's ego. 'How do they get away with it?' I thought.

I stared skyward in disgust, when I heard a voice that cut me like a Stanley blade.

'Hello, Angus.'

I lowered my gaze. 'Mam.'

She stared at me wide-eyed, a look that said she'd just seen death wakened before her.

'God, you're thin, son. Are you well?'

'Yeah . . . yeah, I'm fine, Mam.'

'There's hardly a pick on you. Are you eating?'

'Yes, Mam, I'm fine.'

She gathered up her bags, fidgeted before me. Her eyes looked the deepest of blue as she took me in.

'It's been a while, son.'

'It has that.'

'I saw, whatsisname – the fellah from the pub.'

'Col. He said you spoke.' Earned myself another flash of those eyes. 'I've been meaning to . . . well, you know . . . what with one thing and another.'

'He'd have told you that your father's none too well.'

'He did.'

She shook her head. Her hair was iron grey now and hollows sat in her cheeks, 'Yes, he's not a well man at all.'

I looked away. It felt like the only thing I could do to hide my utter indifference, said, 'That right?'

'He can't leave home. I think he might be, oh, what do you call it? Homophobic.'

I couldn't laugh. 'Oh, he's that all right,' I said, 'and other things besides.'

She tucked her handbag on her elbow and reached out to me. 'It's good to see you, son.'

I smiled. This was my mother, I'd no quarrel with her. She looked to be in pain at the sight of me. Her own son, who she'd been forced to grab a few moments with in the street.

'It's been such a long time, you know,' she said.

'I know. I know.'

'It would be grand to sit down and have a proper chat, but of course you'll be, likes as not, too busy . . .'

'Would you like me to come and see him, Mam?' I hardly believed I'd said the words.

I'd taken her shopping bags off her and began to call out to a taxi before I knew where I was. Something jabbed at me, goaded me. I'd let her down for so long that I had to do something about it. If I walked away, God, those eyes would have followed me for the rest of my days.

The house smelt stale and damp, like something was rotting beneath the floor. The carpet was worn away and the boards beneath poked through.

It was the same carpet I remembered from childhood, my eyes jumped to see it still in place.

'The scene of so many crimes,' I thought.

I saw myself, seven or eight, just back from the Boys' Brigade and settling down to Findus Crispy Pancakes and an episode of *Monkey*. I'd be lost in joy, copying Monkey's moves and shouting at the screen. Then I'd remember who was coming home. It always started with glances at the clock. Then Mam started to chain smoke. After a while, it didn't seem like home at all.

We went through to the front room, sat down.

'Not changed much,' I said.

'We're not millionaires,' said Mam.

'I didn't mean . . . I mean you have it nice.'

'It's how we like it.'

She stood up. Left me to check on him.

'He's sound asleep. I'd wake him for his soup, but I think it might be better to let him rest.'

I knew I should ask what, exactly, was wrong with him. But the words wouldn't come. Somehow, my mother seemed to sense this.

'It's his heart, Angus. He's not a well man at all.'

'You said.' It came out harsher than I'd meant, backtracked. 'I remember he'd some strength.'

My mother's lips quivered, she seemed so gentle. Just as I remembered her, but a shadow of frailty stalked her now. 'His heart is very weak – it's a terrible strain for him to move about.'

'And you, Mam? How are you coping?'

'I'm fine. I'm fine.' She stood up again, brushed down her skirt front. 'Will you have a bite to eat? Oh, say yes, I won't have you fading away under my own roof.'

'Yes. Okay then, I will.'

My mother thought she was feeding the five thousand. Eggs, bacon and chips. Real chips, crinkle cut, and deep-fried in Echo. I'd been so long away from home cooking that one taste of it and I lapsed into ecstasy. She brought out some fresh rolls from the baker's, proper Scotch morning rolls, I piled on the chips and smothered the lot in brown sauce.

'Will you take a drop of stout, Angus?'

'If you've any in.'

My mother returned from the kitchen smiling, a can and a pint tankard on a tray.

'Sweetheart stout. God, do they still make this?'

'I used to let you have a sip of that at New Year when you were a laddie. I remember you loved it.'

'I did that.'

The stout tasted like memories. I downed six in under an hour and gently passed out. Around ten I woke to find my mother loosening off my laces.

'I thought to let you sleep, son. I hope that's okay.'

'Och, sure. Leave those boots, Mam, I'll get them myself.'

'As you are,' she stepped away. 'I brought you a blanket, I was going to put it over you, but if you're awake you could go up to your old bed if you like.'

'I'm not ready for moving back in, Mam.'

She looked away, embarrassed.

I said, 'Why don't you just leave the blanket? I'll pitch down on the couch.'

A smile. 'Grand. I'll leave you to get settled then.'

'See you in the morning, Mam.'

She closed the living-room door softly. I felt trapped, but I knew I'd done some good and that made me feel better.

I settled down again. This definitely wasn't part of any plan of mine. I should have been staying with my old friend Hod by now.

Called him up.

'About that room offer . . . gonna have to put it on hold.'

'No problem. You clicked?'

'God, no. Back home.'

'At the auld dear's! Christ, things must be rough, Gus. Are you sure you wouldn't sooner stay here?'

'It's only tonight. I bumped into her on the Mile, she persuaded me I needed fattening up.'

'Well, don't sweat it. I'll see you tomorrow.'

'Cheers, mate.'

Thought I'd struggle to find sleep again, so I switched on the telly.

Channel Four had on a round-up of Bush-isms. A lookalike did the States' dumbest fuck to a T: 'The French don't have a word for entrepreneur.' Loved that. *Spitting Image* used to joke about Reagan's brain being missing. Christ knows what they'd have done with this mentalist.

I flicked for a while. Found a rerun of the *Jeremy Kyle Show*.

'Puffed-up little prick,' I muttered to myself.

Took great delight in zapping the fucker – if only I'd three-thousand volts handy.

I dug down for the night.

GOD KNOWS I'VE TRIED TO shut this stuff out. But it's a losing battle.

I must be eight or nine. It's the middle of the night and he's home roaring the house down after match day. I've a brother now, baby Michael. He's crying in his mother's arms, but I stay quiet in my bed.

My father roars, 'Gus, raise yourself.'

There's the noise of furniture being moved about, knocked over. Then there's the sound of my father's heavy boots and curses chasing round the house.

'I told you to get out of that fucking bed.'

I'm lifted by my hair from beneath the blankets. I'm terrified. My father's face is scarlet, his hair wet to his brow.

'Down them stairs,' he shouts at me.

In the living room there's scarcely a stick of furniture or picture on the walls that isn't disturbed. Then I see the cause of the ruckus flash before me like a ghost.

My father's earned another gift from one of the men in the Steamboat pub. He's always being given things, says it's a great advertisement to have the mighty Cannis Dury as a fan of your tyres or your shoes or your bacon.

This time the gift is a lively young lamb. It's come home with a rope round its neck, but is none too happy to see it tightened.

'Grab it up, boy,' yells my father. There's no need. It jumps into my arms the moment it sees me.

The rope is wrapped round its little snout. When I loosen it, the lamb grabs for breath.

Cannis is rolling drunk, knocking a lampshade about face. 'Good – now follow me, we have a job of work to be done.'

I follow him to the kitchen. He steadies himself over the sink, reaches for his razor strop. The sight of the strop being taken makes my heart gallop. But not for myself, I've felt its lashes too many times, I'm wondering what my father plans for the lamb.

The little creature seems to sense it too. It squirms in my arms.

'Hold that bastard steady,' roars my father.

'What'll you do? What'll you do to it?' I say.

'I'll cut its throat, what d'ye think?' He grabs the lamb and hangs it over the sink by its back legs. It struggles and squeals. My father has to use both hands to keep from losing it again. All the while the lamb looks at me. Great black eyes, staring.

'Angus, boy, get my razor, you'll have to do it!'

'No.' I say. I don't believe I've uttered the word.

'What do you mean, no? You *will* do it. The razor now, cut this bastard's throat before it has me on my back.'

I look at the lamb, upturned and struggling in my father's great hands. Its black eyes plead again. He takes down the razor, hands it to me, and then there's an almighty struggle as though the lamb knows it's on its own. The squeals are the sound of terror. I feel them reaching into me.

'Cut its throat, hear me, cut it! Cut it, now!'

I stand with my father's razor in my hand. I'm motionless. I know I'm disobeying and what that means. But I can't harm the animal.

The razor slips to the floor; there's a sharp pain in the front of my head when it falls. I realise I've been struck by my father. I lie on the floor beside the razor and when I see him reach for it I fill with panic.

As I get up I feel the cold flap of skin where his knuckle struck bone. There's blood running from my head, going into my eyes and mouth.

I feel no pain as I watch my father run the open steel across the lamb's throat. The squealing reaches a higher pitch for a second and then blood chokes its mouth and spills over its flesh into the sink.

I watch the blood pour from the dying animal. Its black eyes are still staring into the heart of me. As I watch the blood flowing, I feel like it's mine, like the blood I can taste in my mouth from the wound my father made.

A DROOL OF SALIVA STUCK me to the arm of the couch. Sweat lashed off my body. I ached all over. 'Christ, where am I?'

For a moment I thought I replayed the heady, early stages of alcoholism. Days when I greeted every morning in strange new surroundings. But I knew I was past those now. It takes a serious effort to negotiate a kip for the night. My times at the bar had long since been devoted to more serious matters.

I stood up, tried to straighten my back. Hunched over like Yoda, I said, 'Soon will I rest. Yes, for ever sleep. Earned it I have.'

I realised where I was. Recognised the wooden star clock above the fireplace. Red bulbs twirled behind the black plastic coals, someone had been in to turn on the fire.

I looked around. Felt shocked to find myself here, facing a trophy cabinet full of my father's sporting achievements. When I was a kid, my friends would come around to stare at them for what seemed like hours. It gave me bags of kudos on the street. They didn't know the real cost of those trophies.

I heard movement in the kitchen. Plates and cups being laid out on the table. When I went in, my mother stood at the stove stirring some porridge. A vast pot bubbled away.

'Oh, you're awake, son.'

'Good morning, Mam.'

'Did you sleep okay?'

'Yeah, I slept just fine,' I lied. 'Bit stiff, but got a few hours, you know.'

'Can't be too comfy on that couch. You should have went up to your bed . . . Tea?'

'Eh, no. Have you any coffee?'

'Sorry, son. Nobody drinks it since you went. I could nip next door. What time is it?'

I looked at my watch. 'Just after nine.'

'Aye, that's early enough, Dot will be up and about. Hang on, I'll get some coffee next door.'

'No, Mam, there's no need. I'll take whatever's going.'

'Och, no. Sit yourself down, son.' She beamed, looked delighted to have me home. It seemed to be a real treat for her. She acted like an excited child.

I asked myself how I could ever have denied her this.

As my mother put on a headscarf to nip out the back door she said, 'Will you go in and see your dad?'

'Eh, I don't know.'

'He's not eaten yet. You could take him in some breakfast.'

'Mam, I—'

'Oh, never mind, son. It's no matter. If he shouts though, go in.'

'Does he know I'm here?'

'Yes. I told him last night. He's fair over the moon.' She left, showering me with smiles.

What had I done? I'd no right to be playing with her emotions like this. I knew if I laid eyes on my old man – weak heart or not – I'd be liable to lamp him. I'd stored up a hail of misery for my mother by coming here and the thought wounded me.

I fired up a tab. The smoke filled the kitchen in an instant. I opened up a window, tried to encourage it out into the yard. As I leant over I caught sight of myself in the mirror. It had hung on the kitchen wall since I was too short to see into it. Now, I had to crouch to see myself. I looked rough as all guts. Red rings round my eyes, three days of growth. I needed serious attention.

'Gus, just take a look at yourself.' That's what Debs had said to me. I looked, stared, but I saw nothing. Well, nothing I wanted to see.

'Ella!' I heard a roar from upstairs.

It had been years since I'd heard that roar, but it hadn't changed much. 'Ella. Ella.'

What was he calling for this time? Another drink? Helping off the floor? A pot to piss in?

'Ella.' The roar came again, followed by a thump on the floor. Then another. Three or four in quick succession.

'Shut your hole . . .' I said. I felt my voice trail off. I didn't want to alert him to the fact I stood in his kitchen.

More thuds. 'Ella! For the love of Christ, where are you woman?'

'That's it. I'm outta here.'

I stubbed my tab in the sink. Ran the tap to clear the ash down the plug hole, and dropped the dowp in the bin.

'Ella. Ella.' He roared from upstairs as I put on my jacket. I was doing up the buttons when my mother walked in.

'Angus? Where are you going?'

'I'm sorry, Mam.'

She stood open-mouthed, holding up a jar of Red Mountain. 'But I've got your coffee.'

I wanted to go to her, curl her up in my arms. But I couldn't.

'*Ella – Ella.*'

'I have to go.'

She put down the jar, got into a panic.

'Your dad . . . have you been up to him?'

'No, Mam. I can't do that.'

She put a hand to her mouth. 'Oh, son.'

'I'm sorry, Mam. I have to go.'

I turned away, went for the door.

GRABBED THE *EVENING NEWS*. The front page splash was a police raid on a house full of illegal immigrants. I'd read the story a couple of times before it struck me why it seemed so unusual. They'd raided Marchmont. The price tags on houses there carry a long row of Bobby de Niros. I saw we were now talking big business in this racket.

I dipped into R.S. McColls, asked for a pack of Mayfair. Cheapest tabs on the shelf. Yellow-finger specials. I was on a Presbyterian guilt trip, aware I was the only smoker left in Scotland still buying fags from reputable retailers. Christ, what had become of this country? When Joe Public starts buying daily essentials like tabs on the black market, we're in trouble. Was like the war years.

Sparked up outside. Wasn't a bad smoke. But knew I'd wake up tomorrow reeking like pub curtains.

I felt a cold snap coming. Suited me fine, took the edge off the craving. And I needed my wits about me if I was gonna press Fitz the Crime for anything useful. Since Milo's killing, I needed him more than ever.

I'd been besieged by nightmares. They played like this:

I'm back at the Fallingdoon House, flames everywhere, and screams ... young girls crying their hearts out. I burst through the door, hold out my hand.

'Come on! Quick, give me your hand,' I say.

The flames lap all around us, but the girls look like they did the night I saw them, pale-grey ghosts. Half starved, frightened. They recoil from me.

'Come on! Give me your hand,' I roar.

I rush into the room, flames lap at the walls, all around thick black smoke chokes us.

'Christ, I'm not the enemy!' I say. 'I'm not the enemy.'

The girls run screaming, huddle in the corner, terrified.

Suddenly, I feel a tap on my shoulder and I turn. It's Milo, but he's changed. His face is battered to a bloody pulp. Two dark sockets sit where his eyes should be. As he begins to speak, I see flames creeping up his coat tails.

'Milo, Milo you're on fire!' I call out.

I slap at the flames, try to push them back. The heat is intense now, the palms of my hands smoulder in agony.

'Milo, move would you!'

The girls' screaming increases in pitch. Everywhere there's flames and fear. It's the worst fear I've ever known.

'Milo, you must move. We *have* to get outside.'

At once, he tips his head down to face me. He begins to speak, and as he does so, the flames engulf his body. He cries and taps at his chest, then speaks but his words are in a language I don't understand, except for one: 'Latvia.'

Nadja's revelation about Billy's get rich quick plan had been unexpected. It gave me a few bargaining chips to tempt Fitz with. But he was filth, and unpredictable. I'd have to lay it out finely. Make it worth his while.

The bus was packed.

A young jakey barfed in the aisle as we drove down Leith Walk. On a bus full of Leithers, only one woman held her nose.

'Out,' roared the driver.

'Och c'mon . . .' said the jakey, 'It's pishing doon!'

'Out now or it's the polis!'

The driver stood up, tucked himself behind his perspex screen as the jakey pulled down his baseball cap and rolled off the bus. He kicked out at the doors as they closed behind him. Then fell on his arse in the wet street.

The bus pulled out from the kerb, but stopped suddenly in the middle of the road. 'Just stay in your seats, please!' said the driver as he opened the doors to let two cans of Omega white cider roll onto the street. After the cans, the jakey's vomit followed down the aisle and slid over the steps.

I shook my head. Don't know why, had seen this all a million times before. Somehow, today, things seemed that little bit more annoying. This place was riding on my nerves.

An old boy leaned into my space. He took of his cap, slapped it off my seat. 'I'd bring back National Service for the likes of him,' he said.

I turned, faced him, said, 'I'd bring back hanging for the likes of him.'

I ORDERED UP A COFFEE.

'Is that a latte or a mocha or—' The waiter sounded Polish, one of the latest wave of legal migrants. They'd just about wiped out the Aussies in the bars, and now they staked a claim on the cafés.

'Hold up,' I cut in, 'just make it black and strong.'

'An Americano?'

Was I hearing things? This was Leith. Last bastion of old Edinburgh. There wasn't a Continental-style piazza for at least 500 yards. The yuppies had redrawn the battle lines.

I waved the waiter off with the back of my hand, said, 'Whatever.'

He eyeballed me as he went, probably to add some of his home-made gravy to my coffee.

In five minutes he came back, handed me a receipt on a little saucer, two white mints on top, 'That will be two fifty, please.'

For that kind of poppy, I expected the best coffee of my life. Truth told, it sucked balls into a hernia. I loaded in the milk and sugar, tried to focus on why I was still sat here.

For a while now, I'd been rolling around a quote from Bowie: 'It's not really work, it's just the power to charm.'

Sound advice. If I was going to get anything from Fitz – anything other than an introduction to Mr Nightstick – I'd have to suck shit. I'd probably been too forceful at our last meeting. I'd got him riled. In the past, way back, Fitz had been known as a hothead. He was quick with his fists, coulda been a contender, or so I'd heard.

I'd been on the end of one of Fitz's kidney punches before, and I wasn't keen to repeat it. If only for the reason that he could be very useful to me now. Getting him to believe I was doing him a favour would be the key.

Fitz appeared on time. Tearing down Leith Walk in a white heat.

'Shit, he's mad as hell,' I said under my breath.

I stood up, waved a tenner in the air. 'Waiter, a pot of tea please.'

As I saw Fitz approach the café door, he spotted me through the window and glowered. His face looked scarlet, anger shone out of every pore. If I had to pick his match, it was Yosemite Sam, guns blazing.

I got the door for him. 'Fitz, glad to' – he stormed past me – 'see you.'

I watched him remove his coat and take a seat.

I bit down on my back teeth. It went against the grain to go crawling to plod. But, at this stage, what choice did I have? Without the file on Billy, I'd be bust.

'Okay there, Fitz?'

'Cut the shite, Dury.'

The waiter brought the tea. I handed over the cash without looking at the bill. Waited for him to leave, said, 'Consider it cut.'

Fitz's lower lip pointed at me, his grey teeth on show as he spoke, 'Have you completely lost the fucking plot, boyo?'

'Fitz.'

'No, don't you *Fitz* me – when I think about the ways, the thousands of ways, Dury, that I could hang you out to dry.'

I stopped him in his tracks, pointed a finger. 'Cool the beans, Fitz.'

He poured his tea, looked around. 'This place has gone to the dogs.'

'Haven't we all.'

I passed the milk and sugar. Watched him stir them in.

'What's your game, Dury?'

I tried to clear the air. Played up to his ego. 'Look, about that earlier stuff – just forget it. I was a bit . . .'

'Pissed?' He laughed at his own joke.

A wry smile. 'Well . . . let's leave it that I was wrong to abuse the friendship.'

He burst into uproarious guffaws. 'Friends? You and me?' The thought brought a tear to his eye.

I had him blindsided, hit him with: 'Yeah. Who the fuck am I kidding? Let's keep things on a business footing. I've something for you.'

He pushed aside his teacup, leant forward. 'What's this bollocks you're talking, Dury?'

'Now, now. Nothing for nothing.'

'Fuck off.'

I went for the kill. 'Fitz, I'm onto something here, something big.'

'Billy Boy?' I knew by the tone of his voice he'd already done his homework.

'You know what I'm on about? For Chrissake, Fitz, he was tortured to death in a public place.'

'So?'

'So — these days, a wee lassie falls over and scrapes her knee and there's cops running around kitted out like Dustin Hoffman from that *Outbreak* movie. But Billy's taken out good style, and your lot sweep it under the carpet!'

He leant back, took a sip of his tea. Topped up the cup from the pot. I saw he was thinking things through.

'What have you got?'

'Uh-uh. First the file.'

'Arrah, there's no way. No way, Dury.'

'Why not? You know I'm not messing about.' I looked him in the eye. 'Fitz, if you help me out, I could put you back on the K-ladder. This isn't just about Billy, there's been another murder, one of your countrymen as it happens.'

He took a slow sip of tea.

'Think about it, Fitz. Do you want that DI's badge back?'

He stood up, went for his coat. 'Not in here.'

I followed him out. Lit up a Mayfair. It seemed to hit the spot.

'Look, I can't just remove a file. What world are you living in? It's all computerised these days, a printout sends warning lights flashing. What exactly do you need to know?'

'Who's behind this?'

'By the holy, Gus – is that something anyone would put on a file? All I can tell you is there's a, shall we say, tacit agreement to lay off this one.'

'From who?'

'The top.'

'Why? Do you know why?'

'Let's just say our Billy was dealing with some very unsavoury characters.'

'Zalinskas.'

'Vice are all over him.'

'So, they hung Billy out to dry?'

'Bigger fish to fry.'

I took my turn to deliver the goods. I told Fitz about the Latvians at Fallingdoon House. About Milo's calls, and the fire. I left out Nadja's involvement; she could still be useful to me.

'That's it? You wouldn't be holding out on me here, Dury?'

'Never. I get any more you'll be the first to hear.'

'I better be.'

'But, Fitz, go back to that file. I'm not buying any of this.'

'How do you mean?'

'There's more to it.'

'Go way outta that.'

'No, I mean it . . . someone's feeding us a cover story. You need to find out who's at the back of it.'

IF YOU FOLLOW THE LONDON Road out from Meadowbank, you come to Portobello. Not as glamorous as it sounds, but, like every other district of Edinburgh. On the up.

When I come to Porty now, I always think of George Galloway. He said that when he was a kid his father had wound him up about a trip to Portobello, thought he was off to the Italian coast the way the name sounded. Bet he felt disappointed when he hit the beach and got a waft of the sewage outflows. Still, you have to love Gorgeous George. Have to love anyone who sticks it to Bush and Blair in such a high old fashion.

In parts, beyond the Bedsitland-by-the-Sea fringe, Porty maintains a moneyed air of old Victorian mansions. Hod's place, however, is new money. A top-floor apartment in one of the front's eyesores. Plenty of chrome, plenty of glass. Not one ounce of class.

I pushed the buzzer on the front door. The factor was nowhere in sight so I scanned the residents' names. Went for Clarke.

A woman's voice, said, 'Hello.'

She sounded posh, it threw me. I didn't want to come over like I'd an eye to burgle the joint.

'Hello, there. My name's, Dury, I'm er . . .'

'Oh, you must be here to look at my box!'

I spluttered, 'Excuse me?'

'The television thingie.'

Suddenly things began to making sense.

'Eh no, I'm staying with Hod – Mr Dunn.'

She said no more. Think I'd embarrassed her into opening the door.

My friend had offered to put me up for a while. The combination to his flat's door had always been a simple one: 1745. For a rabid nationalist like Hod, it could be nothing other than the date of the Jacobite Rebellion.

I took my boots off in the doorway. Hod's anal fixation for tidiness struck me straight away. If he wasn't a builder I'd have said some dumb doctor's wife had been hard at work, filling her home time by polishing the ceilings.

The thermostat in the hall read 25° Celsius. I scrunched up my toes in the deep, cream-coloured carpet and thought, 'Now, this is the life.'

Seemed a shame to pollute the atmosphere, but I'd made a visit to the tobacconist on the Mile, stored up on some quality smokes. Gitanes, the ones with the dancing gypsy woman on the pack. They're a dark baccy, too tough to get through a whole pack. How Bowie managed to chain them in his Thin White Duke days can only be admired.

For balance I'd picked up some Luckies. Said on the pack: 'Lucky Strike means fine tobacco.' I fired up, said, 'Fine indeed!'

Hod had splashed out on a flatscreen telly, recessed into the wall. Must have been six feet wide; I'd seen smaller pool tables. I nosed around a bit but the ON button evaded me. Would be staying OFF for now.

I threw myself down on the couch. It swallowed me in an instant. 'Oh yes, Gusie boy, could definitely get used to this.'

I praised Hod for letting me crash. Would definitely be making the most of my stay.

A few more belts on the Lucky and I found myself holding on to a handful of fag ash. I got up carefully, trying not to drop any on the carpet, and poured the lot down the cludgie.

The seat gleamed. 'Christ the place is spotless!'

I looked around the bathroom, another telly had been fitted in the wall. He'd racks of lotions: Armani, Mugler, Gucci, even an old favourite, Fahrenheit by Christian Dior. I took off the cap, it smelled as I remembered it – just like Parma Violets. Took me back to the days of Pacers and Texan bars.

Splashed some on, said, 'God, I love this stuff.'

There's a scene from the Westerns. Must have seen it a million times. Some wizened old cowpoke, face as leathery as his saddle bags, dust-caked from the trail, gets into town. Before you know it, he's hit the swing doors of the knocking shop, picked out a Bobby Moore and – bizarrely – demanded she fills a tin tub with bubble bath.

I turned the taps on full. Bliss, steam filled the room. I ferreted in Hod's cabinets for some Matey. Found a remote doofer for the telly. Behind a pile of scented candles, some Radox, muscle-relaxing bath salts, thought, 'Will do just dabber.'

Taps gushed like a power hose. Had me a bath in no time.

Got the 501's off. 'Bucking the old eighties ads there, Gus!'

Was about to dive in when a thought grabbed me to light a few candles. Why not? I needed some serious relaxing, take that as given. Took the lighter from my jeans, had a bit of trouble getting the wick to take, then – '*Arrghh!* Sweet mother of Christ!'

Candle wax splashed on my best mate.

'Holy fucking hellfire! Christ! Jesus! Mother of God!'

I dabbed at the wax. It peeled off like Sellotape. Seemed to take the pain with it. Checked my old fellah – no damage done. Another lesson learned the hard way.

As I sank into the bubbles, I thought, 'God this is good. Those Radox fellahs know their business.'

I hit heaven for all of ten minutes before boredom began to set in. I grabbed the doofer, switched on the telly. *Scotland Today* was on, with all the usual stories. Fishermen in Peterhead moaning about having to cut quotas. Thought, 'Arseholes – get over it, you've cleaned out the seas.'

The parliament reeled out the usual numpty, the environment minister, who blamed the situation on Europe. 'That's the way, fellah, don't isolate those voters.' Another arsehole. God, wasn't the world full of them? Though the parliament seemed to have more than their fair share.

I was ready to flick when a late item, just before the 'and finally', caught my attention.

Any sight of the home town on the telly tends to grab me, but this had an extra edge. A ruckus outside the High Court. The camera spun wildly out of control for a moment and I caught sight of a few press packers.

'Hendo, get that camera up, you tool!' I shouted at the screen.

Then came the voice-over. 'Scenes of mayhem greeted the spectators gallery at the High Court in Edinburgh today . . .'

'No shit,' I said, 'was mayhem on the street too.'

'. . . as city crime lord Benny Zalinskas made his first appearance in what is expected to be a lengthy trial.'

I shot up to the screen, dislodging a flood of bath water onto the floor. He wasn't what I'd expected: squat, stocky, sovereign-ringed. Zalinskas looked slight. Silver hair swept back in a carefully blow-dried manner. His face was unmoving, except for the eyes. Can honestly say I'd never seen a pair like them, they bulged out of his head so much he could have carried an *Evil Dead* remake.

Singular appearance apart, Zalinskas did, however, carry the requisite gangster's camel coat over his shoulders. A biffer, whose arse was no stranger to the steroid needle, removed the coat just outside the court room. He stood holding it over his arm, until Zalinskas gave a little nod and the biffer moved to stand by the wall.

'Holy fuck. Is this Chicago? It's Al Capone on trial, surely?'

I dripped with water and shivered, but the scene held me. I couldn't believe the way this city had changed. Just a few years ago, this would have been the headliner on the news, now it was barely getting billing ahead of the weather.

Back in the studio the newsreader quizzed the reporter by a link-up. 'So what can you tell us about the trial, Polly?'

The blonde with the china-blue eyeshadow flashed up, the one who only a few years ago could have been seen trotting down the street in a pair of her mother's five-sizes-too-big heels.

'Mr Zalinskas faces charges of living on immoral earnings in the city, the charges relate to a period between January and March of this year, where it is alleged he headed up a vice ring of some hundred-plus sex workers.'

'Sex workers? Jesus, even the brassers have gone PC,' I said to the screen. 'Can we have the meat of the issue please, Polly?' I shook my head, there was work for me as a trainer out there.

Back in the studio the newsreader managed to shoehorn in the more significant charge of tax evasion. How the case came about remained a mystery. Already they had shifted to a story about a rehomed sheepdog that only answered to its master in Gaelic.

Said: '*Pòg mo thòn.*'

Flicked off. Sat back down.

I reached out the bath to my jeans, pulled them over the floor. I'd a paperback in my back pocket, *A Nietzsche Reader*. Basically, pocket Nietzsche for simpletons, but it did fit in my pocket.

Read: 'He who breathes in the air of my heights must know it is the air of the heights he is bracing. A man must be built for it. Otherwise, it will kill him.'

I read on, said, 'So, join the queue.'

LAUNCHED A RAID ON HOD'S kitchen. Found fun-sized Crunchies in the fridge. Fancied a coffee to chase. A tin of illy espresso called from the shelves. Picked it up, but it didn't look or smell like instant. I read the tin. 'Caffé macinato.'

'So, what's that? Do I need a machine?'

Read on: 'Only the finest Arabica beans . . . selected with care and passion . . . an experience that will involve all your senses.'

'I only want coffee, for Chrissake! Has he no Mellow Birds?'

Saw Jules in *Pulp Fiction* saying, 'This is serious gourmet shit.' Didn't rate my chances of getting the espresso machine working. Opted for a bottle of Stella. Tasted fine. Reassuringly expensive, like the ads say.

On my third, I crashed on the sofa listening to the Dirtbombs doing 'Got to Give it Up'. Had just discovered them, they were outta Detroit as they say Stateside. Their album covered some amazing tracks; the attitude had me hooked. A real edge that wailed, 'Don't fuck with us.'

Was punching the air and moshing to 'Underdog' when my phone went.

'Hello.'

'Well, hello yourself.'

'Amy?'

'Who else? How's it hanging, Gus?'

I made my apologies for not calling. Seemed to work. Said, 'So what have you been up to?'

'Well, that's the thing. What you told me about Billy, I thought I could be of some help and—'

'Whoa there! *Help*?' I'd told her about Billy to warn her off. To dig myself out of any commitment and to excuse myself from future dates. 'What do you mean, help?'

'Gus, I know what I'm doing.'

I felt myself coming over all paternal, don't know why, it's definitely not a role I'm suited to. 'What exactly have you been doing, Amy?'

'When you told me about the—'

'*Killing*?'

'And the girls and all that stuff.'

'Back up. You heard the *killing* bit didn't you?'

'Eh, yes. Hello? Am I like retarded or something?'

'I'm trying to stress these are not people to mess with, they've killed someone already. Look, just tell me where this is leading. What have you been doing?'

Her tone changed. 'Where are you?'

'Amy?'

'I think I should come and see you. I know you're not at the Wall, I've checked, so—'

'I'm in Porty.' I gave her the address.

'Right, I'll be round soon. Gus, I know you're worried about me, and that's cute, but I really am a big girl. I've got some information for you – it will help the case, I'm sure of it.'

She hung up.

Cute? Christ, what had I done to her?

I tanned another Stella. Hit the Luckies good style. Had the place reeking like a lum. I opened up the french doors and walked out on to the balcony. As I looked over the sea, the sky turned blacker than a dog's guts all the way to the horizon.

I wondered what Amy had been doing. I couldn't quite get my head around her actions. I mean, was I a catch? No chance. I had Debs to confirm that, she wouldn't even talk to me now. I'd read somewhere that Bill Gates communicated with his wife mainly via email, even when they were in the same house. After my last talk with Debs, I'd settle for that.

The front door opened and in walked Hod. 'Hello, honey, I'm home!' he roared. Not quite what I was hoping for, but, hey, glad to have company.

'Hodster – how goes it?'

We did the usual gut-barging welcome, slaps on back to follow.

'Any more where that came from?' said Hod, nodding at my beer. 'My mouth's as dry as a nun's muff.'

'Sit down, I'll get you one.'

'Gee, honey, you sure know how to please a man,' said Hod, trying to plant a slap on my arse.

'Piss off,' I said, mincing off for comic effect.

Got a beer for myself too. 'You hungry?'

'Hungry? I could eat a horse between two pishy mattresses.'

'Whatcha fancy?'

'Ruby Murray?'

'Agreed. My shout. In or out?'

'How about a wee sit doon? I can be ready in five.'

'Cool.' I remembered Amy was on her way. 'Och shit, no.'

'What is it?'

'Got to wait for a friend. You don't mind do you?'

'Bit of stuff?'

'Sort of.'

'Gus Dury, you old dog. She got a pal?'

I shook my head. 'It's a tricky situation, Hod.'

'You've not got her up the pipe have you?'

Shook again. 'No. Christ, no. It's just . . .' I didn't want to get into the whole story with Hod, at least not right away. If I stopped under his roof I knew it would come out eventually, but now wasn't the moment.

Hod gave me a get out. 'Tricky, like you said.'

I nodded. 'We'll call in a Ruby then.'

'Suits me. Number's over by the phone. Set meal for two for me.'

'You greedy bastard!'

Hod stood up, tapped his gut. 'Cheeky prick, I'm a fine figure of a man.'

'Aye, a nice round figure.'

'Plenty to go around. And you'll be seeing me in action tonight.'

'What?'

'Got a night out planned for us. Take that dour look of your fizzer, mate.'

'Oh yeah? Come on then, spill.'

'Later – you'll see.'

Hod went to have a shower. I called the curry house. As I waited I read the paper Hod brought in. Had to laugh at Hugh Hefner's response to Kelly Osbourne's desire to become a *Playboy* centrefold – 'We can't airbrush that much, honey!'

The Dirtbombs CD reached 'Your Love Belongs Under a Rock'. I heard Hod joining in from the bathroom. Thought, 'I'm gonna enjoy living here.' Had been years since I'd been deep in bachelordom. The constant patter was just what I needed to distract me right now.

As the track finished I heard the buzzer go.

'That was quick.'

I jumped up to open the door. 'They better not have microwaved the naan bread!'

Pushed the button, said, 'Hello.'

'Hi, Gus, it's me.'

'Amy – you better come up.'

AS I STOOD IN THE hall, waiting for Amy, a door opened. A barnet of curls that would put Leo Sayer to shame popped out. Tried to do the neighbourly thing, said, 'Hello, there.'

Head yanked in and door shut tightly. The woman with the box? Started to feel the beers hit, had a wee snigger to myself.

I quaffed away as the elevator doors opened at the other end of the hall. They don't play music in there but as Amy appeared I thought Ravel's *Boléro* came on. You know the one? Think, Bo Derek, golden bikini, getting out the water and running to Dudley Moore – yeah, that one.

Amy looked phenomenal, she'd have given Bo a run for her money any day. Until now, she'd been a kinda conservative dresser. Classic looks, nothing to attract too much attention. But here she stood in a black mini-dress, thigh-high kinky boots and a choker. Her hair splayed out, back-combed, bit of a Cousin It thing going on.

'Jesus,' I thought, 'what's with the man-eater look?' Wondered if I was in for trouble.

She came close and I saw her make-up had been trowelled on. Spanish eyes, pillar-box-red lipstick and false eyelashes.

She clocked my expression, cocked her elbow on her hip. 'Looking for business, love?'

'How much will you pay me?'

She laughed and handed me a rain-splattered black PVC coat.

Inside, she said, 'It's pissing down out there.'

'I see that – drink?'

Brought through two more Stellas, as Amy eyeballed Hod's apartment.

'This is some joint, Gus.'

'Yeah. It's . . . er . . . a friend's.' I nodded in the direction of the shower.

Amy winced, looking like Beyoncé on a warble. 'Male or female?'

'Jealous?'

Another wince, facing the other way this time. 'Gus, check the kip of me.' She held out her palms, flicked her boot tops. 'I'm in no nick for a cat fight!'

'It's a bloke. My mate, Hod. He's sound.'

'Phew.' She threw herself on the couch, foot tapped to the music. 'Who's this?'

'Dirtbombs.'

'I like them.'

'I'm delighted – Look, what's with the get-up?'

'Let me get these off first.' She unzipped her boots and kicked her feet up beside her on the couch. 'Christ, that's better – bloody medieval torture they are.'

I sat down too. 'So?'

'Any chance of a foot massage?'

'None.'

She pouted. 'Aw . . . Gussie, and I've been such a good girl.'

'Enough games, Amy.' I felt uneasy watching her making eyes at me with all that slap painted on her face, even if she was joking.

'It's Pepsi.'

'Come again?'

'When I'm dressed like this, I'm Pepsi.'

It was worse than I thought.

'Pepsi? Why?'

'It's a . . . you could call it a stage name.'

My mind raced into overdrive, thoughts ran around like rats down the docks.

'A stage name, right. What have you been up to . . . Pepsi?'

She smiled. 'Remember I said I wanted to help with the Billy thing?'

Nodded. A frown waiting in reserve.

'Well, I had an idea when you said he worked in some clubs.'

'Oh Christ, Amy, what have you done?'

'No. No. I've only been dancing, I promise.'

'What?'

'At the Pleasure Garden. I've been pole dancing.'

I stood up. My gob was smacked.

'I don't believe I'm hearing this.'

'Gus, chill out. There's plenty of girls at college doing it, it pays good money – and I've been able to find some information.'

Shot her a stare, said, 'I doubt it, you're more likely to find yourself in grief.'

'Sit down.' She patted the chair beside her, made a show of fluffing up a cushion.

The CD stopped. Hod's singing ended too, I heard him getting out of the shower.

I sat down. 'Let's hear it.'

'Right. Well, to begin with,' she rubbed her hands together, leaned forward, 'Billy wasn't exactly mammy's little angel. The nicest description I've heard of him so far was cocky little prick.'

'Who from?'

'The girls. I've been getting to know them all.'

'Charming are they?'

'Shut it.' She pointed in my direction, a bright pink fingernail wagged at me. 'Nobody liked him, but they said he knew the score.'

'How do you mean?'

'He played the Big I Am all over the place, but when Benny showed up – different story. He crawled right up Benny's arse.'

'So what? Brown-nosing the boss goes on all over.'

'No, this was more. Billy was his protégé until recently.'

'And?'

'It's all a bit sketchy. Have you any fags?' I lit a couple of Luckies, passed one over. Amy blew on the end of hers to get it going. 'There was some kind of row, big bust up at one of the clubs, a couple of the girls saw it. It was pretty full-on. Billy was in tears.'

'What was it about?'

'That's the thing . . . nobody knows.'

'I find that a bit hard to believe, you telling me the rumour mills just ground to a halt after a flare-up like that.'

'There's a few stories going about. That Zalinskas was giving Nadja one, that Zalinskas was giving Billy one – a big no to that, by the way, Billy definitely wasn't AC/DC – so, just the usual jangling, I wasn't buying any of it.'

'Hold on. Back up there. What's that about Nadja?'

'Ice Queen?'

'Oh, she's frosty, yeah.'

'All, and I mean *all*, the girls hate her guts.'

'No shit.'

'Really, it's like . . . primal, a pack fear thing.' Amy dragged deep on her tab, swiped at the smoke. 'She's bringing in all this Eastern European gash and—'

'Say what? *Gash*?'

'Industry term.'

'Gotcha.'

'So she's like, created all this resentment among the girls, and, at the same time, she's shagging the boss.'

'Volatile mixture.'

'I tell you, Gus, she's the alpha bitch in Benny's empire. Everyone knows it.' Amy stood up. 'Mind if I put on another CD?'

I waved her on.

None of Amy's information struck me as real news. Yeah, it was good colour. It added something to the overall picture but there was nothing concrete, nothing to latch onto. Except for the row between Zalinskas and Billy.

'Amy . . .' She spun round, swept her hair over, and pouted again.

'Sorry. Pepsi . . . about this barney.'

'What about it?'

'Did anything come of it?'

'What do you mean?'

'I mean afterwards – did the girls say there were any, I dunno, changes?

Did Benny start coming in for the takings? Did Billy get moved? Any girls sacked?'

'No, I don't think — Oh, hang on, there was. It's probably nothing, but apparently a day after the row, they ripped out all the security cameras.'

'They did?'

'Yeah. I didn't think anything of it though, I mean, cameras in a place like that, bad idea to begin with, right?'

THE CARRY-OUT ARRIVED. I paid the delivery guy and laid the
tinfoil boxes out on the table. Amy put on the Manics. 'Motorcycle
Emptiness', she said, 'I just love this old stuff.'

Had no answer for that.

'We need plates, Gus, and cutlery.'

'Sure, I'll get some.'

I called out to Hod and he came in, hair wet, reeking of Obsession,
Ted Baker shirt open but for a couple of buttons.

He grabbed me. 'Christ, Gus . . .' he whispered, 'who the fuck is
that?'

'Oh aye, Hod, this is . . . er, Pepsi . . . Pepsi, Hod.'

Amy tucked into some chicken jalfrezi, mouth full, she gave a wave.

'Christ,' said Hod again. 'I'll take the Pepsi challenge any day!'

I slunk off to the kitchen, to grab myself another Stella. Had been
knocking them back and now began to feel like mixing in something a
bit harder. For some reason, gin called. I never touch the mother's ruin,
but my mood told me it would fit. You sit behind a bar, staring at those
optics for long enough periods of your life, sooner or later, labels you've
never even tried start to call you.

I went back to find Hod and Amy deep in conversation.

'Gus, Gus, this is out of order!' said Hod.

'What is?'

'Billy Boy. Pepsi's been telling me you're going after his killer.'

'Oh, has she now?'

'I never knew him very well, in fact, when I did meet him I thought he was a bit of a septic tank to tell the truth, but his father's brand new. God, old Col must be in bits.'

I took a plate, spooned on some rice. 'He's none too good.'

'Pepsi says you've narrowed it down to this Zalinskas guy.'

I dropped the spoon in the tinfoil box. 'Just hang on a minute. I've narrowed down bugger all, and I wouldn't be taking anything she says as gospel, her real name's Amy for a start.'

'Yeah but,' said Amy, 'we're getting close.'

'Amy, is it? I like that,' said Hod. 'I say we go all out tonight – screw hitting the town. I know where Zalinskas has a casino on George Street. We could—'

'No way!'

'Hang on, Gus,' said Hod. 'I'm only saying we could go and have a word, try pushing his buttons.'

I put down my plate, cutlery; threw myself back in the chair. 'Am I hearing right? Have you two completely lost it? The man's a gangster. I saw him doing the full Don Corleone bit on the news tonight. It's a non-starter. I mean, thanks, both of you, for the suggestions. But, no. No way. Outta the question.'

'Looks like it's you and me then, Pepsi, er . . . Amy,' said Hod.

They high-fived.

I stood up. 'He'd have my nuts in a cocktail shaker if I even set foot in one of his places, and as for anyone with me . . .'

'Well, if you're chicken, Gus,' said Hod, grinning at Amy.

'This is no joke, you know. *Hello*, read my lips, the man's a *gangster*!'

Hod walked round the table, put his hand on my shoulder. 'Okay, we'll be careful. Just a look about the joint, a few sneaky wee enquiries. Test the water so to speak. You never know, we might hit pay dirt.'

'You'll get put in the dirt.'

'Gus, look, I've been to this casino a million times, I'm a kent face. No one's gonna say boo to me turning up, I'll sign you and herself in as a couple and we'll play it cool.'

I saw they were set on it. I couldn't let them take a chance like this on their own. Sooner or later I'd have to confront Benny the Bullfrog, maybe sooner was better than later in the circumstances.

'Okay,' I said. For the first time, I wished I'd taken Mac's shooter.

They both cheered. Hod shook his fist in the air. Amy danced, made a mixing-bowl motion.

'But, we do this my way,' I said.

'Absolutely,' said Hod.

'I mean it. You go in there looking for a pagger, Hod we're all coming out like this . . .' I picked up a piece of pakora, dripping in red sauce and dropped it on the table.

They watched my face.

'I'm not joking,' I said. 'You especially, Amy . . . there'll be no going back to the Pleasure Garden after Benny's lot see you with me. You'll be marked.'

Nods. Sighs.

'Okay then, let's do this,' I said.

'Suicide is Painless' began to play.

Not a bad option, I thought.

THE SKY LOOKED BLACK AS a gypsy's curse, throwing down rain that felt personal. Hod crammed himself under Amy's umbrella; his one concession to the cold and wet to put up the collar on his Ted Baker shirt.

'Aren't you freezing?' said Amy.

'Hell no. I've a second skin, see . . .' Hod played peekaboo with his shirt buttons, Sean Connery chest hair made a bid for freedom.

'That's gross!' said Amy. 'Get to a chemist, you get creams for that.'

'Pray there isn't a dance floor in this joint, he'll have the medallion on show,' I said. 'Tony Manero doesn't get a look in.'

Hod undid a few buttons.

'Oh, no – put it away,' said Amy.

Hod laughed. 'That's not what the last one said!' He launched into some sick-making dance moves, finger shooting in the air, hips jutting, the whole nine yards.

We turned away, but got drawn back in.

'Night fever . . . *night fe-v-er* . . . we know how to do it . . .'

He danced and made a show of himself until the taxi arrived.

In the back of the cab I tried to rein Hod in, reminded him what we'd set out to do. He got the message, seemed to settle. Locked his jaw and looked mean.

Amy looked more pensive, fingers worrying at the rim of her boots.

'You okay?' I said.

'Yeah, oh yeah.'

'You sure?'

'I want to get to the bottom of this as much as you, Gus.'

Hod cut in: 'We both do, we know the score.'

Yeah right. Christ, I didn't even know the score. I cursed myself again for not taking Mac's shooter, then remembered the words of John Lennon: 'Don't need a gun to blow your mind.'

We got out the cab at the wrong end of George Street, Edinburgh roadworks playing mischief with my plans. As we walked a succession of pimped-up cars roared past the road-closed signs, beat boys who a few years ago were fitting Spokey Dokeys to their BMXs.

'Twats,' said Hod. 'Don't know what's worse, them or students!'

'I'm a student,' said Amy.

'Definitely them,' said Hod, then changing the subject sharply, 'Here we are!'

Benny the Bullfrog's casino stood inside one of the New Town's old Georgian buildings. At one stage it had been a town house. These days, you needed to be multinational to get the keys to a place like this.

Hod stuck his chest out and frowned at the ape on the doors. A classic pintdown man, he frowned back. Good to know they treat you like shit if you're well-off too.

Inside a scrawny-necked Victoria Beckhamalike, bling a go go, greeted us with an elaborate smile and handshake onslaught. Hod got air kisses. It looked to be histrionics, a job to rival Rada's finest.

'Party of three, absolutely delighted to welcome you, and if I may ask the guests to sign in.'

In the slot for name and address, I opted for Mr and Mrs Smith. Amy smiled, gripped my arm tightly. I saw she still harboured fantasies of us re-enacting the potter's wheel scene from *Ghost*.

'Right, let's hit the bar,' said Hod.

'You'll get no arguments from me.'

My craving for gin had passed. Went for a J&B over ice.

'So what do you do now?' I asked Hod.

'What the big wheel does – circulate.'

He moved to the tables, shoulders set hard, poker face on. A look that said, 'I've worked fucking hard to deserve my place here, have you?'

I wished I could say the same thing. The words fish and water sprang to mind. The casino was a league or two above my own.

I'd heard the late Australian billionaire Kerry Packer had been in a casino once when some Texan oilman started mouthing off about his millions.

'So, how much are you worth?' asked Packer.

'Oh, about a hundred million,' said the oilman.

'Really?' said Packer. 'I'll toss you for it!'

Beat that for a fuck you.

I felt a tug on my arm, turned to see Amy at my side.

'I'm going to look about,' she said.

'Ah, no. Don't think so.'

She stuck her head to the side, rolled her eyes at me. 'I'm a big girl.'

Thought, 'Who's gonna argue with that?'

'Well, be good.'

'And if I can't be good?'

'Just be good.'

I returned to the bar, ordered another J&B. I tried to get a handle on the place. It looked plush, first time I'd seen walls carpeted. And the punters certainly had plenty of poppy. A mixture of old Edinburgh and parvenu trash. A lot of green and tweeds clashing with the Prada set. Champagne in full flow all around, raised voices. I eavesdropped.

'Another bottle of Bolly, darling?'

'Yaw-yaw . . .'

'Oh moy Gawd . . . Oh moy Gawd!'

'What is it, darling?'

'Kitten heels with culottes, darling.'

'Oh, that's so last season!'

Felt my brain softening, more than it had already. Phone suddenly went off. Saved by the bell.

'Hello?'

'Hello, I'm sorry to call so late, but—'

I didn't recognise her voice. 'Who is this?'

'Oh, of course, my name's McClair. I'm with social services.'

'Uh-huh, and who are you looking for?'

'Ehm, is that Mr Dury?'

'Yeah, that's me. Is there some kind of problem?'

Silence on the line, then: 'It's about the remains of, Mr Milo Whittle.'

To hear his name again thumped at my heart. 'Milo, yes . . . God, yes – his remains.'

'Mr Dury, you seem to be the only contact we have. Are you family of some sort?'

'No, I'm not family. I'm, eh, all he had though.'

'In that case, will you be claiming the remains, Mr Dury?'

I felt my heart freeze over, my mouth fell open. The sight of that heap of ashes would stay with me to my dying day.

'Mr Dury, are you still there?'

'Eh, yeah . . . yes, I'm still here.'

'It's, well, the remains have been released now. There will have to be arrangements made.'

I felt my mind slowly clicking over. 'Oh, I see.'

'We can take care of the funeral expenses, if needs be.'

That terrible expression 'pauper's grave' entered my thoughts.

'Eh, no.'

'I'm sorry?'

'I'll take care of it. The funeral and so on.'

'That's very generous, Mr Dury. Are you fully aware of the costs?'

'Fuck the costs. I'm sorry, I mean, I'll manage.'

'Well, we'll be taking him to the crematorium soon, so . . .'

'That's fine, I'll get down there now.'

'I think tomorrow would be better.'

'Yes, look, tomorrow it is then.'

'Okay, Mr Dury. Goodbye.'

My legs buckled, standing became difficult. I summoned the courage to order another whisky. I threw it over, sensed right away I'd reached the magic number.

My blood thumped in my veins as I headed for the cashier.

I threw down all the money Col had given me, said, 'Change that.'

'How would you like it, sir?'

'What?'

'Hundreds, twenties, tens.'

'Fuck do I care?'

As I headed for the roulette wheel Bobby Darin sang 'Moon River'. God, my mother used to play that. The past seemed like happier days to me now.

Put a pile of chips on black.

Croupier spun the wheel. 'No more bets, please.'

As I watched the ball jump Bobby Darin changed his tune, started on 'Call Me Irresponsible'.

Like I needed that.

AS I WATCHED THE WHEEL, my guts turned over. I'd been throwing money around like one of those Indian statues with four arms. It had to end. It might be soon.

I watched the ball begin to slow, popping in and out of the little brass slats. I couldn't take it, turned away.

Amy appeared at my side. 'What's going on?'

'Is it black?'

'What?'

'The wheel . . . I've put it all on black.'

I slouched, she towered over me as she pitched herself on her toes. 'Still, going . . .'

'Christ on a crutch. Keep watching.'

'How much have you put on?'

'All of it – everything I have.'

''Bout ten bob then.' She laughed at her own joke.

'Bit more than that.'

I turned around to see the wheel's silver handle make a final wink in the glare of lights.

'Number twenty-two,' called out the croupier.

'Holy shit, it's black! I've won!'

Amy jumped up, put her arms around me. Before I knew what had happened, we were kissing, Amy leaned in hard, pressing her tongue on the roof of my mouth.

'That was nice,' she said when we finished.

'I didn't see it coming.'

'We should do it more often.'

'God, no, my nerves wouldn't take it.'

'I was talking about the kiss,' said Amy.

'So was I.'

A little crowd formed as the croupier wrote out a chit for the cash office.

Hod appeared.

'I thought you'd never been to a casino before.'

'Beginner's luck,' I said. Amy wrapped her arms round my waist and smiled.

Hod tipped his head, winked towards her. 'I wish I had half your luck, Gus Dury,' he said.

'How do they pay out?'

'Cash. How much is it?'

I showed him the chit. Hod's eyes widened, he whistled through his front teeth. 'Drinks are on you, buddy.'

I felt his words like a lash, I didn't feel like celebrating after the call about Milo, said, 'Look, guys, I've had a bit of news tonight. I hate to piss on your parade but a friend of mine's died and . . . I've to collect the remains.'

'Oh my God,' said Amy.

I managed a limp smile for her as she put her hands on my face. 'Thanks. He was very old and I hadn't known him long, but we connected, you know?'

Amy nodded, eyes widened by my misery.

'Let's get your money,' said Hod. He walked us over to the cash office.

As I handed over the chit, the girl behind the perspex took one look at the amount and reached for the phone.

'What's going on?' I asked Hod.

He shrugged. 'New territory for me too, mate.'

The girl put the phone down. 'You'll have to take this upstairs, sir.'

'Come again?'

'We don't keep that much cash on the floor. You'll need to go up to the manager's office where the safe is. Mr Zalinskas is expecting you.'

I swore I heard Amy gulp. I looked at Hod, he wore a face like a Rottweiler, opening and closing his fists. 'Looks like you're going to see some action whether you like it or not, Dury,' he said.

'Down boy,' I cautioned him.

'What?' Hod's brow dropped, I swore it smacked his lower lip. The look was now confusion.

'If you think I'm going up there looking for a cuffing, forget it.'

'But, Gus, this is your chance to get some answers.' He put an arm on my shoulder, raised a fist to within an inch of my nose. 'Just a bit of persuasion and you never know – could have this wrapped up in no time.'

'Are you off your head?' I slapped down his fist, grabbed him by the collar. 'See those?'

'Cameras.'

'And what do you think they're for?'

'Robbing – stop folk taking him at the tables.'

'And do you think he won't have them up there? What use do you think we'll be to Col inside?'

'Fuck it. Let's do him anyway, we'll take the tapes.'

I saw I was getting nowhere fast. 'Okay.'

'Gus!' said Amy.

'No. No, it's fine Amy,' I said. 'Hod wants a pagger, I'm all for it.'

Hod smiled. 'Well, let's go then.'

'Right-oh,' I said. 'One thing, though.' I eased Hod towards the security guard who was heading over to lead us up to Zalinskas' office. He made the boxer Nikolai Valuev, the seven-foot-plus heavyweight, look like a pillow-biter. 'Who's going to take care of the Beast from the East?'

Hod stepped aside, nibbled on his lip. 'D'you think I could take him?'

I laughed out loud. 'Sure. Without a doubt.'

'He's a big bastard, aye. But they're the easy ones to take out, never felt a good punch, every bastard's too scared to land one on them.'

I did up my jacket, placed a kiss on Amy's cheek, as I walked towards the security guard, I shook my head at Hod. 'If he tests that theory, Amy, be sure to take a note of the ward number.'

THOUGHT IT BEST TO AVOID conversation on the way to Benny the Bullfrog's office. Got the impression the pug had a limited vocabulary. Probably expressed himself best with, on good days, a baseball bat, on bad ones, a crowbar. My bones twitched. Knees and shins especially. Wondered, would I be walking back this way again?

Jean Cocteau said: 'Life is a horizontal fall.' Knew for sure mine was. But every fall had to be broken.

We passed through what seemed like a never ending tunnel of richly carpeted corridors. Chandeliers sparkled above foot-high skirtings edged in gilt. It took serious wedge to put a look like this together. Hod runs a calculator in his head to these things, me, the impact's personal. I want to chuck out the owner, give the place to the scores of families living in B&Bs up and down the country. I replayed the scene in *Dr Zhivago* when the Reds take over the big house. The owners get forced into the attic . . . until it's decided a few more families could live there too. That's redistribution of wealth for you. Say you want a revolution? Bring it right on.

My face slipped into a grimace without even trying. As the goon brought me to Zalinskas' door I wiped it away. He knocked once, I readied myself to meet the man.

After a few seconds the door unlocked and slowly opened. I peered through the gap, nobody there.

I walked inside.

'Hello . . .'

No answer.

A wall of monitors flickered at me. Some of them showed scenes from the casino floor, others spewed statistics – cash taken, payouts, the sums were eye-watering.

The decor here took a departure. A Siberian tiger skin covered a large section of the floor, glass eyes dead to the world but the coat still glossy. I stepped over the head of the poor beast, said, 'Sorry, buddy.' Felt like I'd stamped on a grave.

In the centre of the room a circular seating area was set into the floor. I'd only ever seen this in movies, it looked very *Carlito's Way*. Got the idea Zalinskas wanted to make an impression. The vibe was: 'This is my lair.'

A chrome rail skirted the room, glass bricks beneath lit up. Felt like I'd stepped into the *Billie Jean* video as I paced the joint.

I touched the walls. Red suede. Then I saw it.

'No way!'

Zalinskas had a wolf.

Sunk in the wall, like a giant fish tank, was a glass-walled cage. Inside, the wolf prowled back and forth, back and forth, raising its nose to the airholes and picking up a new scent.

I touched the cage. 'You poor bastard.'

I wanted to find something to smash the glass, let the creature out. But I didn't rate my chances against those fangs.

I felt appalled, shook my head, then a haughty voice cut the air, 'He's a killer, don't you know. *Canis Lupus*!' said Zalinskas.

I recognised him at once. He glided across the room towards me, wearing a black silk shirt, open at the neck. White, what can only be described as 'slacks' sat above a hint of belly. As he came closer I saw his shoes were white too, except for some snow leopard detailing. I'd seen something similar on punky brothel creepers, but these shouted a whole other message.

'You like my companion?'

I kept a lid on my thoughts, I said, 'He's . . . impressive.'

Zalinskas liked that, smiled, a vicious barracuda smirk.

'An amazing predator,' his voice betrayed little of his Russian background, he'd had good voice coaches, I'd give him that, 'almost six feet long, seventy kilograms.'

'Not to be messed with.'

The smirk again. 'Indeed.' Zalinskas moved towards the glass cage, leaned forward. 'Are you au fait with the pack mentality, Mr . . . ?'

I let his question go unanswered. 'Dury.'

'The wolf has a highly developed social structure, Mr Dury. Only one dominant male – ' he tapped the glass – 'will ever be allowed to mate, he will always eat first, and all challengers to his dominance are banished or killed.' Zalinskas ran a finger down the glass, then turned towards me.

'Survival of the fittest,' I said.

'Quite.'

'The strong preying on the weak.'

He flung back his head, laughed to the heavens. His teeth looked neat and straight, bone white. 'Have you ever heard the howl of a wolf, Mr Dury?'

'Close up? Can't say I have.'

'It's not a warning to take lightly.' He turned from me, took his hand along the rail for a few steps then raised both arms in the air. 'A drink, I think. I believe we have a rather substantial win at my tables to celebrate.'

I followed Zalinskas to his desk; it had a black marble top, supported by giant bronze eagles, wings spread. Strange how all these petty despots like to surround themselves with this kind of symbolism. I imagined I'd seen him in some of those holiday snaps Adolf Hitler took after the Third Reich captured Paris – here's me and Benny at the Eiffel Tower . . . the Arc de Triomph . . .

Zalinskas held out a brandy glass, said, 'Armagnac?'

'I won't say no.'

He swilled the liquid about in the glass, sipped.

I shot mine, handed over the chit. 'About this.'

Zalinskas glanced at the piece of paper, I waited for an eyebrow to be raised. His face remained calm as he opened a drawer and handed over two banker's rolls.

'Should I check it?' I said.

'Don't you trust me, Mr Dury?'

'You might have given me too much.'

Zalinskas smiled, those teeth! I thought they must play havoc with the ultra-violet lights in his clubs, he said, 'I don't make mistakes.'

I trousered the cash. Now it was time to really start gambling. 'Is that so?'

Zalinskas sat back in his chair, reached for the bottle and topped up our glasses.

I dived in. 'I believe we have a common friend – sorry, *had*.'

'Really?'

'Billy Thompson.'

If Zalinskas changed his expression, I missed it.

'Such a tragic soul,' he said. He flipped the lid on a cigar box, took one and slid it towards me. 'They're Cuban.'

I closed the lid, ferreted for my tabs. 'I smoke my own.'

'As you wish.'

Clouds of smoke gathered between us. Zalinskas seemed content. If there was any enjoyment to be had in this situation, I wasn't getting it.

'Was certainly dramatic, the way Billy went,' I said.

'Such a loss.'

'To whom?'

'I'm speaking in general.'

'What exactly did Billy do for you, Mr Zalinskas?'

'He was what you might call a factotum.'

'He certainly seemed to juggle a lot of jobs from what I hear.'

For the first time, his ice-cool appearance cracked. 'Billy was ambitious, I like to reward such types.'

I stood up, helped myself to more Armagnac. 'Good stuff this. I could see how a taste for the finer things might turn a young lad's head – Was that it, Mr Zalinskas? Did Billy get greedy?'

'I'm sure I don't know what you mean. He was a valued employee, his death was a loss to all of us. Myself especially.'

I chanced my arm. 'That's not what I hear. Some say you had good reason to get rid.' I moved over to the wall of monitors. 'Quite a dust-up the pair of you had before his death. Did the cameras capture that?'

Zalinskas kept shtum. Rolled the glass between his palms.

I slammed my hand on the marble top. 'Nothing to say?'

'Calumnies are best answered with silence.'

'Ben Johnson.'

'You're obviously an intelligent man. Why are you pursuing such rumours, such lies?'

I played him at his own game. 'What's a lie but a truth in masquerade?' He looked up, obviously not a Byron fan.

He faced me, I thought he might crack, but then he smiled. 'Dig away, Mr Dury. I can assure you there is nothing to implicate me in Billy Thompson's death.'

'Maybe not – but a little mud sticks, no? You're already being dragged through the courts. Two cases would be very messy.'

'A tenuous connection, don't you think?'

His cockiness pressed on the bolts that held in my anger. I felt tempted to slap some information out of him, but he seemed too secure for that.

Zalinskas rose, moved back to the wolf. 'You know, only the pack leader is ever allowed to raise pups,' he said. 'I can assure you, Mr Dury, I take my responsibilities to my pack very seriously.'

'And when the time comes for the pup to challenge the leader, what happens then? Sorry, we've been there already, you explained. Of course. Look, Zalinskas, I know what kind of an outfit you run here. I know about Billy's plans. I know about the . . .'

Zalinskas' eyes widened. I had him where I wanted him, rattled. But I'd get no more from him, I knew that. The result I wanted depended on his next move outside this room. I'd made him sweat, now I needed to step back and observe.

He drew a curtain over the wolf's cage, turned and walked back to his desk. 'I see you have been talking to Nadja, Mr Dury.' He pulled deep on his cigar. 'I warn you now, her word is not to be trusted.'

'Thanks for the friendly advice. I'll store it away.'

'Nadja has her own . . . agenda.'

'Haven't we all?'

'Indeed we do, Mr Dury.' He pressed a button on his desk and the door I'd come through clicked open, the pug and two uniformed filth walked in.

'I believe this is the man you're looking for officers,' said Zalinskas.

ZALINSKAS SMIRKED AS HE WELCOMED in the filth. A glare in my direction said he'd been messing with me, but now he'd tired of the game. I'd seen the look before, on Hannibal Lecter, waited for the, 'Do you hear the lambs, Clarice?'

Tried to stand my ground.

'This is all very cosy, fellahs,' I said as the cops approached me, 'but if you don't mind indulging me a few moments – what's the charge?'

One of the cops touched six feet, carried a build that said he was no stranger to the police gym. He seemed to take my query as a personal slight, lunged at me.

I took a killer punch to the gut. Then a knee to the kidney that splayed me on the floor like the dead tiger. I felt my insides scream. I tried to cry out but my breath deserted me. For more than a few seconds I believed my next move was going to be onto a mortuary slab.

'How about resisting arrest for a start,' said plod.

I found a dim light ignite some strength, it felt like courage. 'Nice try. What am I supposed to be resisting arrest for?' I rolled onto my haunches, each breath felt like acid poured in my lungs.

'You cocky cahnt.'

Plod was London. It only made me more determined to mess with his head.

'Come on, I'm trying to help, I wouldn't want you to get into any trouble with your superiors – your porcine brethren who walk on two legs.'

He went for his baton. It flashed in the air above me, I saw this turn was well practised. I couldn't move, braced myself for bone-shattering.

'Stop!' Zalinskas stepped in. 'Not here – take him away.'

I felt myself lifted by the collar, my arms jerked round to my back as I was cuffed.

'Gentlemen, please, you'll damage those bracelets if you're not careful.'

'Shut it,' said London.

I managed a last glance at Zalinskas, a smirk of my own. 'Nice one, Benny, I love your work!'

He mulled it over. I thought he might answer, show some kind of emotion but he merely turned away from me, went back to his desk, lit another cigar.

As plod led me away Zalinskas blew smoke into the air. He had no more words for me.

'Goodbye, Mr Zalinskas,' I shouted, 'no doubt I'll be seeing you again.'

'Move your fakhin' arse,' said London, sticking his baton in my shoulder blades and twisting it, hard.

All told, I thought, not a bad little result. Sure, I wondered what awaited me at the station, but I'd made an impression on Benny the Bullfrog. I'd taken his casino for a few grand and, most importantly, let him know I was very definitely onto him. I'd given the bastard something to think about.

On the floor Amy and Hod waited by the door.

'Gus, Gus!' cried Amy. 'Oh my God, what have they done to you?'

'It's nothing,' I said.

'Shift,' said London, he moderated his language now we were in the full glare of the public.

Amy threw her arms around me, 'Oh Gus, Gus . . .'

'Quick – the cash – it's in my pocket.'

'Miss, leave the suspect alone, please,' said Plod. He clutched her arms, lifted her away from me.

'Gus, I have it,' she said, waving the rolls of cash.

'Great. Hod, the cash, take it to the crem. Milo Whittle, that's my mate, you have to pay for the funeral expenses tomorrow.'

'Move,' said London. Another prod in the back, he'd lost patience with me.

'Hod, did you hear me?'

'Milo Whittle.'

'That's it. The works, do you get me? I want him sent off in style.'

I saw Amy raise a hand to her face and start to cry. It was the last thing I saw before plod threw me into the back of a meat wagon.

'Wait till we get you down that fakhin' station, you saucy little cahnt,' said London.

THE FILTH WASTED NO TIME throwing me down the stairs. Sorry, I slipped of course.

London had a thing for punching me on the head, probably imagined it would be harder to spot the injuries. He had a fair punch too, knuckles like the pattern on Charlie Brown's jumper, and plenty of energy. I prayed he'd tire himself out, bust a hand. But this was Robocop. He'd stop when he was told.

I spat blood, but I'd been worked over before. After a dozen or so blows a numbness settles in. I watched the punches coming and relaxed into them, he couldn't dent me. I imagined myself as Ali on the ropes to Foreman; I could take the punishment. What was the worst that could happen? He'd kill me. Well, I'd no fear of death, that's for sure. I thought, 'Bring it on – give me your worst.'

'You're gonna need a mop and bucket in here soon,' I said.

'Shut your lairy little hole.'

'Will you do it yourself? Can see you in a set of Marigold gloves. Have you got a tabard too?'

He stood back from me, panting. He showed his bottom teeth. London had borrowed this look from Lenny McLean, the Guv'nor, but he was no bare-knuckle fighter. A few good jabs would put him to bed. He looked like every filth I'd ever known, could only handle a fight with the odds stacked in his favour. It's the old story all over. Weak fucks join up because they know it's their best chance of getting on a winning side.

A green light flashed above the door and London straightened his back.

'That you off then?' I said.

He pulled back his arm, a fist hovered in the air.

I smiled at him. I felt the blood squelching. I'd lost some teeth. But I felt no sense of defeat, and he saw this. I'd taken the best he had to offer and I still smiled.

London lowered his fist, saw I wasn't worth the energy.

'You're fukhin' mental, d'you know that?' he said.

'Whatever – the green light's flashing. Time to get the kettle on for the DCs.'

He looked at me like I was seriously tapped.

'Proper mental, that's what you are.'

My smile sat in place as I threw back my head and roared with laughter. Quite a victory, it felt good. Bring on round two.

For an hour they left me to my own devices. Then brought in a bucket of water and a scrubbing brush.

'Clean this shit up,' a lad in uniform told me, must have been twenty tops, hair still parted with his mother's spit.

I walked to the bucket and kicked it over. 'Bite me.'

Uniform didn't know what to do. Walked out, leaving the bucket behind him.

Inside a minute two gut-huge inspectors appeared. They took an arm each and dragged me out the door.

Together they said, 'Walk.'

They took me to another cell. Table and chairs, camera in the corner. 'Sit.'

'Don't mind if I do.' I knew they were the real deal. I also knew I'd already been through the worst. From here on in, we got down to the meat and potatoes.

'Gus Dury,' said the heavier of the two, Markies shirt, Farah trousers and a Freddie Mercury tache.

'That's what they call me.'

'Lose the fucking attitude.'

I leaned forward, said, 'Lose the fucking tone, you've nothing on me.

Whereas I've a delightful tale of police brutality to splash over the papers tomorrow.'

They both laughed. Looked at each other, I expected back slapping.

'Who'd print anything from a piss-wet old soak like you, Dury?'

The second doughnut-muncher stood up. He looked about five-eight in his comfortable Clarks shoes that squeaked on every step. 'We have a stack of witnesses to your resisting arrest, Mr Dury. I'd recommend you cooperate, it's to your advantage.'

'Christ almighty. Spare me the good cop bad cop routine, eh?'

Silence. Then: 'Cigarette?' said Clarks shoes.

'Silk Cut?'

'I'm cutting back.'

'Have you no real fags?'

The pack went down. I picked out a tab, the cop lit me up.

'Like a breath of fresh air,' I said.

'That's how I'm hoping this, shall we say advice, will greet you, Mr Dury.'

'Come again?'

'Stay away from Mr Zalinskas.'

'Am I hearing right?'

The cop with the tache leaned forward, banged on the table. 'I'm warning you, you'll take this—'

'Is that what you say to your men friends? You charmer.'

He had to be held back after that, it was like *Hill Street Blues* all over.

'Mr Dury, I'd take my partner's advice.'

'Partner, so that's how it is. Tell me this, I've always wondered, is it better to give than to receive?'

Moustache got out his seat again, managed to land a slap on my face. 'You cheeky pup, I'll hang you the fuck out to dry, do you hear me?'

'Reg, Reg . . . control yourself.'

'Och, I'm fucking through with this.'

'Reg . . .'

He headed for the door. 'Dury, I swear to Christ, you'll be in the Forth if I hear your name in the same breath as Benny Zalinskas' again.'

He left.

'Excitable chap your partner.'

'I wouldn't treat his advice so glibly. Mr Zalinskas is a very influential person in this city.'

'With both criminals and the police, I see.'

'Mr Dury, please . . .'

'Please? Fuck off. What's he got on you? Some pictures of you two fags in flagrante delicto?'

A shake of the head. 'I can see you're going to cause us some trouble, Mr Dury. I'm very sorry to hear that.'

'Oh, I bet you are.'

'I'm prepared to ignore your actions on this occasion. Put them down to, shall we say, misplaced chutzpah.'

I laughed.

'But, I can assure you, if we have cause to speak again, you will regret it – most assuredly you will.'

I SPENT THE NEXT TWENTY-FOUR hours in a cell. When they let me go I got handed a polythene bag holding my watch, wallet, phone and some change.

Guy on the front desk said, 'That'll be you off to get hammered.'

I'd never seen him before. 'What?'

'The booze is oozing out of you.' He shook his head, slammed closed the black diary he'd been writing in, said, 'Fucking alkies.'

On the way out the door, I started to shiver. My mouth felt like an open wound. Missing teeth catching the cold air of morning. I had managed a hundred yards when I heard my name spoken under breath.

'Gus – Gus, over here,' was called out from a dark vennel along from the police station.

I looked about. I wasn't keen to venture into more trouble.

'Gus, come here, would ya?'

I recognised the voice this time. Tried to make it look casual as I walked into the narrow street.

'Christ, Fitz, this is a bit close to home for you, isn't it?'

'I had to grab you.'

'Why? What's wrong with the caff?'

'Why do you think? You're a marked man, Dury. By the Christ, aren't ye ever!'

I let out a sigh. 'Tell me something I don't know.'

Fitz eyeballed me. 'Jaysus, they did some job on ye boyo. Was Rambo, no doubt.'

'What?'

'London fellah. Built like a brick shithouse. He came up here about six months ago, playing the Big I Am, so he was. No one was afraid of him, mind. Christ, haven't we Celts been sending them home to think again for long enough?'

'Yeah, sounds like him.'

'Ah, he's a gobshite, I wouldn't sweat over him.'

'I'm not.'

'Arrah, I wouldn't give the likes of him the steam off my piss.'

I saw Fitz had a personal animus for this cop, but knew he hadn't pulled me up to have a wee office bitch. 'Fitz, did you have something for me?'

'Have I ever.'

'Well, let's hear it.'

'I've done a bit of digging about, like you said I should.'

'And?'

'You were right. If vice are interested in Benny Zalinskas, I've started taking it up the Gary Glitter.'

'So someone was feeding you a cover story. Who?'

'Not so fast, Dury. Remind me why I should tell you anything?'

I had Fitz on side, that much seemed clear. But it didn't mean he wouldn't make me work for any information he had.

'Because, Fitz, when this blows, you're the main beneficiary and you know it,' I said. 'I won't bullshit you about being a good cop and doing right. Fuck, I know you're as bad as the rest. This is your chance to settle some old scores. Think of all those bastards who laughed at you when you hit the slide. Give me the name behind this and I'll make sure the ship sinks. All you need to do is get in the lifeboat when I give you the nod.'

'I don't know . . .'

'Fitz, let's put Billy's death aside for a minute. There's one thing you can tell me that means nothing to anyone except me.'

'The old fellah?'

'I need to know what happened to Milo.'

Fitz took off his hat, smoothed down his crown. 'I'm afraid, that's one you'll never get to the bottom of.'

'There's a connection. You know it, and I sure as hell know it.'

'I'm not saying there isn't, but it could well have been an accident that got covered up. Maybe he saw something he shouldn't have – these people cover their tracks, it's what they do.'

'So, that's it? Another fucking suicide verdict.'

'Misadventure, is the term,' said Fitz, as he looked to the sky.

The urge for justice and revenge ratcheted up inside me.

'Who're the two bufties in there, bloke with a moustache and his soft-shoe shuffling mate?'

'Matching beer guts?'

'Yeah.'

'That's Collins and Roberts. Why?'

'They've promised me a second round. I need to get moving on this or I'm finished. It's now or never, Fitz.'

He peered into the street, took his hands out of his police-issue over-coat, pointed at me. 'I swear by the Holy Mother, if this comes back to haunt me, I'll cut yer throat.'

I'd had so many threats lately one more wasn't going to scare me. 'Scout's honour.'

'There's a racket – you know about that.'

'The girls from Eastern Europe.'

'Yes. But it goes deeper than you can imagine.'

I'd seen so much already. It would have to be something to beat a wolf in a glass cage, but I played along, said, 'Try me.'

'Billy had been, oh . . . what's the word, *procuring* girls for some of the top brass.'

'Police – the Chief Constable?'

Fitz, raised his eyebrows. 'Higher than that.'

'What?'

'I tell you, when this comes out, heads will more than roll.'

I wasn't convinced. As if this kind of thing hadn't been going on for ever. I couldn't believe Billy got offed because he had some top-flight customers. Public execution just wasn't their style.

'Who is it, Fitz?'

He wiped his face. 'I don't know yet.'

'What?'

'It's a conspiracy of silence. There's names being thrown about like you would not believe, but no one's putting their finger on it. I've got it narrowed down all right.'

'To where?'

Fitz took a deep breath, held it for a few seconds. 'The First Minister's Cabinet.'

I WENT BACK TO THE Wall and showered. Tried to keep the spray on my mouth for as long as I could bear. The pain seared my gums. Burns knew what he was talking about when he wrote of 'the venom'd stang that shoots tortured gums alang'.

I hit the painkillers. Double-strength jobs, two fiery arrows on the pack to emphasise the point. As I waited for them to kick in I dressed. Faded cords from the late eighties. We'd been through a lot together but they'd held in there. Lost a few belt loops and carried some sheen on the arse and knees. But I wasn't trying to make any statement with them, other than, 'Hey I'm comfortable, get over it.' Finished the look off with an old grey Levi's sweatshirt, soft as down. It sat under a blue checked lumberjack shirt, what the Seattle Sub Pop guys called 'a flannel'.

I checked myself in the mirror. I looked like a Nirvana roadie. Then I opened my mouth. Nup, I looked like a Redneck, some trailer trash from the Georgia woods. I heard the cries of Ned Beatty in *Deliverance*, as the hillbilly shouted, 'Scream like a pig, boy.'

I was out of gel. Most of my day-to-day stuff was at Hod's, but I didn't want to put in an appearance there until I'd checked in again with Col. I knew Amy would stick about there and I didn't want her to see me with missing teeth and a set of racoon eyes. I'd already fired off a quick text, just to let her know they'd let me out, but I needed to switch off my phone afterwards. She was in safe hands with Hod, but had become more of a worry to me now.

I ran my fingers through the few strands of hair that sat up on the top of my head. Could do with cropping I thought. Maybe make a trip to see Mac again. He might still have the shooter, after all.

I tried to down a pint of water, but the effort was too much. I needed alcohol to stop my nerves rattling. This felt like the longest period I'd been without my drug of choice for at least three years.

I needed to go on a skite. Picked out all the familiar indicators. The room closed in on me. I paced up and down. Visualised a row of creamy pints lined up on a bar. My mouth dried over.

It's always been about breaking the monotony for me. The skite's just a purge. Life piles up, you get fed up, and so you go out and try to change everything. That's where the alcohol helps. You want to be a different person, you want to blow your world up. And for a little while, alcohol lets you believe this is possible. Time stops as you rattle from pub to pub in an alcoholic haze. Slowly, the world as you know it ceases to exist. You've broken the cycle, you're off the trodden path. It's what it's all about, keeping normality at bay. For a little while anyway.

The next day it's like being woken by a ghost when shame settles on you. You wonder why you did it. Fear the consequences. Fear you'll do it again. But, you've broken that cycle of boredom. And no matter how much you abhor the person staring back at you from the mirror, you know you'll do it again because it works like a charm.

I strolled down to the bar. Col polished glasses with a small towel. 'Holy Mother of God, what's happened to you?'

I waved him off, said, 'Pint. Chaser.'

The old gadgie with the drinker's nose stood in place, smelling of piss, he approached me and spoke: 'Howya doing, pal?'

'You still here? Becoming a bit of a fixture.'

'Better than a bit of a prick.'

I'd no comment on that.

Col placed my drinks down in front of me. 'On the house.'

'Thanks.'

I drank deep. Belted back the chaser.

'Man, that's a thirst and a half,' said the gadgie.

I felt in no mood for conversation, said, 'Is that piss I smell?'

He got the hint, said, 'When you get to my age, no matter how much you shake, the last drop always ends up in your pants. Remember that.'

Dumbfounded, I watched him walk off and take a seat at someone else's table.

'What's happening to the clientele?' I asked Col.

'He's a lost soul.'

'Aren't we all?'

Col flicked the bar towel over his shoulder. 'You look like you've had an accident.'

My mouth was too occupied to reply. I motioned to the empty shot glass, sunk back the pint.

'Would you like another?' said Col.

'Would I ever.'

He poured out a Famous Grouse, left the bottle on the bar.

'Have you eaten lately?'

'I've been a bit . . . preoccupied.'

'If this case is proving too much—'

I slammed down the glass. 'No. Col, everything's fine.'

'That's clearly not so, Gus. You've been beaten, badly beaten. What's going on?'

I filled my glass up, right to the brim.

'Let's grab a seat. I've something to tell you.'

'Oh,' he said.

'Yeah, I, eh . . . well, you might not like what I have to say.'

Col called over to his part-timer, told her to mind the bar. She popped out a Hubba Bubba bubble, teetering on heels as she walked over.

'We'll take the snug, I think.'

'Would be best.'

'YOU WANT TO GET THOSE teeth seen to, Gus.'

'What teeth? They're all knocked out.'

'Have you a dentist?'

Christ, a dentist. The days of me having a regular dentist, doctor or gym membership sounded like a lifetime ago.

'Debs used to look after all that kind of thing. No, I don't have a dentist.'

'I'll give you the number of mine. He's good, a German fellah, very good.'

I drew on the Grouse. Felt like it heated my soul, had forgotten how much I actually enjoyed a Low Flying Birdie.

'So, you said you had something to tell me.'

I put down the glass. 'I do, yeah.'

Col sat quietly, closed his fingers together. I'd never noticed before, for such a gentle guy, his hands were huge.

'It's all got a bit more . . . complicated.'

'Uh-huh.'

'It seems Billy was up to his neck in more than I first imagined.'

'I knew it.'

'Sorry?'

'How that boy could have done this to his poor mother, I'll never know.'

I hadn't even told Col what I knew and already he'd fired up.

'But, Col, we don't know the extent of Billy's involvement yet.'

'Gus, I raised him. I know my boy.'

I waited for him to continue, but he seemed to be finished. I took up the story as I knew it. Mentioned all I'd found out. It seemed to me Col's eyes glazed over. I wondered if he really did want to know the whole truth behind Billy's death.

'Col, is everything all right?'

'Yes, fine – why do you ask?'

'You seem a bit distant, that's all.'

He shook himself, unclasped his hands. 'I'm sorry. What you said the last time we spoke has, well – you know . . . it upset me a bit, I guess.'

I flattened my tone, said, 'I told you, right at the start, Col, you don't go digging like this without unearthing a few skeletons.'

'I know. I know. It's been hard to believe, though. He was my son. To hear he was involved in the likes of this – it hits you here.' Col thumped on his chest. 'I just want this concluded for his mother's sake. Nothing else matters. She must know how it ended, she needs to see why Billy went the way he did.'

I sensed a colder side to Col than I had previously known. This whole episode had hit him hard. I hoped he'd be tough enough to take it the distance. I knew nothing good would be turned up from this point; there was no fairytale ending coming soon.

'It's only going to get worse. Are you up to this? The picture's not a pretty one.'

'Oh, yes.' He perked up a little, managed a stock smile. 'Yes, I wouldn't worry about me, Gus. None of this is much of a surprise.'

'*None* of it?'

'A figure of speech. What I'm saying is, I knew Billy had his . . . moments – always did. When he hitched up with that Nadja one, I saw there would be trouble. It was only a matter of time. I've been following his fall from grace you know.'

'But like you say, he's your son, it must be painful to hear it.'

'*Was* my son.' Col stood up, his mood flipped again, he looked rattled. 'By the way, I took down *all* those pictures of your father.'

I got the message loud and clear. I'd crossed the line. Took the swipe.

I stood up to face him, said, 'Think I'll go and get a cigarette.'

'Okay.'

'Look, I'm sorry if I, you know, said anything that's . . . I know this is very upsetting for you.'

He collapsed back in his chair, shook before me. 'Oh, God . . . what have I done?'

'Col,' I tried to coax him round, 'come on, you're made of strong stuff.'

'God, I'm so, so sorry . . .'

'Come on, here have a drink of this.' I tried to get him to sip the whisky.

'No, no – I'm fine, I'm fine really.'

'Are you sure?'

'Yes.' He trembled a little, then seemed to go completely calm again. 'Gus, I've no right to put this pressure on you.'

'I've good broad shoulders for this kinda thing.'

'I've placed you in terrible danger. Billy's sins are not your concern. I should never have asked you to take this up.'

The guy looked ruined. He'd taken himself to hell and back several times. I put a hand on his shoulder. 'I'm glad to help.'

'No, Gus . . . I've a terrible feeling that this will all end badly. Very badly indeed.'

I squeezed his shoulder. 'How bad could it get?' I said.

SOMEONE ONCE SAID LIFE'S ALL about letting things go. I wish I could let some of this go.

It's 1982 and I'm fourteen. My father's had the call up for the World Cup squad. The *Evening News* has him on the front and back page. My mother keeps a scrapbook, tapes *Scotsport*. He's a Leith boy made good, now it's official.

There's traffic stopped in the street, men hanging out of car windows to shake his hand. I stand watching as my father is surrounded by people. They swarm to him, clapping and shouting, screaming for a word from the man himself.

I have my own minor taste of fame to deal with too. The Schools League Cup Final. I have the sweeper's role – same as my father's – everyone tells me I have a hard act to follow.

But I've invited only shame.

It happens like a dream. The ball floats down from the heavens, lands at my feet. There's no one between me and the goalie, it's a clear run. I've only to cross the field, then hit the ball.

Cheers and roars go up as I take off like a scalded dog. The rest of the players behind me can only watch. I run for goal and as I look up I see all that stands between me and my first taste of mythic success is the scrawny frame of the goalie, Ally Donald.

Then, I freeze.

Something stops me. Twice I draw back to strike the ball, but can't. I hear my father shouting for the whack of the ball to follow but I can't move. It's as if I know that if I score, I'll never escape his influence.

I look at the ball, black and muddied below, but no matter how hard I stare I can't summon the force to move it, and then the moment passes.

The scrawny Ally Donald appears before me, running, his feet already making their way to the ball, which he clears back to the halfway line.

I know at once I'll never play again. As I walk off the pitch, my world shifts.

'You worthless coward,' says my father. He follows me into the changing rooms to tell me, over and over. 'Too yellow to face a runt of a boy like wee Ally Donald, a streak of a lad without the strength to hold up his own socks.'

I say nothing.

'Aye, he got the better of you,' says my father. 'Ashamed to show your face again you should be. You've cost the team the game, the cup, you spineless wee bastard!'

I don't care about the game. I hate being in the team. He's put me here and I hate being watched by him, hearing people say, 'There goes the next Cannis Dury.'

'They'll be laughing long and hard after this day,' he says. 'I'll never forgive you for the shame. It's me they'll be laughing at! Not you – who are you?'

I look at him, his face is red, eyes bulging.

'And what the fuck are you looking at?' His fist comes from nowhere. It catches me on the temple and knocks me to the floor. I feel the cold of the ceramic tiles as I land. The floor's white but by my eye, where I lie unable to move, it's turning red.

I don't know how long I lie there. My team mates call the coach and I'm carried out to an old Austin Allegro and driven home. For the next four years I hear Ally Donald's name mentioned on an almost nightly basis.

'My, he got the better of you,' says my father. 'Ashamed to show your face again so you should be.'

His playing days are well and truly over now, but he still thinks he's someone, calls me a 'worthless coward' at every chance.

I put up with it until Debs appears on the scene. I take her home to see my mother. She stands by the mantelpiece. Those stupid red bulbs twirling behind the plastic coals, lighting up the backs of her legs. She looks so out of place, so uncomfortable.

Then in he walks, hanging off a tin of Cally Special and says, 'Yes, very good son. A great wee bobby-soxer you've got there, but what's she doing with you?'

I let it go. Take Deb's hand and lead her away.

'I met Ally Donald's father today,' he says as we go, 'he's in London now, a big job in the government, so he has, the English working for him. You'd be better off with him than with this worthless coward.'

I walk Debs home. Tell her I'm sorry. She places a hand on my face, cries. She says she had no idea how awful it was for me.

On the road back I decide to take action into my own hands. I wait outside until my mother's bedroom light goes out. As I go in he's still sitting in his usual chair, watching *The Benny Hill Show*. He's laughing his guts out as the wee baldy guy's slapped on the head.

I walk in front of the television. Turn it off.

'What do you think you're playing at?' he says.

'On your feet.'

He curls up his brow. 'Fuck off with yourself. Off to your bed.'

'I said – on your feet.'

He tries to stare me out, but I'm unflinching. Then he says, 'What are you doing, laddie? You calling me out?'

The blood pumps in my veins, a strange copper taste comes to my mouth as I say, 'That's right.'

He laughs.

'Called out by a coward like you. A wee coward that Ally Donald got the better of – that scrawny wee streak of piss.'

My mouth dries over, I wet my lips. 'That's not going to work any more. Up, on your feet.'

He puts down his Cally Special, places his hands on the arms of the chair and raises himself. He's a fearsome sight stood before me. But as he puts his glare on me I don't move, he walks forward.

Clang.

My fist catches him cleanly. He goes down like a pack of cards. He's shaking his head, patting the floor with his palms.

'Up,' I say.

He struggles to find his feet. His great ego won't let him be felled. He swings at me, it comes from below the hip and I walk past it. I swat him on the back of the head and he goes through the washing my mother has drying by the fire.

He thumps on the ground with his fist and raises himself again. He runs at me, head down, but he's too slow. I kick out and the heel of my boot stops him dead. He drops to his knees, blood pouring from his head.

I give him a moment, then: 'Up.'

He touches his wound. 'Look what you've done!'

'I've done? You brought this on yourself.'

'I'm your father.'

'That's no excuse.'

He stands up. Faces me. I look into his eyes, I'm ready to strike him again if he moves an inch. But he stands still before me.

I walk past him to my room. Pack my things. On my way out he doesn't look up.

'Don't let me hear you've ever raised so much as a bad word to anyone in this family again,' I warn him.

He still doesn't look up as I close the door behind me.

ANOTHER LETTER FROM DEB'S LAWYER. I didn't think it worth opening. I mean, what was it going to say?

'Congratulations, your last call was such a success that Ms Deborah Ross has decided to halt all formal divorce proceedings . . .'

I doubted it. Scrunched the letter into a ball and launched it to the trash. My heart felt scalded but maybe it was time to move on. What's the phrase? Oh yeah, flogging a dead horse.

A catch, I wasn't. My career was washed up. I had a serious alcohol problem and, on top of everything else, I'd lost most of my top row of teeth. I mean, who'd rate *me*?

Debs deserved better, deserved to start afresh. It would take a cruel bastard to stop her. Much as I wanted to think she'd always be there, I knew I'd blown it. There may come a time I'll be able to face her, tell her I was sorry, but it wasn't right now. I turned to George Burns for support, he'd said: 'Do you know what it means to come home at night to a woman who'll give you a little love, a little affection, a little tenderness? It means you're in the wrong house.'

I waited for the bus on Leith Walk. A man carrying a canoe strolled up behind me. I turned, thought about asking, then turned back. I didn't want to know.

When the bus came the man with the canoe tried to follow on after me.

Driver said, 'You can't get on here!'

'Why not?' said the canoe guy.

'Cos you can't walk on a bus with a canoe.'

'Would you prefer I paddled?'

I liked that, but the driver didn't, got out his seat and looked ready to lamp the guy, before he took off. A man running down a busy street with a canoe is not something you see every day, even in Edinburgh.

I sat beside some geezer with a stookie on his arm. He'd a tight T-shirt, a toast-rack chest poked from beneath.

'You look like you've been in the wars,' he said.

This from a guy with a broken arm, I lied: 'Car crash.'

He winked. 'Aye sure.'

'Excuse me.'

'Had a bit of soapy bubble, big man?'

I tried to laugh it off. Left at the next stop. I couldn't go around looking like part of the body count from a Steven Seagal film, so called Col's dentist. By some kind of miracle he gave me an appointment right away.

In the waiting room I picked up an Ikea catalogue. Was full of happy couples, rosy-cheeked children and friendly-looking dogs. They all had perfect teeth. Even the dogs. For a moment, I wanted to live an Ikea life. The moment passed.

I turned to the free paper, the *Metro*. A picture showed a six-and-a-half-stone cyst that doctors recently removed from an obese woman. The article said the cyst weighed the same as Paris Hilton. Now, if they could cut her out, that's a story I'd like to read.

The receptionist called out my name.

My nerves twitched.

As I sat in the chair, I felt my knackers tighten.

The dentist was called Klaus. 'There's quite a considerable amount of damage,' he said. 'How did you do this?'

For the second time in under an hour, I lied: 'Rugby match.'

'You should be more careful.'

'Yeah, it's a rough game.'

'I mean at your age. Playing rugby. It's suicide.'

Right now, if I got given the option of playing rugby or suicide, I knew which one I'd choose. But what got me was the 'at your age' bit. I'm only mid-thirties, but it struck me, maybe I look like I'm carrying a few more years on the dial.

Klaus fixed me up with a set of temporaries. Promised me a full new top row, bridgework, the lot, by the end of the month.

He handed me a mirror.

'Wow,' I said. They looked Ultrabrite white, arrow straight. I couldn't believe that my mouth looked so good.

'I could live with these.'

'They'll come out in a week or so, then I'll do the bridgework proper.'

'Great. Well, I'll settle with you when the job's done.'

To my shock, he bought this. Figured I'd be good for it in a week – if I lasted that long.

I had to check in with Hod, called him. 'How goes it, man?'

'Christ, you're still with us, then?'

'Oh yeah, no danger. You'll have to try harder to edge me out the scene. How's Amy?'

He stalled, changed subject. 'Look, you coming round?'

'Why, what's up?'

'Nothing, shit, all's hunky dory here, compared to what you've . . . you know.'

I sensed cracks in Hod's voice and his cover story, but I'd too much to think about right now to be delving further. 'Right, sound. I'll be in touch soon as . . . keep an eye on Amy for me.'

'It's done.'

'But, not that close!'

'Gus . . . c'mon, I'm on the job here.'

'That's definitely not what I want to hear . . .'

A laugh. 'Sorry, just a slip.'

'Make that your last. See you later.'

On the street I kept trying to catch a look at my teeth in the reflections of shop windows. Were they really mine? Well, no. But God, they looked good. With teeth like this, a bit of a tan, perhaps I could pass myself off as a regular guy.

Maybe not.

I dropped back to reality, remembered I'd things to take care of. Nadja could expect a second visit from me soon. But before that, a visit to Mac the Knife called.

ON MY WAY TO GRAB a coffee I purposely passed two Starbucks. Finally settled on a place at the end of a side road leading out to Tollcross. Very low-rent. Gave it a month before the place got a revamp.

Browsed a chick's magazine and found one of those top ten worsts – on celebrity quotes. Jade Goody's gormless utterances dominated the top five, but Mariah Carey had it as far as I was concerned: 'I'm jealous of Ethiopian kids. I'd love to be skinny like them, except for the flies and the deaths.'

A case for bitch-slapping if ever I heard one.

As I flicked through the magazine again I felt a presence at my shoulder. Turned to see a bearded jakey stood over me. He looked old-school, herringbone coat and trousers held up with a length of rope. What was once referred to as a gentleman of the road, a paraffin lamp. He could have passed himself off for one of Van Gogh's Potato Eaters.

'Can I help you?' I said.

'Marks and Spencer's.'

Not a clue what he was on about, said, 'Come again?'

He leaned closer, I got a waft of him and moved in the opposite direction. 'That,' he said touching the magazine with a hand in fingerless gloves.

'The magazine . . . ?'

'The advert for Markies, that's my pitch. Paying a pretty penny now I tell you.'

I offered him the magazine. 'Here take it.' I hoped he'd get the hint and nick off, but he merely folded it down the spine, and expounded.

'Now, you see yon Twiggy there?'

I nodded, Christ why did they always flock to me?

'That's the look they're all after in there. They want the lot, big baggy jumpers, trendy trousers – och, even the hats!'

I lost patience. 'Great – but can I ask, is there a reason for this?'

He looked stunned. 'Is there a reason for anything?'

A jakey gets philosophical on you, you listen.

'What I'm saying is my pitch has started paying out. I'm on a winner since Twiggy started on these ads. The women buying the clobber and the hats and that, they're not short of a bob or two. They see me sitting outside after they've just got their hands on some big fancy outfit and they're splashing the cash.' He lifted up the magazine. 'I've a lot to thank Twiggy for.'

'I'm sure she'd be delighted to hear it. Why don't you write her a fan letter?' I stood up, drained my coffee cup. 'On second thoughts, you better not, she might ask for a percentage.'

Outside the caff two uniformed garbage inspectors photographed a pile of wet cardboard boxes dumped beside a row of wheelie bins. They gave me a look I'd seen a million times before, it said: 'We've got authority, you got a problem with that?'

I gave them a flash of my new teeth, said, 'Good morning, officers.'

Totally threw them, they didn't know if I'd just ripped the pish out of them or been sincere. I wanted them to ask me if I knew anything about the boxes – so I could have a go at them, show them how much authority they really had, but they took one look at the teeth and ignored me.

I walked to Mac's shop. Through the window I saw the place was empty of customers. Mac sat on one of the vacant barber's chairs, reading a book.

As I walked in an electronic beep sounded. I'd never heard it before and it made me look over my head. When I lowered my gaze again, Mac had risen to his feet before me.

'That's new,' I said.

'Holy shit,' said Mac, 'I thought you'd shot the crow . . . or worse.'

'Worse?'

'Went the way of Billy Boy, come on, out the back!'

Mac ushered me from the window, stuck a head out into the street and looked left and right, then hung up the closed sign.

I picked up his book as he pushed and prodded me through a narrow corridor to his office.

'Lawrence Block,' I said. 'I didn't have you down as a reader.'

'He's the top.'

'Matt Scudder series?'

'What else?'

'Have you read—'

He cut me off. 'Gus, I've read them all.' He took the book from me, placed it with a pile of others. The bookshelf heaved with crime novels. I name checked: Derek Raymond, Andrew Vachss, Ken Bruen, Horace McCoy, David Peace and on top, Barry Gifford's *Perdita Durango*.

'Quite a collection.'

Mac bridled. 'Have you come here to talk about books, Gus?'

A bashed leather couch was opposite me. 'Mind if I sit down?'

Mac waved up a hand, said mockingly, 'By all means.'

'Suppose a cuppa's out the question.'

'Don't push it.'

As he went to put on the kettle, I delved into some Thomas H. Cook.

People were lost and helpless, even the smart ones . . . especially the smart ones. Everything was vain and everything was fleeting. The strongest emotions quickly waned. A few things mattered, but only because we made them matter by insisting that they should. If we needed evidence of this, we made it up. As far as I could tell, there were basically three kinds of people, the ones who deceived others, the ones who deceived themselves and the ones who understood that the people in the first two categories were the only ones they were ever likely to meet.

Heady stuff.

Mac appeared with two cups, a packet of caramel wafers held in his teeth.

I took my cup from him, tasted it. 'That's good coffee.'

We supped in silence for a minute or two, then Mac stood up, said, 'Och for fucksake.' He was on edge as he went to his desk, took out a bottle of Grant's. 'Here . . . get fired into that.'

I topped up our coffees with the whisky.

'Where have you been?' said Mac.

'Hod's place.'

'Portobello — I thought you might have went a bit further than that. Porty, *Jesus*, Gus.'

'Mac, I'm still working the case.'

'Och . . . I dinnae want to hear any more.'

'I'm close.'

'Close to a hiding, one you won't forget.'

I showed him my new teeth, said, 'I've already had one of those.'

He shook his head. 'I'm on about a proper one — the kind of hiding they put the full stop on. Do you hear me?'

'I hear you. Look, what's new? You told me all this the last time. You must have picked up some more details.'

Mac reached for the Grant's, filled his cup to overflowing. 'It's been pandemonium since the trial kicked off.'

'I saw him on the telly.'

'Pissing show trial.'

'Come again?'

He raised the cup to his mouth, gulped deep, and winced. 'Did you not think he looked a little bit too cool?'

'Does he ever look otherwise?'

He filled his cup again, offered me more. 'From what I hear they've enough to put Zalinskas away for good, only he's covered his back.'

'He's protected?'

Mac nodded. 'Friends at the very top, so high nobody saying who.'

This wasn't a town to keep secrets in. 'Nobody? Come on . . .'

'Gus, if I knew, I'd spill it. I'm already up shit creek. Have you seen the nick of my shop? The business is on its arse. I've nothing to lose.'

I wondered if Mac connected our friendship with his loss of trade. 'You don't think . . . ?'

'God no, Gus . . . it's this city. Trends change so fast I can't keep the pace any more.'

I drained my cup. Poured in a power of whisky. Drank deep.

'About the murder – any ideas?'

'Don't know.'

'I'd heard Billy had something on Zalinskas.'

'Like what?'

'That's it, I'm as much in the dark as you, although . . .' I had my doubts about putting this out but knew Mac to be a good enough friend; if I couldn't trust him, who could I trust? Said, 'The night before his death, there was a fight between them.'

'No shit.'

'Pretty full-on apparently. Spooked the girls in the club – goons running around ripping out security cameras. Then a few days ago, I heard Billy was supplying brassers to a Cabinet Minister.'

'Are you saying what I think, Gus?'

'If that's Zalinskas' armour suppose Billy got a bit too greedy?'

'The old story.'

'Dipping his nib in the company ink.'

'Benny wouldn't like it. I can tell you that for nothing; the Bullfrog would not like that.'

I took a final swig from my coffee cup, said, 'I'm gonna need one last favour from you, Mac.'

'I don't know. I'm already hurting here.'

'I plan to do something about that real soon.'

I HAD ONLY ONE WAY to get some answers. And it wasn't going to be pretty.

I took a long walk, tried to figure things out. At Holyrood Park the sky turned grey, shot through with red. The queen's wee bit hoosie provided just the dark overtones my mood needed. The royals used to hold court up the road at the castle. Legend has it they moved down to Holyroodhouse because it was less draughty. In the gardens is Mary Queen of Scot's bathhouse, where she used to bathe in goat's milk and white wine. Every time I pass I see it as a nice reminder that the upper classes of this city have always been first with their snouts in the trough.

As I crossed the road to Arthur's Seat, a swan sat on the tarmac.

'Off . . . come on, move yourself,' I told it. I waved my arms about, but it wouldn't take me seriously. Stamped my foot at it, jumped in the air. It took the hint, waddled off.

'Nice work, Gus,' I thought. And not a broken arm in sight.

I followed the tourist trail, even on a day like today with the wind sharp enough to cut glass, they were out in force. You want to practise your French, or German, Italian – Japanese even, this is the place. All nationalities brave the elements to get a view of the city from on high. It didn't seem much of a way to spend your vacation, but then this place did have some undertones for me.

At the top, I lit up. Straightforward Benson and Hedges this time.

I scanned the skyline. Picked out Calton Hill, the parliament, the schemie eyesore of Dumbiedykes. I knew, from where I stood, any one of these sights could have been Billy's last.

I was close to the spot where he'd met his end.

I felt no ghosts here. Maybe my own demons held them at bay. Maybe there's just too many fighting for attention. It is, after all, where they found the Murder Dolls.

Seventeen minute figures in their own coffins. Eerie artefacts. Two schoolboys out rabbiting found them in 1836. At first the authorities thought they belonged to some sick practitioner of the black arts. Then someone pointed out that the grave robbers, Burke and Hare, murdered exactly seventeen people.

To this day, the Murder Dolls remain one of the city's mysteries. One of the many. To take a stroll down the Mile and see the ghost tour guides grabbing punters, you'd think the streets perpetually ran with blood.

'And some of that blood would have been Billy's,' I whispered to the hills.

The wind picked up, threatened rain. I looked at the tourist trail, they still streamed all the way up to the summit.

'Come on, Billy, give me a hand here. Do right by Milo and those girls.'

I put up my collar, stuck my hands in my pockets. Inside I felt the Glock I'd taken from Mac. A 10mm auto, it felt unusually light.

I'd seen Bruce Willis with a Glock in *Die Hard 2*, he called it a porcelain gun made in Germany, said: 'It doesn't show up on your airport X-ray machines, and it costs more than you make in a month.'

I'd asked Mac if this was true. He'd said, 'No. It shows up on X-ray and it costs more than you make in a year.'

I told him I'd give him it back in one piece, hopefully unfired. But I couldn't promise anything.

THE ROBOTICS DANCER ON PRINCES Street began to pack up his Gary Newman tapes as I passed. A Goth with black lipstick and platform trainers put a camera-phone on him, asked, 'How about a few moves for the camera?'

A single-digit salute, then another. 'How's that?' said the robotics guy.

'No need to get aggressive.'

'No offence, your get-up just brings out the worst in me.'

The Goth put the camera away, slunk off. I thought, 'When a guy who wouldn't look out of place in Woody Allen's *Sleeper* slams your dress sense, it's time to pick another look.'

I needed courage to put my plan into action, stepped into a new super-pub that had opened on George Street.

'Today's special, sir, Strawberry Blonde,' said a Geordie girl in a two-sizes too small T-shirt. She handed me a piece of card, smiled like she had my night all planned out.

'Sorry?'

That smile again.

'Strawberry Blonde!'

I'd got this bit, but something seemed to be missing, she was blonde all right, but looked like she'd been dying her roots black, said, 'I like the collars to match the cuffs.'

Inside the barman tried to take the card. 'Strawberry Blonde, sir?'

'Christ, not you too.'

'Is it a pint, sir?'

'Yeah, Guinness. No Strawberry Blonde. Got me?'

He nodded, backed off to the pumps.

I shouted out, 'And a Dewar's to chase it. Double.'

When the drinks came, the barman knew better than to try and sell me anything else. I took my pint and chaser and sat in the corner. Speakers above my head blasted out KT Tunstall. It seemed to fit the place. I'd tanned my pint before KT had got through telling us about her 'Black Horse and the Cherry Tree'.

The Dewar's I sipped slower.

Thought some things through, wondered if I'd been asleep at the wheel.

It all began to look so straightforward. Sure, I needed Nadja to fill in the blanks, but could that be so hard?

I knew it could. She was smart, wily. Cocking the Glock in her phiz wasn't going to cut it.

The words of Vyvyan Basterd, of *The Young Ones*, didn't seem out of place here: 'Now this is going to require a subtle blend of psychology and extreme violence . . .'

I'd tried the violence bit already. It was time to play Nadja at her own game.

'Yeah, good luck with that, Gus,' I heard myself thinking, 'like you're such a great success at second-guessing women.'

The example of Debs sprang to mind again. Could I even make a comparison?

Scottish women, it must be said, are unlike any others. Impossible to impress, for starters. There's a bullshit detector built into every one of them. In my youth they had a phrase, 'Do you think I came up the Clyde on a banana boat?' Subsequent generations refined this to a look. If it comes with a nod, you've crossed the line and should expect to be told so.

The other thing is they're all plain speakers. You find yourself on the end of one of their tongue lashings you might expect to learn more about yourself than perhaps you'd ever really wanted to.

I've a past littered with blastings from Scottish women. Usually delivered in a nightclub after the last dance. Any later, say in the taxi rank, we're talking hell cat. Guaranteed, an experience not to be repeated.

I returned to the bar.

'Same again.'

Barman thought a moment. 'Right away.'

For some reason, all this introspection began to latch on to my conscience. Thoughts of Debs and the impending threat to my mortality made me reach for my phone. Always a bad move when a drink's been taken.

Deb's number went straight to voicemail.

'Aw, shite!'

I toyed with hanging up, then the beep.

'Hi, Debs . . . me again. Look, I just wanted to say, sorry, you know, I've been a bit on edge lately.'

I struggled to pad out the message.

'Oh, and I, er, got your letter . . . but I had a bit of an accident with it. Was it important? Sorry about that too. If it's important you could maybe get your lawyer to send it again. Oh, and, I'll be at Hod's place in Portobello, all his details should still be in the address book. Bye, Debs, and sorry again.'

I didn't feel good lying to her about the letter, but what was I to do? I told myself it was only a white lie.

'Christ, you've told worse than that, Gus.'

Would the call cut any ice with her? I doubted it.

I LAID MY PHONE ON the bar. Inside a second it started to ring.

Picked up, said, 'Debs?'

'Eh, no, it's not Deborah, son.'

Was my mother, I'd never had a call from her on my mobi before, I felt a bit shocked. 'What is it, Mam?'

I heard her snivelling on the other end of the line.

'Mam, what is it?'

The snivelling gave way to full-on tears, then I heard the phone taken from her.

'Hello, hello,' I said.

'Hi, Gus, Mam's gone to sit down in the kitchen.' It was my sister, Catherine.

'What's up? Why's she calling?'

A pause, then: 'It's . . . Dad.'

I felt my lungs empty with a loud sigh, 'Oh yeah? What's it this time? Broke his hand on her again has he?'

'Gus . . . he's not well.'

'Yeah, I heard.'

'He's sick, Gus.'

'Oh, I know that. Should have heard him roaring at her when I was there a while ago . . . really, really sick he is.'

Cathy's tone changed. 'No, Angus he's . . . dying.'

I searched for sympathy, found none in me.

'Did you hear me?'

'I heard.'

'Well?'

'Well what? I don't perform miracles you know.'

I heard her snap her teeth together. 'The doctor says he won't see out the night. Mam – your mother, remember her? – thought you'd want to see him.'

'One last time, eh?'

'Yes, before he goes.'

She made it sound like he was getting ready for a holiday. Like he'd be back, sunburned and gagging for a proper pint and chips with broon sauce. I couldn't take her seriously. I'd blocked him out of my life for so long that the news he was finally dying made no impact on me.

'Oh, but goes where?' I said.

A long pause filled the line, I thought she'd hung up, but she'd only given me time to think about what I'd said. Families can do this, they know the buttons to push.

I said, 'Who else is there with you?'

'Everyone – the whole family. Look, I know you might not like the idea but it would mean a lot to Mam.'

'Is that why you're there?'

She didn't answer.

'Why should I, Cath?'

'You know she wants you here, it would give her peace of mind.'

'Peace of mind? She should be singing from the rooftops. *Christ*, she'll be free of the bastard.'

Cathy let out a gasp. I'd been venting, but it was too soon for a remark like that.

She stormed me: 'You shouldn't do anything you don't want to do.'

Clunk.

I'D STAYED IN THE PUB longer than I should have. The place filled up, got into party mode. Stretch limos dropped off loads of hen-night scrubbers. The choicest Scousers and Cockneys – munters that had seen more action than Chuck Norris.

They yelled at the barman: 'What about a Slow Screw? Can you do that?'

He lapped it up. Had them all buying pints of Strawberry Blonde.

Some of these old pterodactyls were clearly on a mission to play away from home. To a one, they were old slags. Tarts in microminis and white stiletto shag-me-shoes, fishnets that hardly disguised the network of Stilton-like veins. And plunging décolleté necklines that offered eyefuls of wrinkly DD cleavage.

The worst of it though was they all had tans. Sunbed tans. Tans that tighten and brighten younger skins but on older ones, merely darken the tractor tracks that have been driven all over their faces through the years.

'What about a Creamy Punani? Can you give me one of them?'

The Irish had arrived. Joined by a mob of Geordies. Green leprechaun hats jostled for attention with giant inflatable bottles of Newcastle Brown.

It was time to leave.

I got up, made for the door. The bar staff changed CDs, put on Steely Dan's *Reeling in the Years*.

I listened to the first line as I walked. The rest of the crowd joined in, shouting more than singing.

'Your everlastin' summer you can't see it fading fast.'

I thought, 'Was I the only one in the place getting the message?'

Outside I fired up a B&H. Not a bad smoke. I wondered if I could stick to these. 'Christ, can I stick to anything?'

I only had a few hundred yards to go to the Shandwick. The wind cut like bad memories as I plugged my mouth with the cigarette and crossed the road.

On the way up the steps a bloke in a top hat, grey overcoat, put out a hand.

'Yeah? You got a problem?' I said.

No words. Just the index finger of a black leather glove pointed at the tab.

I took it out, crushed it underfoot.

'I could have given you an ashtray,' he said.

'I could have given you a slap.'

Inside I turned down my collar. An open fire blazed hot as a blast furnace. Keeping this temperature must have been pushing up the cost of coal. I swerved past the main desk and headed for the stairs to Nadja's room.

Sure, the bar called. When did it not? But I'd put this off for long enough. I kept a hand on the Glock as I climbed.

I wanted to make an entrance, thought about blowing the lock off the door. But it was only a fantasy. Likewise, I knew there'd be no Puerto Rican maid in the hall, a set of keys conveniently secreted about her person.

'Calm, Gus, calm,' I told myself. 'Remember why you're here.'

It was time to get with the programme.

I MADE A GENTLE KNOCK on the door, the kind room service might use; stepped away from the spy hole.

No answer.

A light shone under the door. I heard movement. A bath running.

I knocked again. This time, an answer. Nadja kept the chain on the door.

She wore sunglasses, her hair tied back tightly.

'Hello, Nadja,' I said.

'Why are you here? I have told you all I know.'

I said nothing. Tried to appear calm, I didn't want to spook her before I got inside.

She moved to close the door, in a second I jammed in my boot, applied a shoulder. The chain snapped, spraying weak links on the floor.

'What was that? "Come in." Glad to.'

I walked into the middle of the room, turned to face her. She wore a short white bathrobe, the hotel's initials stood out above her left breast.

'I was preparing to bathe.' The robe fell open to her waist, exposing an expanse of taupe skin.

'I see that.' I also saw she was changing tactics.

'Let me turn off the water.'

As she walked away from me I noticed her legs. Long and shapely, what was once referred to as a finely turned ankle.

'Help yourself to a drink, Mr Dury,' she called out from the bathroom.

I didn't need to be told a second time.

The whisky decanter was unmarked but before I even tasted a drop I had it pegged as Johnnie Walker, Black Label. Call it one of my many skills, I've a nose for these things.

When Nadja returned she'd taken the pins out of her hair; it hung wildly on her shoulders.

'What's with the shades?' I asked.

'I have a little bit of a migraine.' She sat opposite me, crossed her legs. My eyes fell on a tranche of thigh.

'Walking into a fist will do that.'

'What? No, it *is* a migraine, that is all.'

I threw back my whisky, walked towards her.

'Stand up,' I said.

'No – No, I will not.'

I put down my glass, jerked her by the arm and pulled her to her feet. We stood facing each other, I held her close enough to feel her heart beat.

I removed her glasses. 'Who was it – Zalinskas?'

She nodded. Slumped into me. 'He knows . . . he knows you were here.'

'He does?'

'Yes . . .' She gripped me so tightly I felt her nails in my back. 'You must protect me. I have no one else.'

'Stop with the tears,' I told her. 'I'm not buying into the little-girl-lost act.'

Nadja composed herself, stared at me. I put my hand to her face, moved her eye towards the light. 'I think you'll live.'

As I let down my hand, her mouth opened. She threw back her head, showed me her neck. Her breasts slid from beneath her robe. Then the robe slid from her shoulders.

She turned, stood with her back to me, arms round my neck, grinding her rear into my crotch. I smelled expensive perfume on her wrists as she clawed at my head with her nails.

'Nadja,' I said.

'No words.'

'Nadja, stop this.' I knew I had to pass it up. Every fibre of me yelled, 'Stop now, Gus! Walk!' But reason had left me the second her robe hit the floor.

'Come . . . follow me.' She lowered her arms, walked slowly away from me, her long legs crossing each other like she'd taken to a catwalk.

At the bedroom door, she turned, ran her hand up the jamb, and with the other summoned me to follow.

I TRIED TO TELL MYSELF there wasn't a man alive could have passed her up. But I was hurting now. I knew I'd jeopardised my position, relinquished the upper hand.

As Nadja ordered room service, I put the Glock out of sight, stuffed it between the mattress and the bed springs. I looked for a way the situation might work to my advantage, but found none. Women like her, in situations like this, hold the aces. Christ, Billy was proof of that.

She came back, said, 'My, my, you are quite the cowboy.'

I had to laugh. 'Cowboy?'

'With the gun in your pocket.'

I touched the rim of the bed, where I'd hidden the Glock.

'Weren't you about to have a bath?'

'You are right. I will take a shower. Would you join me?'

'Rain check. I'll wait for the food.'

She climbed over me, lingered on a kiss, then slipped off to the shower.

Dressed, I poured another whisky. Got halfway through my second when room service arrived, closely followed by Nadja.

'Ah, now we eat,' she said.

'Yeah . . .'

'Come, sit by me.'

She'd ordered eggs Benedict, not my usual fare of choice.

'You like it?'

'It's very . . . rich.'

'That will be the Hollandaise, dar-ling.' She lingered on the dar-ling.

'That's not what I meant.'

She laughed. 'We can have the concierge call out for McDonald's if you prefer.'

I tried to get the conversation back on a business footing.

'Nadja, I went to see Zalinskas.'

'I know.'

'You do?'

'How do you think I got this?' She waved a hand over her eye. 'He knows about us.'

If Zalinskas thought there was an 'us' he was misinformed.

'Us?'

'He . . . heard you were here.'

'Yeah, you said.'

She put down her knife and fork. 'I have lost all appetite.'

'Nadja, it's time you laid your cards on the table.'

She stood up, walked over to the window and picked up my cigarettes. 'Can I take one of these?'

I nodded.

She looked out, blowing smoke onto the windowpane. 'Benny found out about Billy's plans.'

'Plans?'

'He had big plans, he was going to break away from Benny. He was tired of . . . how do you say? Playing the second fiddle. He knew he could make enough money to leave Benny for good and set himself up.'

'What were the plans, Nadja?'

'I do not know.' She turned away. 'I do not know anything.'

I walked over to the window, placed a hand on her shoulder and turned her around. 'You can tell me. We're on the same side, remember.'

She sat down. 'I do not know everything, but I do know some. Billy, he had . . . knowledge. He had some . . . information.'

'And . . . ?'

'It would pay him. He was going to make someone pay him.'

Things suddenly clicked into place.

'This was a government minister, wasn't it?'

'I think so, yes.'

'Who?'

Nadja stood up again, started to walk around. 'That I do not know. I promise I do not.'

'Then, Zalinskas . . . how did he sus this?'

'Benny knows everything. He finds out by . . . he has many friends. Perhaps this person found out and went to him, like you say, out of the blue. For help perhaps. It happens all the time, all it takes is for Benny's name to be put up and things happen or don't happen.'

So, Billy had got greedy. Saw himself as the Big I Am. But he'd decided to put the make on the wrong man. No wonder Zalinskas was sore.

'Billy was blackmailing this minister?'

Nadja nodded meekly.

Just what Billy had on the minister was anybody's guess. The obvious old favourites sprang to mind, it mattered for one reason alone – to point me to Billy's killer. I needed to know who the minister was.

'Does that work?' I pointed at a laptop on Nadja's desk.

'Yes of course.'

'Internet connection?'

'Yes.'

'Then log on.'

I KNEW MY WAY ROUND the government site from my reporting days. Found the Cabinet Ministers in no time; went to their mugshots.

The page threw up a list of past achievements, education and portfolios held. All I wanted was a clear picture Nadja could identify.

I took them one by one.

'If you see someone . . . anyone you might have seen with Zalinskas, sing out.'

I put up the first picture.

'No.'

The second.

'No.'

Third, fourth, fifth and sixth.

'No . . . I do not recognise any of these faces.'

'What about Billy? Did he mention any of these names, or anything at all related to the government.'

'No, never . . . Except . . . well, sometimes he would make a rant at the news, but I never heard him name anyone, or single anyone out.'

I continued to scroll down the screen.

'No,' said Nadja. 'No. This is all so hopeless.'

'Keep going.'

'No . . . no. Wait! Yes.'

'This one?'

'Yes.'

'You know this one?' I double-clicked on the picture, opened up a bigger shot. I definitely knew the face, it was Alisdair Cardownie, Minister for Immigration.

'I think . . . but, wait, no. No, I cannot be sure. I think I may only have seen him on the television shows.'

My pulse had raced at the sight of him, to hear her change her mind like this put ice in my veins.

'Are you kidding me?'

'No, I am sorry. I do not think I have seen this man, other than on the television . . . he is on television a great deal, is he not?'

I nodded. 'Oh, he is that.'

'You know him?'

'After a fashion.'

'I do not understand, what does that mean?'

'It means . . . let's just say I've run into him on the odd occasion.'

'There is the bad blood between you?'

'He cost me my job.'

Nadja looked back at the screen. 'This man? He doesn't look capable.'

The sight of the smug arse-wipe turned my stomach, I closed down the laptop. This line of enquiry had got us nowhere. It was time to change tack, go to the root cause.

'The fight between Billy and Zalinskas.'

'What about it?'

'That's just it. What *was* it all about?'

Nadja shuffled in her seat, looked uncomfortable. 'I do not know, entirely. Some security issue I think. I did not have any interest.'

'Nadja, I know Benny ordered a sweep of the clubs after that row. It's common knowledge.'

She took another one of my B&H, lit up. 'I think some tapes had went missing. Benny is very particular about, how you say, running the tight ship.'

'The tapes went missing on Billy's watch?'

'Yes, of course. Why else do you think they argued?'

'Tapes of what?'

'Just tapes. From the security cameras. Benny keeps them all in order, the tapes went missing and Billy had the hell to pay.'

'Tapes from the casinos?'

Nadja squirmed. 'And the houses.'

'Houses?'

'Where the girls work.'

'Hah! You mean bawdy houses.'

I saw why losing some of the tapes from the knock shops wouldn't be good for Zalinskas' business.

I knew why the cameras were in place. They were Zalinskas' insurance policy, or, maybe just for a rainy day. Billy had obviously got the same idea – only he'd decided to cash in Zalinskas' chips a little bit early.

'What else was Billy working on?'

'Nothing.'

'Come on – ambitious guy like Billy, he must have had umpteen irons in the fire.'

'Nothing I tell you!'

I didn't see Billy going too far down this track, he wasn't building a second empire that's for sure. But I knew if he thought of striking out on his own he'd need some kind of legit cover.

'Motors . . . Billy liked his motors,' I said, thinking out loud. 'Did he have a workshop, garage somewhere?'

'No. Never. He liked cars to drive, but he was not that kind of a man – you know, macho.'

'What *was* he like?'

'He liked the finer things in life.'

'So, he liked his luxuries – clothes, scent?'

'Yes.'

'Did he ever bring in, say, a batch of designer gear from the Continent? Or anywhere else for that matter.'

'Not that I know of.'

'But say he did . . .'

'He did not.'

'Christ! Paintings then, Louis Vuitton handbags, mucky books? Where would he keep them? Where would he store them?'

'I do not know. I really do not know. I tell you, he never had such business that I knew of.'

I was getting nowhere. I needed to know what Billy had been up to. Now, either Nadja was in the dark too, or she was holding out on me again. I wasn't about to let her away with that for a second time.

I ran through to the bedroom, picked up the Glock. Stuffed it in my belt.

'Right, on your feet,' I said.

'Why? Where are we going?'

'Billy's gaff. If he's left a hint of what he's been up to we'll find it.'

'But Benny's people have already been over it.'

'I'm not Benny's people.'

BILLY KEPT A YUPPIE APARTMENT down on the waterfront.
I'd read an article by Irvine Welsh where he'd queried what it was with
yuppies and water. I'd never found the answer to that myself. The water
down here, looking out to a sea black to the horizon, is far from calming. Byron Bay it ain't.

Whoever came up with the saying 'worse things happen at sea' had
the Scottish coast in mind at the time. There's a spot in the north called
Cape Wrath. Says it all. A name like that, you don't need to see the
pictures. Safe to say, it hasn't made any holiday brochures.

Robert Louis Stevenson's family fortune came from building light-
houses to warn against the harshness of the Scottish coast, he had the
right idea nicking off to Samoa. As a teenager on a trip up north, he'd
described the coastal town of Wick as 'one of the meanest of man's
towns, and situated certainly on the baldest of God's bays'.

As I looked out of Billy's floor-to-ceiling windows I couldn't find one
word of praise for the view, said, 'What *were* you thinking, Billy?'

'What, what did you say?'

'Nothing. Just admiring the view.'

Nadja looked at me as though I'd fallen into apoplexy.

'Are you serious? It is like the end of the world.'

What do you say to that? I said nothing.

'Can you hurry, please,' said Nadja. 'I don't like it here.'

'Why? Bad memories?'

'I've never liked it here.'

She stood in the centre of the floor, arms folded. Her eyes darted from me to the door and back again. She looked cold. I expected to see her shiver, but then it dawned on me – it was a deeper cold, a visceral chill. She'd carry this cold with her wherever she went.

Coming back here I'd expected tears from her. At least, some stirring of emotion. Maybe pick up one of the pictures dotted about the place. Pictures of her and Billy in what looked to be happier times. But she seemed unmoved by the return visit. Worse than that, the place unsettled her.

I asked, 'Why?'

'Why what?'

'Why did you never like it here?'

She gave out a loud huff, moved away from me, propped herself on a bar stool.

'Can you please get what you came for? I want to leave.'

The place had been turned over by Zalinskas' goons, but I guessed it was a week since anyone had been there. A layer of silver dust covered the dining table and a stack of unopened mail sat on the mat.

'Cleaning lady on holiday?' I joked.

Saw a set of drawers turned out onto the floor, packs of cards, *TV Times* and Sainsbury's coupons everywhere.

'Billy clipped coupons?' I said.

'Ohh . . . that man!'

The DVD player lay smashed to bits on the floor. A set of size tens stomping on the casing will do that. A stack of empty shelves, left untouched, confused me. 'Why are these shelves empty?'

Nadja shrugged her shoulders.

I got behind the DVD player, poked about on the floor, found an empty CD case and another empty CD rack.

'They've taken all the disks.'

'Yes, so what? Can we go now?'

I tramped through the debris to the kitchen, placed a hand on Nadja's thigh. 'You'll have my full attention soon enough. Why don't you make yourself a coffee?'

She rose, threw up her hands. 'I am going to wait outside.'

'No, I don't think you are.' I lowered my eyes and she went back to her seat.

'Can you hurry – please.'

'All in good time.' I handed her the pile of unopened mail. 'Here, look through that.'

In the bedroom, Billy's clothes covered the floor. He had some expensive gear, but no taste. Ties that the guy off Channel 4 news wouldn't give the nod to.

Inside his wardrobe more shelves had been removed, I say removed, torn out more like. But his shoes seemed untouched, lined up on the floor in two neat rows. Had a brainstorm to tip them out. Instantly, glad I did. A key for a mortise lock fell out of a Reebok runner.

I picked up the key. 'Hello, what's this?'

It seemed like an old key, rusted over. Certainly not well used. I called out to Nadja, 'Hey, come in here, would you?'

No answer.

I stood up, went back through to the lounge.

'Nadja,' I called out. Then again, louder, 'Nadja . . . Nadja.'

The place was empty. She'd run out on me.

I LOOKED IN THE HALL and out the window, but saw no sign of Nadja. She'd cut out with the pile of mail.

I paced the house looking for something that the key might fit. I spotted a couple of linen chests, a drawer on Billy's desk, but the key I'd found fitted none of them. It looked like an old door key, probably for an exterior lock of some kind. I pocketed it and, on a hunch, decided to check the one room I'd left out so far, the bathroom.

Call it a cliché, but I reckoned the cistern was still a safe bet to find stuff people don't want to put out on open display. Especially, I thought, if Billy was keeping something from Nadja – there was no way she'd risk breaking a nail poking about at the shitter.

I lifted the lid, depressed the ballcock. Nothing. The cistern held only water. I put back the lid, turned for the hall. On my way, a board beneath my feet creaked. I looked down, the floor was carpeted, but at the wall there seemed to be a few tacks missing.

It took some work but I managed to loosen the carpet, it was rubber-backed and moved freely once I'd taken out the grips holding it down.

'Bingo!'

One of the boards had recently been lifted, nails removed, chips at the edges where it had been prised up.

I banged on the edge with the heel of my hand and the board shot up. Hidden beneath was a small Nike holdall. I reached in, pulled it out. Inside, I found Billy's passport, bank books, a heap of unsigned credit cards and about twenty gees in used notes.

'Planning a quick getaway, Billy Boy?'

I put the boards down, stamped down the carpet and slung the bag on my back.

I tried to leave Billy's apartment as I'd found it – think Hiroshima aftermath.

Outside I strolled along casually. Not an easy task when you've twenty large flung over your shoulder. I'd never been mugged in my life, I prayed it wouldn't be my turn today. Not because I feared losing the cash, but because I still carried the Glock. Didn't want to be caught warding off a hoodie with such a serious weapon, had a feeling the consequences might be disproportionate.

At the Wall, the same old faces were in residence. The gadgie spied me, got to his feet. If I'd no time for him when we last met, I'd less now, greeted him with, 'Fuck off.'

His face, skin as patchy as kebab meat, failed to detect any hostility. He swayed about, looked far gone, then sat down again and drooled into his pint.

'That's a bit harsh,' said Col. 'That's a customer you're talking to.'

'I've no time for pleasantries.'

A frown, shake of the head. 'I know we're hardly the Ritz, but a man deserves a bit of common courtesy.'

Felt in no mood to debate the fineries of Edinburgh's carefully culti-vated class system; I threw the holdall on the bar.

'What's this?'

'Open it.'

Col tipped the bag on its side, struggled with the zip fastener on the pocket.

'Here,' I said, grabbing it off him, undoing the cord at the top, 'have a look at that.'

Col peered in. 'By the cringe, there must be—'

I put my hand on his mouth. Some of these people would do a lot worse than kill for half this amount.

'Picked it up from Billy's gaff.'

'You went round?' Col ferreted further into the bag, removed the pass-port. As he saw the page with Billy's photo on he touched his lips.

'Col, the place has been turned over. It seems Billy had got his hands on something that attracted a lot of interest.'

'Like what?' Col was genuinely confused. I wondered if this episode might be the one to tip him over the edge.

'Something he shouldn't have.'

Col's features stiffened. He flared his nostrils then yanked the cord closed on the bag. 'Here, take it.'

'Uh-uh. If anyone's due some of Billy's earnings, I think it's you.'

He forced the bag into my hands. 'I'll never touch it.'

'Think about it. You take it or Nadja does.'

A dog barked outside, Col vacillated.

I said, 'Take the money, Col. Dump it in the collection plate the next time you're at church.'

Slowly, he slid the bag off the bar. His hands trembled as he tucked it underneath the till.

'This is all very unsettling, Gus.'

'Tell me about it.'

'If I'd known . . . Well, I'd have found a way to intervene, sooner.'

'Sooner?'

Col touched his brow, looked like he'd just remembered something burning in the oven. 'Christ, listen to me! Here's you chasing all over the place on my behalf and – will you have a drink?'

I nodded. Col poured out a Guinness, and a chaser.

'We're a bit quieter tonight, I think,' he said.

'How so?'

'*Big Brother* . . . it's eviction night.'

'Holy shit, even your punters watch that garbage?'

'Oh yes, it's like an obsession with them.'

'Where's the attraction of recording every cough and fart of a bunch of nobodies?'

'I agree. I think it's like watching lab rats myself.'

'We're all of us guinea pigs in the laboratory of God.'

'Is that a quote?'

'Tennessee Williams.'

'I like it. Do believe he's right you know.'

I drained my whisky, Col picked up the glass, raised it to the optic behind the bar. As he went, I took out the key I'd found at Billy's apartment.

I turned it over on the bar towel, trying to guess where it might fit. The key looked older in this light, I noticed some ornate markings on the hilt. It looked Victorian.

'Where did you find that?' Col said, as he placed the whisky before me. His voice seemed to suggest he wasn't unfamiliar with the key.

'This?'

'Yeah. It's my old cellar key, isn't it?' He turned quickly from me, went back to the till. A felt board with brass hooks held all the keys for the bar. 'Oh, hang on . . . it's here.'

He brought over his key, placed it next to Billy's. 'My, they're almost identical, aren't they?'

'I found this key at Billy's place. It was tucked away in a shoe, out of sight.'

Col took the key, raised it to the light. 'Do you think he got hold of a spare or something?'

'I don't know. I wondered what it was for, to tell you the truth.'

Col, put the two keys together on the bar towel. 'Well, that's the queerest thing.'

'For the cellar you say?'

'No. No. We've a proper cellar down there,' Col pointed to the floor. 'This is for the old cellar up the back there, it's more like a coal house.'

'What's in it?'

'In it? Nothing, nothing at all. Last time it was used, to my knowledge, was in the war, you know, as a kind of shelter.'

I stood up, took the first sip of my Guinness. 'Have you got a flashlight?'

'Sure. You going to check it out?'

'Och, I think I should. So you coming?'

'No, you go, I've got the bar to mind . . . was near impossible to get staff tonight.'

I huffed. '*Big Brother?*'

'You wouldn't believe it, would you?'

I shook my head, took the flashlight from him.

Outside the cold bit like a bastard. I tested the bulb. It looked to be dimming but would do the job.

The key slotted into the lock without effort. As I pushed the door open a waft of dampness caught in my throat. 'Christ Almighty!' I closed my mouth and descended the stairs.

As I reached the floor, I checked for a light switch. None. The walls had been painted white at some stage and caught the light I shone on them throwing off more into the room. The smell of damp rose like poison gas. I brought my T-shirt up over my mouth and nose.

I moved about, the place seemed to be empty. No shortage of cobwebs, streams of moisture on the walls and general grit and dust blowing about the floor. But nothing worth hiding a key in your shoe for.

'Come on, Billy Boy. What's your big secret?'

The flashlight started to fade. The bulb dimmed to a faint orange glow. I slapped the butt in my hand. It went out.

'Fucking brilliant.'

I searched for my matches, struck a clutch of five or six. The fizzing flame heated my hand, threw shadows on the wall. I lit another batch, raising them aloft. For a good few seconds I'd a fully lit view of the room. It was empty. Not a thing there.

I returned to the stairs, at the top pushed open the door and gasped for breath.

'Jesus . . . that was rough.'

Felt good to taste fresh air once more. So good, I sparked up a Marlboro. First of a new pack. Red top, proper fatal.

A few drags in I clasped the tab in my teeth, turned to lock up. A damp old donkey jacket hung on the back of the door. I'd always wondered how they got the name, I saw now it was because they smelled like them.

I pushed the door, and the hook holding the jacket snapped, dropped it on the ground.

'Oh, shit.'

I picked it up, about to throw it down the stairs, when something fell out of the side pocket.

'Hello . . .'

I bent down to see what it was.

'Billy, you sly old bastard.'

A disk.

I took it back to the pub. Col sat in front of the bar, watching television.

'You're actually watching *Big Brother*?'

'Thought I'd see what all the fuss was about.'

I picked up my Guinness, drained half of it in one go. 'You disappoint me, I had you down as a man of some taste and discernment.'

'Bollocks! Did you have any luck?'

I held up the disk.

'What's that?'

'CD or DVD.'

'And what do you think it's for?'

'I don't know. Will we have a look?'

Col stood up, leaned over my shoulder to stare at the disk. 'What are you doing?' I said.

'Having a look!'

'You're having me on.'

'Sorry?'

'I meant, on a player. I'm presuming you don't have one, then.'

'What's that?'

'A CD or a DVD player?'

'Oh no, no. I've a video recorder, but I never use it. The wife used to hire the old films. Howard Keel's her favourite.'

I was mystified. Drained the rest of my pint. As I did so the phone rang, Col went round the bar to answer it.

'One minute. It's for you,' he said.

'Me?' I wondered who would call me at the Wall when I had my mobile. Took the mobi out my pocket, it was still switched off.

'Will you take it? It's your sister.'

She had no news I wanted to hear. I got to my feet.

'Tell her I've left.'

'I can't do that. I've already told her you're here.'

I buttoned my jacket, pocketed the disk. 'Not any more.'

HOD HAD THE CLASH CRANKED up full when I arrived. 'Tommy Gun' blaring out, felt surprised the neighbours hadn't complained.

'You'll get your door rapped,' I said.

Hod flared out his chest, took a strongman stance. 'Who'd mess?'

Took his point.

The place looked spotless as usual. Even the kitchen shone like a show home, every surface gleamed. The shine as the uplighters hit the stainless-steel kettle and toaster set almost hurt my eyes.

'Do you know what this joint needs?' I asked him.

'What's that?'

'A man about the house.'

Hod took the opportunity to dip into mince mode. He had it down pat, sorta Dale Winton doing Freddy Star . . . Whoa, there's an image.

'Oooh you are *awful*,' said Hod, slapping me on the arm, 'but I like you!'

We cracked a couple of Stellas and went through to the lounge. Joe Strummer wailed, 'Someone got murdered, somebody's dead for ever . . .' I got up and turned down the CD.

'So, the wanderer returns,' said Hod.

I raised my bottle. 'Here I am.'

'*Slàinte*. What's the story?'

I filled him in on my brush with the law and everything I'd unearthed about Billy's demise.

Hod listened carefully. 'What do you think he feeds it on?'

'What?'

'Zalinskas – the wolf?'

'How the fuck would I know? Probably dog food.'

'You reckon, like, just from Tesco?'

I couldn't believe this, after all I'd revealed to Hod, the one thing that had provoked any response was Zalinskas' pet wolf. 'Definitely not. A man like Zalinskas, with all his cash, he's doing his shopping at Waitrose.'

Hod coughed into his fist, made a clearing noise in his throat. 'You wouldn't be mocking me would you, Gus Dury?'

'Never.'

We exchanged some childish dead arms, then Hod fell back onto the sofa.

'Christ, it's good to get you back in one piece, mate.'

'Tell me.'

'You had us worried for a while there. Amy—' Hod checked himself, sat up.

'What about, Amy?'

Hod touched his knee nervously, then looked at his open palms. 'Think you're going to have to set her straight, Gus.'

'What do you mean?'

'She's totally, I mean totally, sold on you. It's not fair on the girl.'

I tried to laugh it off. An involuntary reaction.

'Or fair on you, you sly bastard,' I said.

'No. No way. Seriously, Gus. I like her, for sure, but I'm not talking about that. She's off tapping brassers for bits of gossip in the hope she can impress you. She's gonna get herself in trouble.'

I sucked at the Stella. 'I'll have a word.'

'Will you?'

'I just said I would, didn't I?'

'Should I Stay or Should I Go' finished up and the CD slowly ejected. I reached over to my jacket, took Billy's disk out of the pocket.

'Here, chuck this on,' I told Hod.

'What is it?'

'Billy had it hidden away.'

'Had quite a bit hidden away our Billy Boy.'

Hod took the disk, popped the plastic wallet open and slotted it into the player.

'It's data.'

'Come again?'

'It's for a computer.'

'Do you have one?'

'Gus, for fucksake, does the Pope wear a funny hat?'

Hod left the room. Returned with a Sony Vaio. I should have known better than to ask, the man had a breadmaker in the kitchen for crying out loud.

'Is there a gadget you don't own?' I said.

'Oh yes, there's one I can think of.' He made a buzzing noise, vibrating his Stella bottle in my face.

'You surprise me. Thought that would have been right up your alley!'

'Ha-ha. It was, until your mother borrowed it!'

The old dis your mother joke struck a chord, I didn't want to be reminded of the fact that I'd been ignoring my mam's pleas to visit my dying father.

I grabbed the laptop. 'Let's get this booted up.'

Hod seemed unfazed, left me to it while he went for some more Stella and some munchies, a bag of Doritos and some salsa dip.

'Nice,' I said.

'You'll like it. Though I think Pringles might have been a better option.'

'Hod, I'm not talking about the fucking crisps. Check it out.'

The disk showed a video taken with what looked like a good-quality camera set in the corner of a room. Footage from Zalinskas' club's camera; though the image was anything but the kind of thing normally shown on *Crimewatch*.

'Social Security style,' said Hod.

'What?'

The picture was clear, a brasser straddling some geezer on a double bed. All the scene missed was some dodgy electronic organ music and it could have been sold as a tug movie.

219

'Like I say . . . Social Security style.' Hod pointed to the screen, mirrored the see-saw motion with his finger.

'I don't get you?'

'Well, you see, Gus, this is what you call Social Security style because the girl's getting the *full benefit.*'

He was right about one thing. She was only a girl, no more than fifteen, and at that I was being generous. The face of the guy underneath was harder to make out.

'Can we forward this?'

'Oh yeah.'

Hod's first effort put the video into reverse. 'Och, hang on . . . here we go.'

In no time the girl jumped off, moved away to get dressed. Then we saw the guy's face clearly. My heart tripped.

'He looks familiar,' said Hod.

'I'm not surprised.'

Hod turned to face me, slit his eyes. 'Why's that?'

'He's on the telly every other night.'

Hod grabbed the screen, leaned in close and creased his nose, the look was concentration. 'Who is it?'

'Don't you know?'

'No . . . I mean, yes, I recognise him, but I can't place the face. Who is it?'

I took up the laptop, pointed, could hardly believe I was about to say the words, 'That's our Minister for Immigration – the Right Honourable Alisdair Cardownie.'

I OPENED THE DOORS TO the balcony. Fired up a Marlboro. Hod followed with two fresh bottles of Stella. Neither of us said anything, just stared out at the city, lit up like a fair. A taxi sounded its horn below and two young girls ran out from the flats across the street. The clack of their heels drowned out their giggles as they tried to dodge puddles.

'Look at them,' said Hod.

'Just daft wee lassies.'

'That's it, though – so they should be.'

I knew what he was trying to say, I didn't need to hear the exact words. The girls looked little older than the one we'd just seen with Cardownie. They had their whole lives in front of them, and every right to enjoy them. Somehow they no longer seemed half as annoying as the rest of their age group.

'So what now, Gus?'

Quite a question. I wondered myself. I didn't buy it that Billy had been working to the same set of principles as myself and Hod. I sure as hell knew that Col didn't have a good word to say for his son. Billy had planned to take off; he wasn't thinking about blowing the whistle, shutting the operation down. He wanted to make his pile and shove off, probably take some new skills to another manor and put them to good use. I felt sick to my stomach with everything I had seen: with Nadja, Billy, Zalinskas and all his outfit. But more than any of them Cardownie sickened me.

'Do you remember how I lost my job, Hod?'

'Which one?'

'The last one. Only one I'd ever had worth shit.'

'The sauce, wasn't it?'

'Okay, well you could say that. But the actual incident which caused me to get the boot.'

'Oh yeah. The night you were on the news, you nutted a politician.'

'Not hard enough.'

Hod turned from the view, put his elbows on the rail. 'It wasn't him, was it?'

'The very same.'

'Gus, I'd say you have a score to settle.'

'Fuck that. It's in the past now. I wouldn't want that job back as a gift.'

'Really?'

'Yes, really. Are you trying to say something, Hod?'

'Me? No, never. So what are you going to do?'

I pointed out towards the city. 'Look out there, so much going on. So many people, all trying to screw each other over. Do you think it's possible to plan anything?'

'Hannibal thought it was.'

I looked at Hod, it was the first time I'd ever heard him even approach something approximating sense, learning.

'Crossing the Alps?'

'Must have missed that one.'

'What one?'

'When they were in the Alps – The A-Team.'

'Christ, you're talking about *that* Hannibal.'

'Yeah. "I love it when a plan comes together!" Who did you think I was talking about?'

I shook my head at him, wanted to say 'I pity the fool', but went for 'Never mind.'

I turned to go inside.

Hod followed and put his beer bottle down on the table. He left the room, came back carrying a container about the size of a shoe-box.

'Eh, Gus, I don't suppose there's a good time to do this, so I'll just let you have it now.'

I looked at the box he was holding out to me. 'What is it?'

'It's from the funeral . . . your friend's ashes.'

My breathing slowed, then quickened. 'Milo.'

'I, eh, don't know . . . should I say something?'

'It's okay.' I reached out, shook his hand. 'Thanks for doing that, Hod.'

He turned away again, sat.

'Was it a good . . . do?'

'We did what you said, gave him a proper send off.'

'Was there any . . . family?' It was a stupid question. I realised at once I wouldn't be holding Milo's ashes if his family had shown up.

Hod shook his head. 'Just myself and Amy . . . a chick from social work.'

It sounded a sombre affair. Not something to circle on your calendar. But, God, the guilt. I'd been the only person this man knew at the end of his life and I hadn't even made his funeral.

'You all right, Gus?'

'Yeah, oh yeah – just a bit, you know, gutted.'

'Amy was in floods. She said she never even met the guy but, well, it was a funeral, wasn't it?'

'She's got a sensitive soul.'

'You're right there.'

Hod had an eye on me for a reaction.

'I know. I know. I'll have to let her down gently.'

I COULDN'T SLEEP, SPENT THE night reading *The Legend of the Holy Drinker*. Its author, Joseph Roth, a chronic alcoholic who drank himself to death in Paris at the age of forty-four.

I'd always loved this book, even before I was a drinker, never a holy one. It's about a jakey called Andreas who hits on, the worst of things for any drinker, a run of luck.

In the translator's note at the back of my edition it reads: 'It is clear that Roth for some time had been running out of reasons to remain alive.'

When a line like this strikes a chord, you know you're in trouble.

I read on: 'He advanced a sophisticated argument that while drink shortened his life in the medium term, in the short term it kept him alive – and he worked hard at testing its logic.'

Lately, I'd been crippled by hangovers. Time was, when I could wake up the next day, shake off the night before and start again. Now, only one word described the way I felt: deteriorated.

Heard John Lennon doing 'Living on borrowed time . . . without a thought to tomorrow.'

Phone went.

I sat up in bed, answered before checking the caller ID.

'Hello, Gus.'

Shocked.

'Mam . . . hello.'

Her voice sounded weaker than ever, she sounded frail. 'I know you're very busy, son, but I had to call. I'm sorry to disturb you again.'

Her words sent my heart into spasm. 'No, Mam, don't apologise, I've been meaning to call, I have.' It was a lie, but I'd got used to those recently.

'I know Catherine told you about—'

'Is he no better, Mam?'

'Oh, Gus . . .'

'Mam?'

A groan, actual pain. 'Gus, he won't last another day, the doctor says it's a miracle he's still with us. Oh, son, he's holding on for you, he's holding on for your visit. If you would only . . . Oh, Gus. Oh son . . .'

'Mam, please.'

'I know, I've no right to ask. I'm sorry.'

'Mam.'

'No. I shouldn't have called. You have your reasons. I'm sorry, son. I'll leave you be.'

'Mam, I'll come. Tell him I'll come.' Had I said this? Had I ever. Where was my head at?

I dressed in black cords, nearing on grey at the knees. I looked for a white shirt, had to settle for a white T-shirt. Topped the look off with a navy lambswool V-neck. I'd been reckless with the washing instructions and the jumper had tightened round the shoulders. I pulled at the neck, heard a tear.

'Och, Christ on a crutch!'

The neckband came away in my hand. I tossed it, put on a red Pringle instead. It fitted like a dream, no substitute for quality.

I pulled on my Docs, checked myself in the mirror. 'Bit like a schemie golfer, Gus.'

Still, would have to do. Clothes supply running low.

In the kitchen I tried to make some coffee but my hands shook out of control. I clanged the spoon in the sink and went to the fridge. Hod kept some Grolsch in reserve, the heavy bottles made fashionable by soccer casuals. Along with sharpened umbrella points, the bottles once made for a perfect concealed weapon. The Grolsch hit the spot. I shotgunned two bottles. The shakes subsided, but I felt a long way from medicated.

Hod looked out for the count as I left. I tucked the Glock in my waist-band, Milo's ashes under my arm.

I strolled along Portobello beach, hoping inspiration would strike. My head throbbed with troubles or was that just the sauce calling? Talking to my old man after all this time wouldn't be easy. I knew I was prepared to do it for my mother. She'd borne the brunt of his torture over the years, after all that, how could I refuse her?

'Jesus, Mam – why didn't you get out?' I muttered.

If only she'd taken the steps to free herself from him, she might have found a life. For her though, it just wasn't the done thing. I never under-stood it; was it a generational thing? No woman would put up with it nowadays. Deborah certainly needed a lot less provocation to leave me.

'Bollocks!' I walked off a sand-bar, sank up to my ankles in sea water. 'This is all I need.'

I left the beach. Too close to nature for this city boy. I had thought it might be the place to spread Milo's ashes, but I was wrong. They must be returned to Ireland, I thought. It's what Milo would have wanted. God, it felt painful to think about him, and how he got mixed up in all of this. I knew it would for ever be one of the deepest hurts of my sorry existence.

First newsagent's I hit, I asked the shopkeeper for a carrier, placed the box of ashes carefully inside.

'Twenty Regal as well, please,' I said.

I lit up – one after the other – until I found myself two streets from my family home. As I reached it, the place that held so much hurt for every one of us, I drew deep on my cigarette, then crushed it soundly underfoot.

My sister stood at the window, tucked behind the twitching net curtains.

'Hello, Gus,' she said as I walked through the door.

My soul screamed as I went in. Every fibre of my being begged for alcohol.

'Can I take your coat?' said Cathy.

'Yes. Oh, and can you put this away?' I handed over Milo's ashes.

'What is it?'

'An old friend. Take care with it, please.'

She placed the carrier on the top shelf of the hallstand, waved me into the living room. I stood in the doorway for a moment, my palms gathering sweat.

'Angus,' called out my mother. She stood up, held out her arms.

'Hello, Mam . . . How are you?'

She held my face in her hands, placed a kiss on my cheek. 'You're as white as a maggot!'

'I'm fine, really.'

'When did you last have a square meal, son?'

'I'm okay, Mam. There's no need to fuss.'

'Sit yourself down. I'll make you something to eat. What would you like?'

'Nothing, I'm not hungry.'

'Nonsense, you'll take a sandwich.'

I shook my head. 'Mam, I'm here to see . . . Dad.' The word caught in my throat like a razorblade.

My mother sat back down. 'Of course. You'll want to see him as soon as you can.'

What I really wanted was to turn around and walk out. Wait for the funeral, dance on his grave. Said, 'Sure.'

She stood up again, smoothed down the sides of her skirt, then patted at her hair. 'I'll see if he's ready. The doctor's given him something to make him sleep, but he may be awake again now.'

'All right.'

She left the room. On the stairs, she turned. 'He's been asking for you day and night, son – you know that, don't you?'

I looked up. 'Yes, Mam, I know.'

'I THINK HE'S FIT FOR visitors now,' said my mother.

I stood up. My knees felt weak as I tried to walk. Why was I here? Nothing he could say would change how I felt.

I didn't want to feel like this. I knew my bitterness had hurt me just as much as any of his blows. But here I was, turning the handle on his bedroom door.

'Gus . . . is it you?' said my father.

He looked pale and old now, his skin grey from the weeks spent indoors. There was none of the terror left in his eyes at all.

I stared at him and found the image hard to take in. Had this pathetic man blighted my childhood and continued to blight my life to this day?

As I stared, I couldn't feel any hatred for him. Any hatred I felt was for someone else entirely.

'Gus, come away in,' he gasped.

My father held out a hand to me, motioned to his bedside.

The hand looked feeble, bony and withered, the fingertips purple where his weak heart failed to pump enough blood to keep the circulation going.

I stared at his hand and wondered if it really was the same hand that had made me tremble in fear. As I stared I wanted to find the words to say how I felt. How I felt as a boy, and how I felt right now. But I couldn't find any words at all.

'I'm glad you came,' said my father, his voice trembling over his grey lips. 'I'd hoped you would.' He coughed, spluttered, grasped for breath. 'I'd hoped you'd give me a chance to explain.'

I nodded. I still couldn't find any words. My voice was somewhere else, hidden in the depths of me, to sound a breath felt beyond me.

My father reached out and took my hand, spoke for us both. 'I know why you came, son. It wasn't for me. I don't deserve any visitors. Your sister and brother came, but you stayed away, I don't fault you for that – you were a different case, but I hoped you would come.'

Why was I different? Why was it me sat there and not Cathy or Michael? He'd fathered three children. The idea that he had singled me out hit like a bolt in the belly.

'Why?' I said. The word burned my heart, nearly choked me on the way out.

'You were the firstborn, son, and I was hard on you.' He spluttered when he spoke, his dark eyes looked blood red and circled in black. 'I learnt to be a mite gentler on the others, but the habit with you was hard to break.'

'Why?' There it was again. It had always come down to the same question.

'I had such high hopes for you; my first boy. I wanted you to be *my* boy, but you were always your own man. I thought I could win you round by being hard on you – it was all I knew. I got what I wanted by being hard, a hard player I was . . . I thought you needed the same.'

'You were wrong.'

'I know it. I know it now, son. I see it now, I do, I see what I did was wrong.'

'Why didn't you see it then?' I spoke through my teeth, jaw clamped tight. 'That was when I needed you to see it.'

'I saw what was in you, and it wasn't the same as was in me, Angus. I wanted to change it. I wanted to make you more like me.'

'I could never be like you.' I spat out the words. I wanted to look at him when I said them, but I couldn't face him.

'You are better off being nothing like me,' he said, 'my flower bloomed only briefly.'

'I never missed it . . . and neither did Mam.'

'I know it. But now the Lord's close to his harvesting it feels like I finally understand.' My father brought his hands up to his face, tried to cover the tears in his eyes. 'You are a very different man to me, different entirely, I tried to shape you the only way I knew how, but I was wrong. You cannot mould a child, it's wrong to try. The best you can do is live your own life well and hope the child follows your example.'

For the first time in my life I thought I understood something of him. I saw he felt sorry, I didn't need to hear the word.

'Angus, son, you have a good head on them shoulders. I always knew that. It only confused me though. I never knew what to do with you. Me a muck savage, how could I?'

I looked at him. 'It's all right,' I said.

'No, son, you don't understand. I know I've ruined you. All these years though, it's been too much, too much to think of what could have been.'

'Stop now.'

'I was a coward. It was hurt pride that sent you away, pushed you away like I always did. And why? Jesus, son, I'm sorry. I was a fool then, but we're always learning right to the end so we are. That's why it's never too late, it can't ever be too late to change, to say you're sorry, can it?'

I looked at my father, wasted away in the bed before me. He looked exhausted now, the effort shown in his face shocked me.

'No,' I said.

Wasted. Wasn't that what he had done with most of his life? Wasted it away. Playing for his country, the adulation, it all meant nothing to him now he was dying.

'It's all right,' I said, something in me felt sorry for him, the old man dying before me needed comfort, 'we all make mistakes.'

'Don't make mine, please.' As he closed his eyes it was like watching a light go out inside him.

I gripped my father's hand tight, then left his bedside.

I closed the door and went back downstairs, where my mother sat waiting for me. She rose as I entered the room.

'What is it?' she said.

'I think he's gone, Mam.'

ON THE DAY OF THE funeral my mother hung a black crêpe scarf on the door of the family home. A white card told when the remains would be taken to the kirkyard.

I tried to straighten my tie in the mirror, not easy when you find it hard to look at yourself.

I didn't know how to feel about my father's passing. He felt sorry, yeah, but the memories were still there. Every time I felt sympathy sneaking up on me I had to ask was it really myself I felt sorry for?

All I did know, the person I was wasn't the person I wanted to be any more. My father had tried to shape me with lashings and harsh words, but look what he'd done. Look what I was. A waster, basically. An alkie loser.

Deep down though, I knew I couldn't blame him. I'd been over it a million times. If I'd had it better, who's to say I would be any different? Kids who are showered with affection develop their own problems. They go into the wider world looking for a kind of love they'll never attain. My problems felt like mine alone. For years I'd been nurturing them. Perhaps now it was time to let them go. I knew that was what my father had tried to show me.

The coffin was balanced on the dining-room table, my mother sat beside it, dabbing her eyes with a handkerchief. Cathy stood beside her, a hand placed delicately on her back.

'The others . . . are they coming to the house?' I asked.

'In a while. Michael's talking to the television people.'

'The telly?' I wondered why Michael had been asked to do this, I was the eldest, and Christ, I had the media experience.

'They're doing a slot for the news.'

My mother spoke up: 'Do you think anyone will remember him?'

'Mam, he was a big name in his day,' I said. 'There'll be loads of interest.'

I knew this wasn't the case. Football had moved on. To the fans of today, he was a relic. A strange remnant of a bygone era when men were men.

'Och, I don't know, it's all that David whatsisname these days. One married to the skinny girl off that Spice group.'

'David Beckham,' I said. 'We can be grateful he's nothing like that pretty boy. My dad never once wore shin guards; can't see Becks taking ninety minutes of tackles like that.'

I'd surprised myself. Here I was defending my father.

'Do you know what George Best said about Beckham? "He cannot kick with his left foot, he cannot head a ball, he cannot tackle and he doesn't score many goals. Apart from that he's all right."'

A few smiles were raised. For once, I'd done some good.

'Angus, son,' said my mother, 'I wanted to ask you something.'

I knelt down, beside her. 'Sure, anything.'

'Now, I don't want you to feel you have to say yes – really, I don't want that.'

'Mam, what is it?'

'There are some men from your father's old club coming to help carry the coffin . . . and there's Michael, but I thought . . . ?'

I saw where this was leading, the final thing my mother could ask of me.

'Mam, it's no problem. I'll help carry the coffin.'

She raised her handkerchief again. More tears.

'Come on now, there'll be cameras out there – stiff upper lip remember.'

Cathy put her arm around her. 'Come on, Mam. Why don't you have a bit of a lie down? There's plenty of time before we need to make our way to the kirk.'

The pair looked a strange sight, both dressed in black, as they moved out of the room.

For a moment I was alone with my father in his coffin. I felt uneasy, moved through to the lounge. As I closed the door behind me, Cathy returned.

'She's wearing up well,' said my sister. 'Do you think it'll last?'

'She's a tough old girl,' I said. 'She just needs a bit of a rest.'

'She got no sleep last night.'

'I'm not surprised. What about you?'

Cathy ran her fingers through her hair, I saw a few streaks of grey had crept in. 'I'll be okay.'

'Sit down, would you? You've been running about like a mad thing all day.'

'No, I was going to make some tea.'

'Cathy, I'll get the tea. Put your feet up.'

On my way to the kitchen, I tried to stop myself, but had to glance at the dining-room door. I'd seen dead bodies time and again, but this felt different. This was the home I'd played in as a boy; it shook me up. It's obvious to say death is all about endings, but this really did feel like the curtain had come down on something.

I brought Cathy her tea.

'Thanks,' she said.

'No problem.'

My sister perched on the edge of her chair, blew into the cup. 'Gus, there's something I have to tell you.'

'Uh-huh.'

'I know you and Deborah, well, aren't exactly getting on right now—'

I put up a hand. 'Correction. Debs is divorcing me.'

Cathy lowered her cup, balanced it on the arm of the chair. She took a deep breath, then spoke slowly. 'She came round a few days ago. She'd heard about Dad, and I think it was more for Mam's sake, but she wanted to say goodbye.'

'And?'

'I told her he wasn't expected to see the night out – this was before you arrived.' Cathy raised up her cup, took a sip.

'I know this is leading somewhere, Cath.'

'Well, she asked to be told about the funeral.'

'She's coming to the funeral, that's what you're trying to tell me?'

Cathy put her cup on the floor, a little tea spilled over the side and down the edge.

'Did I do the wrong thing, Gus?'

AS THE SLOW CORTÈGE MADE its way into the kirkyard, my mother wore a brave face. Old women stood up from the graves they'd been tending, gave knowing glances. People I'd never seen greeted us with nods, said they felt sorry for the family's pain.

A few men in black arm bands spoke like we were old friends. I guessed they were from my father's playing days; we may even have shared a word here and there in the past. But I recognised none of them. Names were a mystery.

At the graveside the sun blinded. A yellow oblong led the way to the broken earth, where the minister stood with a small crowd. More strange faces, people I may once have known, but not now.

Even the minister was a stranger to me, a young bloke, with pale blond hair and paler cheeks. He stood sweltering, sweat dripping down his flat forehead. It all looked very difficult for him. He started to speak; 'Cannis Dury was known the length of the country,' he said. 'In his day he knew faith, not only faith in the Lord, for faith comes in many forms, but faith in himself. When he took to the football field, Cannis Dury showed his faith in a strong body and a determination to win. He had skill and he had heart, and, he was an idol to many.'

I tried to block out the minister's voice, every word was a reminder of what I'd sooner forget.

'In these times of change, we see the worship of many false idols, but it is men with faith, in the Lord and in themselves, we can look to for guidance.'

Please. I'd heard enough.

I loosened myself from the crowd, walked away. Under an oak tree I lit a cigarette and watched while they laid my father to rest. My mother scattered earth over the coffin, stepped away. The minister was the first to signal the end of the ceremony, heading off to the kirk's hall.

As the crowd dispersed I lit another Marlboro with the end of the last one. It grew colder, then the brief glimpse of sun disappeared. The sky still looked blue, but grey clouds started to pitch up.

A voice from nowhere, said, 'Hello, Gus.'

She wore black trousers and boots, one of those sleeveless tops that could be worn as a dress. Her hair was the first thing I noticed though. Shorter than usual, and a whole new colour. 'You've changed – gone blonde,' I said.

Deborah took off her sunglasses, flicked back her fringe, then swept the lot back and held it in place with the shades. 'Fancied something different.'

'I like it – It suits you.'

'And you? What about those teeth?'

I dipped my head, felt tense. 'They're falsies.'

Silence, as we both searched for more small chat.

Then, we broke in together. 'I'm sorry . . .'

'No, you,' I said.

'I got your message on my voicemail, I wanted to call but – what with your father being so ill, I thought . . .'

'It's okay. Cathy said you'd visited. That was kind of you. You were always thoughtful that way.'

'I figured you'd have enough to deal with. Last time we spoke, you sounded stressed.'

'Look, Debs, I'm sorry about that. Really, I am. Things have been getting on top of me.'

She looked away, rubbing at her bare arms. I didn't want to stray back into old territory. She'd already spelled out her feelings to me. I stepped back, said, 'What am I saying? You don't want to hear my tales of woe—'

She cut me off. 'Actually, Gus . . . Look, it's bloody freezing out here, can we go inside?'

I looked towards the kirk; most of the mourners had filed into the hall, two men in trench coats, heads bowed, were the last to go in. 'Tell you the truth, I can't face it. But if you'd like to grab a coffee . . . ?'

'Coffee, nothing stronger?'

I shook my head.

'Okay, coffee's good.'

As we crossed the street, the rain started up. Not heavy, but impossible to escape. We took seats beneath an air heater, ordered two large coffees, Debs had a piece of carrot cake. Her expression looked serious. I didn't see us doing the spaghetti scene from *Lady and the Tramp* at the table.

A television played in the background, lunchtime news drew to a close. The arseholes at the parliament had spent the day in serious debate about whether or not to erect a Hollywood-style sign on the Holyrood Crags. Were these people for real?

The news kept one item of interest to the end, again.

'I don't believe it,' I said.

Debs had a mouthful of cake, frowned out a, *'What?'*

'Could you turn this up, please?' I called to the waitress. 'I know him.'

'Who is he?' asked Debs.

'Benny Zalinskas.'

'He looks like a gangster.'

I nodded. 'That's exactly what he is.'

'And how do you know a gangster exactly, Gus?'

'Not personally – not like that anyway. It's the case I'm on.'

'Case . . . you're making it sound like work! It's not a job, Gus.'

I shut her down, said, 'One minute; let me hear this.'

The TV volume rose, Zalinskas' trial was about to draw to a close. The jury, entering into deliberation, were expected to have a verdict inside forty-eight hours.

Back to the studio. 'And now the weather.'

'Fuck me,' I said.

Debs put down her fork. 'What's going on?'

I filled her in on the case, left very little out.

'That's dreadful,' she said, pushing aside her plate.

I looked out to the street. 'I know . . . to think it's all going on right under our noses and we're powerless to do anything about it.'

'That's not what I meant.'

'No?'

'Why are you getting yourself involved?'

'Col's been very good to me . . . I really felt for him. He deserves answers . . .' A cringe. 'He deserves closure.'

'But this isn't your fight. You've let yourself get drawn into this and got yourself into Christ alone knows what.'

Her concern surprised me, but I wasn't knocking it.

'I'm not doing anything else.'

Her eyes lit up, she pointed at me. 'Exactly. You had a name once. A name to be proud of. You were known for your writing, people listened to your opinions.'

I knew what she meant. I'd heard it from Col a million times. I'd even heard it, more recently, from my father. But those days were past. 'Debs, who'd hire me now? I'm a burnt out case.'

'That's just what you tell yourself – keep at it, then that's what you will be.'

I knew she was right, but it didn't alter the end result. What she was selling, I just didn't want any more. My life had grown meaningless. I'd lost the juice to fire any ambition.

'You can change yourself, Gus.'

'Can I?'

'You can . . . you *can* be happy.'

'You sound so sure. I'm not.'

I'd strayed into cloying sympathy. It was the last thing I wanted to do. I wanted happiness for Debs as much as she wanted it for me. I said, 'This is all wrong. I'm sorry.' I called over the waitress, asked for the bill. 'Look, thanks for coming to my father's funeral, I'm sorry I faffed about so much with the divorce. I shouldn't have lost that last letter. Get your lawyer to write again, I'll sign whatever you want me to.'

A siren wailed from the street; Debs' eyes flickered. 'There won't be any more letters.'

She motioned me to sit.

'I don't understand,' I said.

She took a deep breath, exhaled slowly. 'Neither do I.'

'What are you saying?'

'I don't want a divorce.'

'But . . . what's changed?'

'Nothing, though I'm hoping *you* will.'

Her face turned to granite. I wanted to see her smile, to pick her up in my arms, run down the street with her on my shoulders. But this wasn't a cause for celebration.

'I'm not sure I can do that.'

'I'm not asking for much.'

'Deborah . . . this is me, you know. What you see is what you get.'

She looked out the window. 'I don't believe that, Gus. I think there's more to you than this . . . *phase.*'

I wanted to believe her. I wanted to believe a better life waited out there for me. And for her.

She was offering me a second chance and I knew I'd be a fool to knock it back.

'So where do we go from here?' I said.

Deborah's eyes widened as she stared through the window. I turned to see what had her attention – two police cars had the street blocked off. The trench coats from the kirk walked towards us. Now I saw their faces, I recognised them right away as Collins and Roberts.

'Angus Dury?' said Collins.

'You fucking know who I am,' I snapped.

A badge flashed. 'Lothian and Borders Police . . .'

He shoved my face into the table top. I heard Debs scream as my arms got pushed behind my back.

The cuffs went on, Roberts said, 'Angus Dury, I'm arresting you on suspicion of possession of proscribed substances, dealing in laundered currency, aiding and abetting a criminal syndicate, attempting to blackmail a member of Her Majesty's government and living on immoral earnings. Have you anything to say?'

'I think you forgot jay walking.'

AS UNIFORM TOOK OVER FROM Collins and Roberts I yelled to Debs, 'It's a set-up – I've done nothing.'

Debs picked up her bag and coat, turned away from me.

'It's all a set-up – Debs, you have to believe me.'

The wagon doors opened, the filth threw me inside. My last sight, before the doors closed, was of Debs running in the opposite direction. She held her hands to her face, attempting to stem the tears. She couldn't even look at me. I figured the image would stay with me for a long time.

In the back of the wagon I felt a heavy boot to the gut. I curled over, then the batons came out.

I kicked out with my feet.

'Fuck off, you pig bastards,' I yelled.

The batons kept coming.

'You fascist scum.'

A few of my kicks connected, but they piled onto me. As I struggled, hands grabbed at my arms and legs. Out came the plastic cable ties – they trussed me up like a loin of pork.

I could barely move, breathing became difficult, each gasp of air forced cuts in my wrists. The uniforms watched me squirm, then the batons got put away to be replaced by fists.

My new teeth became the first casualty. Spilled like glass beads on the floor.

'Where's the smart mouth now, eh?'

There's no answer to that. Especially when your mouth's full of blood, and you've just lost your second set of teeth in a month.

I tried to curl up, take my punishment. They'd soon tire themselves out.

At the station plod emptied out my pockets. Felt relieved I'd decided not to take the Glock to my father's funeral. As they fingerprinted me, the front door opened again and Collins and Roberts appeared, leading Amy along. Her hands were cuffed, she looked exhausted. Hair everywhere, eyes a mess of smudged black mascara.

'Amy,' I said. My voice cracked, I heard my shock register.

'Gus, Gus,' she screamed, close to breakdown. 'What's happening to me, Gus?'

'Don't worry. They've nothing.' I lunged, tried to get to her, but got held back. 'They just want to scare us. Don't worry, Amy.'

Collins and Roberts moved past. I spat at them, missed by a mile, yelled, 'You weak fucks. Take me on.'

'Oh, we will,' said Collins. 'Patience, patience, Mr Dury.' He threw his head back, laughed. 'We've something special planned for you.'

I spat again. This time Collins took it full in the face. He raged at me like a lunatic, fired an elbow into my solar plexus.

'I'm calling your number, Dury,' he said, looming over me, eyes burning, 'You got that?'

I fell against the desk, slid to the ground.

'Take this sack of shit away,' he yelled.

They left me to dry out in a cell. I hit the wall a few times. Shouted for a lawyer. No surprise, I was ignored. All the while, I feared for Amy. Christ, she was just a girl, 'You've really messed it up for her, Dury,' I told myself.

I knew the filth were leaving me to sweat before the intimidation started. When they arrived, I saw at once I wasn't wrong.

Collins, on fire, roared, 'I ought to rip off your head and shit down your neck.'

'Aren't we going to play good cop, bad cop again?'

He grabbed me by the hair, so tight I felt my eyes popping. 'Test me and you play no more games . . . ever.'

I tried to bold it out. 'If I start trembling, it's 'cos I'm off the drink. Wouldn't want you to flatter yourself that I was scared.'

He opened his palm, pushed it in my face. I felt my nose crack, collapse into my cheeks. At once the room began to spin. My eyes rolled up into my head and blood trickled into my throat. I fell in and out of consciousness for a few minutes.

Water – a bucket full – got thrown over me.

'Don't make this any harder than it needs to be, Mr Dury,' said Roberts. 'Think about the girl, if not yourself.'

'Leave her out of this.'

'Oh, we'd like to but I'm afraid your little friend is looking at a rather substantial charge sheet.'

Collins laughed. 'Like hanging with whores do you, Dury?'

'Amy's no brasser.'

Collins' laugh burst around the cell walls, set my ears ringing.

'Oh, this one's gonna have the conviction to prove it, I'm afraid,' said Roberts.

'What do you want?' I mumbled.

'I think you know what that is.'

'Lay off Zalinskas . . . that it?'

'You still have some memory then,' said Collins. As he stood before me his gut bulged in my face. He lifted an arm, I flinched. He toyed with me, twisting the edges of his moustache into little points.

Roberts butted in. 'That was our advice to you on our last meeting. We've since had cause to believe this advice went ignored.'

'Oh yeah? What makes you think that?'

Collins slammed his hand on the desk. 'We'll ask the questions. You'll fucking listen, laddie.'

Roberts again: 'Let's be clear. We have it on good authority that you've continued to pursue a vendetta against Mr Zalinskas.'

I knew I'd been careful to keep clear of Zalinskas since our last meeting, obviously not careful enough.

I called his bluff. 'And I thought Nadja was only after my body.'

'What?' said Roberts.

'I'm guessing you've been talking to Benny's right-hand man, or in this case woman. It was a man, but then Billy Boy was taken out, wasn't he?'

Collins edged closer. 'I'm warning you, Dury.'

Roberts held him off. His Clarks shoes squeaked on the floor.

I started to smirk. I knew now I'd been had by Nadja, probably to root out Billy Boy's missing footage. I saw that with both Billy and Zalinskas out the picture, she stood to take over the entire outfit. A tidy little manoeuvre.

How much Zalinskas knew about Nadja's scheming was a blank to me. I guessed not much. Both, however, now needed me out of the way. While the court case carried on, I figured, my life was safe. After that I was all out of options.

The pain in my head intensified, felt like my brow might crack down the middle. Who held all the power in the room was obvious.

My only hope, was to chance my luck. 'Let's deal.'

They looked at each other, frowning in symmetry.

'You don't hold any cards, Dury,' said Roberts.

I spat out another mouthful of blood.

'Let's see what the Bullfrog has to say about that, shall we?'

'You're mad, fucking mad,' said Collins. He began to laugh again, this time without the maniacal edge.

Roberts pushed him aside. 'Shut up, would you? Let me talk to the man.' As he leant over the desk, Collins turned away and kicked at the cell door. 'I won't tell you again to shut up. Now, Mr Dury, what, exactly, would you have us say to Mr Zalinskas?'

I sat up, brought my nose to within an inch of his. 'Tell the Bullfrog I have, in my possession, some very interesting footage. Footage that would not do his current position any favours.'

This played right into Nadja's hands – exposing the footage was just what she wanted. Risking the wrath of Zalinskas, though, that felt insane. Being in possession of the footage had cost Billy Boy his life and I'd just declared my ownership. But what option did I have? I needed to get Amy on a plane, somewhere far away until all this blew over.

My only hope was Zalinskas' case would drag on a little longer; if it didn't, Amy's life was ruined. And I was a dead man.

'And if we don't pass on your message?' said Roberts.

I rocked back on my chair, looked under the table. 'I wouldn't like to be in your shoes.'

A WHILE BACK, THE PRODUCERS of the Brits pulled off a coup when they got Paul Weller to agree to appear at their awards ceremony. They had every reason to feel proud of themselves, had been trying to get the Modfather for years. But then, they blew it.

They asked Weller to do a duet with James Blunt.

'I'd sooner eat my own shit,' he was reported as saying.

I felt the same way about my only option.

As I sat in the cell, I mapped out a plan in my mind. But none of it sat easily with me.

I paced up and down, near wore out the floor.

After an hour or so, Collins and Roberts showed their hand and sent in a doctor.

He checked my nose, said, 'It's a clean break but it's been broken before.'

I smelled whisky on his breath. 'And?'

He wiped away the dried blood with a cotton bud, squeezed the bridge. 'You can't polish shite.'

'Is that a medical opinion?'

'It's my opinion.' He stood up, put on his shabby dogtooth coat. 'Don't pick it for a few days, it'll heal itself.'

He tapped on the cell door to be let out. I shook my head at him, he hadn't even asked me how I'd sustained these injuries. Just presumed I'd fallen down the stairs on the way to the cells.

'Another upright citizen. The city can be proud of you, Doctor,' I said.

He didn't bat an eyelid.

I paced for another half hour, then sat on the cell floor, staring at the wall like Steve McQueen in *The Great Escape*. Wished I had a pitcher's mitt and a baseball. All I had was misgivings, fears, regrets.

Occasionally my nose throbbed. I tried to clear out the blood inside by pressing a nostril, one at a time, and blowing out. It helped at first, but soon became too painful to touch. I let it be. Left nature to take its course.

The throbbing settled into a persistent pain in my head and jaw. I learned to stay still, any movement resulted in agony. After a while, pain became the norm and I numbed my mind to it. I found if I concentrated, a Zen-like peace could be achieved. I'd just about perfected this when I heard a key in the lock.

I expected to see Collins and Roberts again, felt ready for them. But this time, shock walked in.

My blood began to race. My heart pumped me up for a whole new kind of fight.

As the door closed I stood up, faced the enemy.

'That looks like a terribly painful injury you've got there, Mr Dury,' said Cardownie. He wore a green sporting jacket, leather patches on the elbows and one shoulder. Tucked around his neck, a cravat, yellow with green paisley swirls. He'd obviously been yanked from a shooting party.

'Funny that, there's nosebleeds every time we meet,' I said.

He laughed aloud. 'I'm so glad not to be the one on the receiving end this time.'

'There's time yet.'

His laugh subsided, he took off his tweed cap. 'Come now ... we can be civilised, can't we?' He squirmed, tucked his hands behind his back and fired a crooked grin at me. He'd been sent by Zalinskas to do his dirty work. I saw now where the real power lay.

'Civilised ... now there's a word. Goes hand in hand with profits.'

'Quite. Coolidge, I believe. You're obviously an educated man.'

He sounded like a character from a Noël Coward play. My fists clenched. I wanted to grab his scrawny neck in my hands, twist the life out of him. Kept seeing the footage of him pushing aside that young girl like some worthless rag after he'd had his fun with her.

'Nothing that's worth knowing can be taught,' I said.

He missed that one, put on his 'what a chippy fellow we have here' smirk. The kind he kept for the below stairs type that I clearly appeared to be to him.

I prepared to deliver the lash. 'Don't you agree?'

Silence. He twisted his tweed cap in his hands. This whole affair seemed such an irritation to him. I mean, for someone like him to be forced to come down here, sort out this mess. To deal with a common grunt like me. I saw I churned his insides, just like the rest of the masses beneath him.

I gunned the pedal. 'I know Billy Thompson knew the value of knowledge.'

Cardownie's face twisted at the mention of Billy, but I wanted a wince out of him. 'What's that you say, Minister . . . an upstart? Och, I'm sure you're right, Billy Boy was definitely an upstart. Son of a publican, the gall of him, thinking he could drag himself out of the gutter, make something of himself.'

'He was a common criminal!' burst out Cardownie.

'Now, now. What's raised your dudgeon, Minister? The *common* bit or the *criminal* bit?'

He put his sleekit eyes on me, then drew them away. I knew he wanted the footage, but while I had it, there was time to play.

'I'm gonna take a guess here – not the criminal bit. No, because we know you have some powerful friends from that particular community, do you not, Minister?'

'I have not,' he barked.

'No? Then who pulled you away from your pheasant shoot?'

Cardownie smacked his hat off his corduroys, then stuffed it in his jacket pocket, pointed a finger at me. 'Now look here . . .'

'I'm looking.'

'Oh, what's the point? You clearly have your agenda.'

'Haven't we all?'

'*What?*'

I seemed to have lost him, felt like it was time to spell things out, said, 'Must be annoying for you to find someone who doesn't share your agenda. I bet that doesn't happen very much in this town, Minister.'

He looked ready to pop. 'I've had just about enough of this. If you want to play silly little games that's your prerogative, Mr Dury. I for one am not prepared to stand idly by and listen to this . . . this, arrant nonsense.'

I raised my hands. 'You done?'

He made towards me, the soles of his expensive brogues slapped heavily across the floor. 'Do not goad me, Mr Dury. I can walk out of that door every bit as easily as I walked through it. You, however, cannot. And neither can your young lady friend.'

Game over. But I'd had some fun with him.

'What're you selling, Minister?'

He lowered his tone, the smile eased back into place. 'Glad you're prepared to see sense. Now, about the matter of the . . . item of property pertaining to Mr Zalinskas' business affairs.'

'Oh, that.'

He stuck a finger under his cravat, took a handkerchief from his pocket and patted the moisture from his forehead. 'Quite. What do you propose to do with it?'

I turned up the heat. 'We are talking about the same item here. I mean, to be doubly certain, we are talking about the footage of some teenage prostitute taking a length off your good self.'

He dropped the handkerchief, turned away. 'Mr Dury, must you, please . . . I really won't hear you—'

'Tell the truth? Oh, don't worry about that, my lips are sealed – or should I say, can be.' I walked round in front of him, looked him in the eye. 'You see I'm just as prepared to be bought as any of your gentlemen's club buddies.'

His jaw tightened. Veins raised in his temples and throbbed like insects burrowing beneath his skin. 'I am, shall we say, in a position—'

'Authorised – let's get the word right.'

'As I say – I am authorised to see the charges pertaining to both yourself and the young lady dropped.'

'Wiped clean. Not dropped to be reactivated at a later date. Wiped clean, or do I need to call in a lawyer to draw up an official agreement?'

He returned to his handkerchief, carefully folded it, dabbed at his upper lip. 'I don't think the services of a legal practitioner will be required. In your, demotic, Mr Dury, the charges will be wiped clean. I can guarantee that. In exchange, of course, for the safe return of said items.'

'*Item* . . . Billy only had one copy, and I didn't make one either.'

'How can I be assured of that?'

I crossed the floor again, stretched out my hand. 'Minister, we're both gentlemen, surely.'

'But there are people who will seek assurances that this unfortunate incident shall never again be—'

I cut in, 'Whoa, whoa, there. I'm trusting you on the charges angle, a little bit of respect in my direction, if you please. Otherwise . . .'

He caved.

'How will you arrange delivery?'

'On the outside.'

Cardownie made for the door, knocked twice then turned back to face me. 'I need hardly remind you, Mr Dury, that you have incurred the displeasure of some extremely powerful people in this city.'

'I guessed as much.'

'Do you really think you can get away with it? I mean to say, one can quite easily have a class of creature like you stamped out.'

'Is that what you told, Billy when he tried to blackmail you?'

The smirk again. Keys rattled outside the cell door. 'Your type never learn, do they? No matter how harsh the lesson.'

'My *type*?'

The door handle turned. 'Make the delivery, Mr Dury, and take your medicine, now there's a good little man.'

COL CLEARED THE SNUG FOR us, made coffee. Amy curled up at my shoulder; she still trembled like a frightened child. I'd sent Hod to make the drop, until he got back with the all clear, we were on pins.

'You should see a doctor for that nose,' said Col. He placed a blanket round Amy's shoulders. 'Drink up, girl . . . Goodness, she's in a terrible state, Gus.'

I rubbed her back, tried to tuck the blanket in tighter. 'Amy, do you want me to take you home?'

Tears started to roll, sobbing. 'No. Can't I stay here with you?'

'Sure, sure,' I said. 'Just relax, it's all going to be fine.'

I checked the clock, I knew time was running out for us. I needed to get Amy away from the city. I couldn't risk any more fallout striking her. But, Christ, how did I tell her that?

I'd dragged her into this, I might not have meant to, but sure as shooting she was here because of me. I fired up a tab, dragged deep. My mind wouldn't function. Ideas seemed like something I used to have.

'Col, a word,' I said.

He left Amy's side, joined me at the bar.

'We need to get her out of here. We've very little time. If she's still around me when they come looking . . .'

'I know, I know.' Col trembled, went behind the bar and poured himself a large whisky; I'd never seen him drink before.

'What's this?' I said.

His face turned ashen, his eyelids dropped. 'Courage . . . I need courage.'

He raised the glass, downed it in one, I grabbed his wrist. 'I don't think you should.'

He snapped, 'Don't tell me that, Gus. This is all my doing, do you think I can't see it?'

I tried to set him straight. 'Col, none of it, not one bit, has anything to do with you.'

He shook my hand off, returned to the bottle. 'What do you know? You understand nothing. Didn't I put you on to this? Didn't I start it all. By the Lord above, wasn't Billy my son!' A tremor passed through him, head to toe, and he started to cry. 'When I look at that girl through there do you know what I see, Gus?'

I shook my head. 'What do you see?'

'Those girls . . . those poor young girls, all of them.'

'Col . . . don't.'

He raged: 'No. Billy brought those girls in, he was a maker of misery – him and all that pack. How could a son I raised be guilty of so much misery?'

'Don't. Don't do this to yourself.' I wanted to stop him. To see him get a grip, because every word he said felt like another drop of acid on my own conscience. 'Amy needs us to be strong right now. We need to get her away from this. It isn't fair on the girl to see any of us folding; I'll take what's coming to me, but for Chrissake, let's keep her out of it.'

Col put down the glass, seemed to gather himself.

'What do you want me to do?'

'We need to get her away . . . do you still have Billy's money?'

'Of course. I wouldn't touch it.'

'Then give me some of it, now.'

I returned to Amy, flicked on the television to try and distract her. She sipped at her coffee, started to come around. She was tough, I knew that, but even still, she'd need some time to get over this. Time, however, was one thing we didn't have.

Col appeared with Billy's Nike holdall, handed it to me. He gave me a look I'd never seen before, imagined it to be the kind exchanged in the trenches of World War One, just before two buddies went over the top.

'It's done,' said Hod. As he walked in the door my thoughts clicked into place.

I grabbed his arm. 'Right, I need a word.'

I led him away to the bar, left Amy with Col, told him to keep the coffee flowing.

'Hod, get her out of here,' I said. I handed him a bunch of notes. 'Get on a flight – Paris, Ayia Napa – bloody anywhere.'

He took the cash. 'So that's it then – it's over, we just cave?'

'There's that word *we* again. It's *me* that's brought this on.'

'And what about finding justice for Billy?'

'Billy found his own justice.'

'Meaning?'

'He wasn't exactly Mr Nice Guy. Go figure, Hod.'

Hod pulled his head in, tried another line of attack. 'And what about, Col then?'

'He knows the score better than anyone.'

'I think it's wrong, Gus, to come this far.'

'Drop it, would you?'

'You're letting them off, Gus. Billy's killer is walking free and nothing's changed, there's still a racket feeding off the misery of those girls.'

'Hod, I'm telling you – drop it.'

He stared me in the eye. I turned away. As he passed, I felt his shoulder cut into my own. I spun around, nearly knocked to the ground.

'I'll be telling Amy what she should really make of you,' said Hod.

'I wish you would.'

'I thought I knew you better than this, Gus. Thought you'd never go down without a fight.'

If an answer waved in my mind, I missed it.

On the TV screen Zalinskas' face flashed up. The case had concluded.

I ran through to the snug, stood under the television.

'I don't believe it,' said Col. 'He's walked free.'

I knew all hell might break out at any minute. 'Hod, get her the fuck out of here . . . now.'

I READIED MYSELF FOR THE WORST.

I told Col all I'd learned about Billy and the case. I filled him in on Nadja and Zalinskas, on Cardownie and the footage and anything else I'd missed out on previous reports. Throughout he sat quietly, listened. He seemed to be recording all I said, storing it away, but his eyes looked dead.

'I'm sorry I couldn't get all the answers.'

'No matter,' he said. 'What does anything matter now?'

'I wanted to give you some closure, you know that, Col.'

'What else could you do? They've drawn in the wagons. You've done all you could, Gus. I'm thankful for that.'

I'd called a taxi, the driver blasted on the horn from outside the pub.

'What will you do?' said Col.

'Get away for a while. I think I might be able to patch things up with Debs – just maybe.'

'You deserve some happiness.' He leaned forward, called me in, hugged me. I thought he felt cold. 'Thank you, Gus Dury.'

I felt tears in my eyes, but I didn't care.

'This isn't goodbye, Col.'

'Och, I think it is.'

He took my hand and shook it. 'I wish my son had been more like you, Gus.'

It felt like the greatest compliment of my life.

The taxi's horn sounded again.

'I have to go.'

'Goodbye, then.'

We'd no time to linger on a lengthy farewell; for that, I felt grateful.

I told the cabbie to take me to my mother's house. I planned to collect the urn and get out of town. The furthest ahead I thought was to return Milo's ashes to his homeland. If I could persuade Debs to come with me, I'd take it from there.

A line of cars stretched bumper to bumper all the way down my mother's street.

'Can you wait?' I asked the cabbie. 'I'll only be a minute.'

A huff. 'I'll have to keep the meter running.'

'Well go on, then.'

'I'll get turned. Can't wait more than five minutes, though.'

I dashed inside. My mother sat in the living room with my sister.

'Gus,' said Cathy, 'what is it?'

'I can't stop. How are you, Mam?' She didn't even look up, just stared at an indistinct spot on the wall.

'She's out of it. Doctor's given her a scrip,' said Cathy.

'Is she going to be okay?'

Cathy turned around, walked me into the hall and closed the door behind us.

'It would be nice to have you around a bit more, you know. She needs her family.'

'Cathy, this isn't a good time.'

'You're her son.'

The cabbie got impatient, another round of the horn sounded. 'Maybe in a while. I have to get away for a bit.'

I turned from her, went to the hallstand and took down the ashes.

'Suit yourself,' said Cathy. She spun around, walked back to the living room, slammed the door.

I wanted to say something, but I knew time was against me. I took the Glock out of its hiding place beside the ashes and stuffed it in my waistband.

As I ran out the cabbie scolded, 'I can't sit about blocking streets all day you know. Lucky I never got a ticket round here.'

My mind buzzed. My hand brushed the handle of the Glock, and I felt tempted to put it on the cabbie, but gathered myself.

'And where are we going now?' he said. 'Well?'

Where was I going? Had I any choices left? I knew if I took off, that was it. I'd be running for the rest of my days. Constantly looking over my shoulder. Worrying about strangers. Did I want that for Debs? Christ, did I want it for myself?

'Well?' repeated the cabbie.

I'd never see my mother again. I'd never see Col again either. And I might not be able to face Hod. I knew the solution was simple. 'You selfish bastard, Dury,' I told myself, 'for ever out to save your own worthless hide – you coward.'

I thought about Billy. The girls. Those poor innocent Latvian girls who didn't know what they had let themselves in for.

Then the footage of Cardownie started to play before my eyes once again.

'Well?' said the cabbie. 'Where to? Tell me or get out!'

'Turn it around again.'

'*What?*'

'Back that way, to the hills. I'll give you instructions on the way.'

Cardownie had a mansion house somewhere in the foot of the Pentland Hills. A place for the city's rich to gather, where backs got slapped and plans hatched to divide spoils. Seemed as good a place as any for me to start.

After a quarter of an hour on the road I got out and tipped the cabbie with a fifty. Immediately, his tone changed.

'Thank you very much, sir. If I can ever help you out again, just holler.'

'Actually, there is something. Have you a piece of paper?'

I scratched down a note to Debs. If I didn't make it, at least Milo would be properly laid to rest. I passed through the carrier with the urn inside. 'Take it to this address and give her the letter – that should explain everything.'

To sweeten the deal, I dropped another twenty. 'And make it snappy, eh?'

THE HOUSE WAS SCOTS BARONIAL. Normally, I go near a building like this, it's a museum or a hotel. To think someone lived here, with the choice of a hundred-plus rooms to rattle about in, made my spleen twitch.

A few generations back, the closest someone like me got to the landed gentry was to muck out their stables. Well, here I was now, ready to rake up some shit.

The pathway scree crunched underfoot, so I moved to the verge, and tried to shrink below the line of the windows. At the building's gable end, I put my back to the sandstone. I saw Cardownie's Range Rover parked beside a Seven Series BMW – the missus's runabout?

At the kitchen window a woman in her bad fifties with bingo-wings, obviously the help, shelled peas. I limboed beneath her line of vision, tried the rest of the windows.

In a small book-lined study I found Cardownie. He sat with his back to me on a chesterfield. My heart raced, pumped fire in my veins. I ducked beneath the windowledge. I sat on my haunches, banged the back of my head on the wall and tried to collect myself.

'What am I doing? How the hell has it come to this?' I wondered. 'Have I totally lost it?'

I felt sweat gather on my upper lip and brow, it dripped in my eyes as I reached for the Glock. I lifted myself to the window again to check he was still alone.

There appeared to be only one door. I figured if I dragged him back through the window, no one would be wise to me.

I took a handful of scree, lobbed it at the glass, ducked back down.

As if on cue, the latch slid open. Cardownie stuck out his head. My hands quivered as I cocked the gun.

'From this range, I believe it would blow your head clean off. Do you feel lucky, punk?'

He looked down, a gasp.

'Where's the shit-stopping smirk now, Minister?'

'I-I-I . . .'

'Why don't you save it? Out.'

The Beemer was good to go. I made him drive, heading for the city.

'Where are you taking me?' he asked.

'Sorry, didn't I mention? I'll be asking the fucking questions.'

'I have every right to know—'

I aimed the Glock at his crotch. 'Maybe I didn't make myself clear enough. This could put a serious damper on your whoring.'

Silence for the best part of the journey. I do believe I'd made myself clear. I'd put him in his place, just where I wanted him. 'Pull over.'

At the side of the road, I ordered he take out his phone.

'I want you to listen very carefully. You're going to ring Nadja and tell her to meet you at Zalinskas' casino.'

'But—'

'No buts.' I cocked the Glock, put it to his head. 'And, you better make it convincing. Your life depends on it, in case you hadn't realised.'

He had the number on speed dial. The call went better than I'd imagined it would.

'You're a formidable liar, Minister. Don't believe I could have done any better myself.'

'I think I should warn you that this is a very costly mistake you're making, Mr Dury.'

'Oh, I think I'll take the chance. Now drive.'

We put in on George Street, didn't worry about feeding the meter. I took off my jacket, folded it over the gun, kept it close to Cardownie's back. 'One false move will be your last.'

I led him up a side street skirting the casino. A rotten wooden fence was all that came between us and Zalinskas' lair. I put my foot to a weak stanchion, it split in two. Another kick and we were in, walking towards the fire escape.

The metal gates were, in contrast to most New Town premises, unlocked.

'Good to see Mr Zalinskas is sticking to the fire-safety regulations,' I said.

Cardownie frowned. 'I'm warning you, you imbecile, if you go through with this—'

I put the Glock to his lips. 'I don't take threats kindly, Minister. *I'm* warning you now. Get up there, tap on Benny's lovely french doors and when he opens up, I'll be right behind you.'

The gun seemed to focus his thoughts. At the top of the fire escape, Cardownie rapped on the windowpane. It took Zalinskas a little time to answer.

'What the hell are you doing here?'

I stepped in. 'Allow me.' The Glock did all my explaining.

As Zalinskas backed into his office, followed by Cardownie and myself, one of his goons showed and reached for a shooter. I dropped him with one shot to the kneecap. As he writhed around in agony, I lifted his gun from the floor.

The gunshot had set off the wolf, it clawed at the confines of the cage, then began to wail. The wolf's cry put the shits up every one of us.

'Now, so we know I'm not messing . . . that's the last warning shot, the next time I fire this gun it'll be pointing at someone's head.'

I sat them on the couch. The pug rolled about in agony, clutching at his knee.

'The wolf can smell blood,' said Zalinskas.

'He's not the only one,' I said.

I helped the goon onto the couch, barked at Cardownie. 'Get your belt off, tie it round his thigh to stop the bleeding.'

As I kept a close eye on them, the buzzer went. On the monitors above Zalinskas' desk, I saw Nadja arrive.

I ran to the door, stood in wait. As she walked through, I closed the door behind her.

'Hello, Nadja.'

'*You?*'

'I bet you thought I didn't have it in me.'

She looked round, first at Zalinskas, then at Cardownie and the pools of blood on the floor.

'Welcome to the party,' I said. 'Why don't you have a seat?'

As they lined up on the couch, I let them simmer. The wolf cries grew louder. I walked over to the cage, shook my head. 'Poor animal. What kind of a sick fuck keeps such a beautiful beast caged?'

Nobody answered, then Nadja spoke, 'Gus, surely we can talk about this?'

'Oh, we're past the pillow-talk stage, honey, or hadn't you realised?'

I turned away from the wolf, strolled over to the group. 'Quite a gathering. I'm sure you must be wondering why I brought you here.'

No one answered. The pug groaned, I put a kick in his back, yelled, 'Shut the fuck up.'

The others flinched as I turned on them. I cocked the gun in their direction.

'It's all very simple. I'm going to ask one question, and I *will* get an answer.'

'Mr Dury,' Zalinskas stood up, 'I'm sure you are a reasonable man.'

I brought the gun across his face, opened up a two-inch gash. He yelled, fell back. Blood streamed through the fingers he brought up to his cheek.

'Whatever gave you that idea?'

I pulled up a chair, turned its back towards the group. As I sat down I kept moving the gun between their heads. 'One question and I *will* have an answer. Do you understand?'

The three of them nodded. 'Yes.'

'Who killed Billy?'

No one answered. Nadja turned to Zalinskas, he turned away.

'Maybe I didn't make myself clear.' I stood up again, put the gun to Zalinskas' head.

'It's not what you think. It's not what you think,' he whined.

'Who pulled the trigger?' I yelled. 'Who killed him?'

I pushed Zalinskas aside, grabbed Nadja by the hair. 'Was it you?

Huh? Did you kill him? Zalinskas found out about your blackmail plot, so you took Billy out to save yourself.'

She screamed. 'No. No. No.'

I threw her down, stuck the gun in Cardownie's left eye. 'You? Go to the source, wipe out the threat?'

He cried like a child. 'Oh my God . . . no. Please, spare me . . . I didn't kill him.'

I took the gun back to Zalinskas. His face was running with blood. I hit him again, opening up a matching wound on his other cheek. He fell to the ground. On all fours he wheezed, gagging for air.

'Get up!' I stood over him, fired a shot into the floor, right between his hands. The wolf's howls rose higher as I grabbed him by the throat. 'Billy was a threat to everything, wasn't he?'

He tried to speak but his words were choked.

'Billy was gonna blow it all wide open, wasn't he? The girls, the connections, everything. You'd have had nothing left, would you?'

I fired the gun into the ground again. 'Who killed Billy? Tell me. Tell me, you fuck. Who killed Billy?'

'It was me, Gus.'

The voice came from behind me. Sweat ran down my spine, I turned and tried to focus.

'I killed him.'

I let Zalinskas fall to the ground, straightened myself, said, '*What?*'

'I killed him. It was me.'

My breath quickened. I wiped the sweat from my eyes. 'Col – what are you doing here?'

He walked from the balcony through the french doors and faced me. 'I killed Billy. I killed my own son.'

My thoughts raced, my mind felt numb, but my heart pounded. 'I-I . . . I don't understand.'

As Col walked closer I felt drawn into his wide eyes. 'He was as good as dead. The life he made for himself had killed him.'

'What are you saying?' The room swayed, everything felt surreal.

'Billy was a thug. A criminal. He preyed on those who couldn't defend themselves.'

'Do you know what you're saying?' I asked.

'Every word.'

It didn't make any sense – any of it. 'But Billy was tortured. They pulled his nails out.'

'That's how I found him – left for dead. I put him out of his misery.'

'Then why, Col? Why did you need me?'

'I had no idea about any of this, Gus. You've led me to them.' As Col moved forward I saw he carried a shotgun in his hand. 'And now, when I do what I have to do, you'll be here to explain to everyone why it had to be like this.'

He raised the gun to his shoulder.

'No, Col, you don't have to do this.'

'I must.'

He steadied the gun, pointed it at Zalinskas.

'No, think about this.'

'I'm sorry, Gus.'

He lowered his eye, stared down the barrel at Zalinskas.

'No, Col! No!' I yelled at him.

I couldn't let him do it. I grabbed for the gun, held the barrel tight. He wrestled me for the firearm. 'Leave it, Col.'

'No it can't be left.'

I heard Nadja and the others screaming, everything blurred as they ran for the doors. I saw the pug hobbling down the fire escape, and then, the gun went off.

The sound of the shotgun echoed round the room, followed fast by the noise of breaking glass.

I fell back with the fierce recoil. Landed on the floor where Zalinskas curled in fear. Nadja and Cardownie were already through the door on the fire escape.

I saw Col take aim at Zalinskas for a second time.

'No, Col . . . put it down.'

'Get out of the way, Gus.'

'No . . .'

As I waited for the second shot to come down the barrel, Col suddenly lunged forward, pushed from behind by the wolf as it leapt through the shattered cage.

The shotgun went flying as Col crashed face first into the ground. By instinct I raised the Glock, for a second I put the wolf in my sights, I squeezed the trigger. The bullet connected with the wall behind.

'No-o-o-o,' yelled Zalinskas. He jumped to his feet and I saw a flash of red, like paint spilling, as the wolf clamped its jaws into his neck.

The wolf tore and tore, pulling out the carotid arteries, ripping the flesh. I was transfixed, unable to remove my eyes. I felt the Glock slip from my hand.

As the second round of the shotgun went off, I snapped back to reality.

'No!' I turned away. Col lay propped against the wall, the gun barrel in his mouth, the back of his head blown out.

'Oh Jesus Christ, Col . . . no.'

THE WOLF'S SNARLING AND THE sound of ripping flesh helped me gather myself.

I closed the doors behind me as I stepped onto the balcony, then descended the fire escape. In the ground behind the casino, the pug tried to squeeze through the fence, he was too big, I forced him out of my way.

'Move it,' I yelled.

He toppled over, whimpering like a beaten dog. As I ran for the side street, I got tangled in some bramble bushes. They caught my feet and dropped me to the road. As I tried to raise myself, my guts heaved, I threw up. I retched and retched, couldn't seem to stop, and then I caught sight of Cardownie and Nadja. They were arguing; Cardownie refusing to let her get into his car.

'It's over for both of them,' I thought. 'I'll make sure of that.'

I found my feet and managed to keep the rest of my stomach's contents in place as I turned on to George Street. I tried to put as much distance as possible between myself and the sight I had just witnessed, but my legs trembled.

I stumbled to a bench, dropped like a stone, and dialled the filth.

'Lothian and Borders Police.'

I got them to connect me with Fitz.

'I'm paying my dues,' I said.

'What? Who is this?'

He played a role, I knew it. 'An old friend. There's a casino owner on George Street. Let's just say someone's taken a bite out of him.'

'And who would this person be?'

'His name's Zalinskas. I believe he's known to police. Is that the expression?'

'Yes. Yes . . . but.'

'No. No more, if you hurry, you might find a witness out the back. But you better take a tranquilliser gun, otherwise it *will* get messy.'

'Ah, now . . .'

'Goodbye, Fitz. Oh and good luck with that promotion. Don't forget who your friends are.'

I hung up.

Starting to walk again I felt the strength returning to my legs. I made it all the way to Broughton Street where I stepped into an Internet café.

Ordered a coffee and connected to the net.

In my webmail, I opened an email I'd sent myself earlier from Hod's computer. Clicked on forward. Keyed in the e-address of my old boss at the paper. In the subject line I tapped in one word: Exclusive.

'No one lies better than a hack, Cardownie,' I said to myself, as I forwarded Billy's footage to Rasher.

I sat back and sipped my coffee. From my window seat, the city went by, oblivious to the momentous events of a few streets away.

Inside ten minutes, police sirens began to wail.

I drained my cup, went outside.

On the street, I took out my mobile phone and dialled Debs.

It rang for an age, seemed like for ever, then: 'Hello.'

'Hello, Deborah . . . it's me.'

'Gus . . .'

'Did you get the package I sent?'

'What the hell is it, some kind of sick joke?'

'No,' I started to smile, it felt so good to hear her voice, 'not at all. For once, I'm deadly serious. So, how about it?'

'How about what?'

'You and me. Do you fancy a trip to Ireland?'

'*Ireland* . . . what for?'

'To lay a lost soul to rest.'